Praise for
A DARKNESS OF DRAGONS

"All the ingredients of a perfect fantasy adventure."
Kieran Larwood, author of *Podkin One-Ear*

"This stunning book reminds us of the soaring joy of adventure, the captivating danger of magic, and of the delight of finding friends in unexpected places."
Mr Ripley's Enchanted Books

"S.A. Patrick builds a quite brilliant original tale whilst also creating an unforgettable magical world…"
Storgy Kids

"Full of twists and turns and full of non-stop adventure."
Chatterbooks Review

"S.A. Patrick has adapted the traditional fairy tale to create a fearsome character and then filled the plot with action, suspense and magic…"
TES

LO · D1584045 · RNET

To my daughter Tilden,
who has waited long enough

First published in the UK in 2021 by Usborne Publishing Ltd., Usborne House,
83-85 Saffron Hill, London EC1N 8RT, England, usborne.com

Copyright © S.A. Patrick, 2021

Cover and inside illustrations by George Ermos

Title typography by Leo Nickolls

Illustrations and title typography copyright © Usborne Publishing Ltd., 2021

The right of S.A. Patrick to be identified as the author of this work has been
asserted by him in accordance with the Copyright, Designs and Patents Act, 1988.

The name Usborne and the Balloon logo are Trade Marks of
Usborne Publishing Ltd.

All rights reserved. No part of this publication may be reproduced, stored
in a retrieval system or transmitted in any form or by any means, electronic,
mechanical, photocopying, recording or otherwise without the prior permission of
the publisher.

This is a work of fiction. The characters, incidents, and dialogues are products of
the author's imagination and are not to be construed as real. Any resemblance to
actual events or persons, living or dead, is entirely coincidental.

A CIP catalogue record for this book is available from the British Library.

ISBN 9781474945684   04820/1 JFMAMJJASO D/20

Printed and bound in Great Britain by CPI Group (UK) Ltd, Croydon, CR0 4YY

A VANISHING OF GRIFFINS

S.A. PATRICK

USBORNE

In a world of dragons, song-spells, pipers and battles, three accidental heroes found themselves thrown into an epic quest which began in *A Darkness of Dragons*.

Now Patch, Wren and Barver continue their hunt for the evil Piper of Hamelyn in a second spell-slinging, shape-shifting adventure…

THE STORY SO FAR

Ten years ago, **an evil Piper** stole the **children of Hamelyn**. They were never seen again. Then the same Piper stole a hundred **dragon children**, and they too disappeared for ever.

Caught at last by a group of heroes known as **The Eight**, the Hamelyn Piper was locked deep in the dungeons of **Tiviscan Castle**.

Patch Brightwater is a trainee Piper who fled in disgrace from his training at Tiviscan. He befriends **Wren Cobble**, a girl cursed into the shape of a rat, and promises to help break her curse.

But Patch has played an illegal Song! Hunted down by

Custodian Piper **Rundel Stone** and his apprentice **Erner Whitlock**, Patch faces the **Pipers' Council** – the highest authority for Pipers – and is thrown into the dungeons of Tiviscan for five hundred and ten years.

From the distant **Dragon Territories**, a vast **dragon army** comes to avenge the loss of their children. They smash the dungeon walls, seize the **Hamelyn Piper**, and burn him to ash!

In the chaos, Patch escapes with Wren. They meet **Barver Knopferkerkle**, a dracogriff – part dragon, part griffin. The three journey to see **Tobias Palafox** at Marwheel Abbey, hoping he can help cure Wren's curse. **Erner Whitlock** also arrives seeking help: **Rundel Stone** has been poisoned and is close to death.

They venture to The Witch of Gemspar Mountain, **Alia Corrigan**. In a trance, Alia gives a terrifying **prophecy,** warning that someone will betray them.

Alia saves Rundel's life, but can only give Wren a partial cure – so Patch, Wren and Barver set out with Erner to confront **Underath,** the Sorcerer who cursed Wren. They find him horribly wounded, his castle overrun by cut-throat mercenaries, and his friend the griffin **Alkeran** kidnapped by a mysterious woman. Underath agrees to cure Wren – *if* she can bring Alkeran safely home.

As they flee from the mercenaries, Erner seems to fulfil the prophecy; in shock, Patch **pushes Erner from Barver's back** into the clutches of the mercenaries below.

Patch, Barver and Wren journey to the Dragon Wastes where they learn the **terrible truth** of why the Hamelyn Piper took the dragon children. Returning to warn the Pipers' Council, they find that the **Hamelyn Piper is alive** and plans to use a **vast Pipe Organ** made of the magical substance **obsidiac**, to control the minds of Pipers!

Our three friends destroy the Pipe Organ; the Hamelyn Piper escapes.

But now it is the Pipers' Council who seem to fulfil the prophecy of betrayal, instead of Erner.

Will Wren ever find the griffin Alkeran, and be cured of her curse? And what of their friend Erner Whitlock, abandoned to the mercenaries? Realizing he was innocent all along, they vow to rescue him. Yet even if they succeed, can the friends track down the evil Piper of Hamelyn and defeat his plans – before he destroys them all…?

1

WHATEVER HAPPENED TO ERNER WHITLOCK?

Erner woke, as he did every morning, from a nightmare: being pushed off the back of a dracogriff, into a cold lake far below. In his nightmare, the face of the person who had pushed him was smiling a terrible smile, cruel and cold, *laughing* as Erner tumbled through the air and into the icy water, his Pipe slipping from his fingers and lost to the depths.

When it had actually happened, though, there had been no smile on Patch Brightwater's face: he had looked utterly terrified.

A question had burned inside Erner ever since that fateful day, and he knew that there was only one way he would ever get an answer.

He would have to find Patch Brightwater, someone he'd

always thought was a friend, and ask him *why*.

Why did you push me into the lake?

Erner's journey since then had been eventful. It had brought him, eventually, to the Islands of the Eastern Sea, and to the court of one of the many Pirate Kings and Queens. Here on the island of Pengersick was an old fortress, where the King of Pengersick had his palace. It was in the heart of that fortress that Erner was imprisoned now: hanging in a tiny cage next to the throne of a Pirate King.

The King snored in his throne. He always slept there when he threw a party, and he'd thrown a party almost every night since taking the crown. The floor of the throne room was covered in sleeping pirates and empty rum bottles.

Erner's legs were going numb. He shifted his weight, working his feet out from under him, trying not to make his cage swing – if the cage swung, the rope it hung from would creak, and the creak might wake the King.

That was never a good idea. Two nights before, one of the pirates had let out a belch that was long and thunderous as everyone slept. He'd woken the King. Worse, he'd *laughed* about it.

In front of the throne were a dozen wooden spikes, and on the top of each spike was the severed head of someone who had displeased the King. The head of the belching pirate was there, the freshest of the bunch.

Yes, waking the Pirate King was never a good idea. He was *not* a morning person.

Arpie Noss was his name – King Arpie to his subjects. He hadn't been King long. Two months, that was all, but it had been a *busy* two months. Pirate rulers didn't tend to last, and it seemed that Arpie Noss had been trying to fit as much as possible into whatever time he had.

Like buying Erner, for a start.

Erner was an apprentice in the Custodian Elite. Held in the highest esteem, the Custodians only accepted the best Pipers into their ranks.

The magical Songs that Pipers played could achieve wondrous things: there were Songs to conjure winds to sweep snow from blocked roads; Songs to make seeds sprout in barren fields; Songs that helped wounds to heal. There were even Songs that could defend against *armies*.

Pipers usually specialized in one kind of Song, but Custodians excelled at them all, using their skills with the Pipe to help wherever they could.

To the poor and downtrodden of the world, the Custodian Elite represented justice and hope, and for Erner there was no greater honour than being part of their ranks.

For many, the greatest honour of all would be to become a member of the Pipers' Council, as they were the highest authority among Pipers, and decided the laws of Piping. But it was the Custodian Elite who *upheld* those laws, and much more besides.

Erner had gone with Patch Brightwater to visit the castle of Underath the Sorcerer, hoping that the Sorcerer would help their friend Wren – a girl cursed into the shape of a rat.

When they'd got to the castle, however, they had found Underath seriously wounded and in hiding, his castle occupied by violent mercenaries. When the mercenaries had discovered them, the Sorcerer had hidden again; Erner and the others had fled on the back of Barver the dracogriff, as the mercenaries gave chase.

Just as they seemed to be out of danger, Patch had suddenly pushed Erner off Barver's back, into the lake below.

Erner had managed to swim to the side of the lake; exhausted, he'd expected the mercenaries to kill him. The moment they saw Erner's robes, however, they realized he was in the Custodian Elite. Killing him wasn't worth the kind of trouble it could bring down on their heads.

Instead, the mercenaries did what they always did: they tried to think of a way to make some money out of the situation. They'd already plundered everything of value from Underath's castle, and the time had come for them to move on; extra money would be welcome.

They considered holding him to ransom, but the Custodian Elite was far too powerful a foe, with far too long a memory. Such a course of action would end disastrously, they decided.

But there were, they knew, criminals in the world who were reckless enough, or foolish enough, to actually *enjoy* the thought of angering the Custodians.

Pirates.

So a letter was sent to the Pirate Kings and Queens of the territories of the Islands of the Eastern Sea, all two hundred and twelve of them. *We have come into the possession of a young apprentice in the Custodian Elite*, said the letter. *For a simple payment of one hundred gold muttles, you may have him as your prisoner, and show how little you fear the Custodians! Although none shall pay, for none would dare!*

The Custodian Elite tended to leave the Islands of the Eastern Sea alone, but it would take a particularly foolish and reckless pirate to think that a captive Custodian wouldn't be a huge risk. Luckily for the mercenaries, one of the Pirate Kings and Queens *was* particularly foolish and reckless.

Arpie Noss, newly crowned King of Pengersick, looking to make his mark in the pirate world. *What better way,*

13

thought King Arpie, *than to do something nobody had ever done before*?

He wanted everyone to see how *fearless* he was!

He wanted everyone to see how *wealthy* he was!

And so Erner was sold. He spent a week blindfolded and chained in the stinking hull of a ship, his stomach heaving with every swell of the sea, and then he was brought before the King.

"Is this what I paid for?" said King Arpie. "Not exactly formidable…" The King prodded Erner with his staff. "Put him in a little cage hanging by my throne!" he said to a tall, skinny man standing beside him. The skinny man looked anxious. "Snap to it, Skreep! I gave you an order!"

"Yes, Your Majesty," said Skreep. "But surely the Custodians will be angry when they find out?"

"Of course they will!" said the King. "That's the whole *point*! Every pirate will know that I, King Arpie, fear nobody! You worry too much, Skreep. Worry less!" Skreep nodded and seemed to relax ever so slightly. "That's an order, by the way," added the King. "Worry less, or I will have you *killed*."

Skreep looked much less relaxed.

And so, they had built Erner a cage. It wasn't quite high enough for him to sit upright, or long enough for him to lie down, and in the weeks he'd been here he had yet to

14

discover a way to sleep without some part of him being numb when he woke. He'd learned that as long as he was quiet, he was forgotten. Sometimes, one of King Arpie's pirates would amuse themselves by throwing insults to see if Erner responded. But Erner did not respond, and interest was soon lost.

He was given the bare minimum to eat and drink. Once a day, he was taken from the cage, manacled, and led outside; there, he would do what needed to be done, and they would douse him with buckets of cold water when he was finished.

Yet Erner considered himself lucky. While King Arpie was eager to show how badly he treated his captive, Erner was a prized possession: no real harm was allowed to befall him.

Eventually, he knew, the Pipers' Council would do all in their power to find him, and they would make an example of King Arpie Noss. It would not be pleasant.

Then, once free, Erner could find Patch Brightwater.

He could finally ask him *why*.

Once Erner had shifted his legs – without making the rope creak – the pins and needles subsided, and he dozed. After a while, the entrance to the throne room swung open; a nervous pirate came inside and woke Skreep, the King's advisor. A few whispers later, Skreep looked very worried indeed. He came over to the throne, and gave a little cough, but the King kept snoring. "Your Majesty..." said Skreep, and then he just threw caution to the wind. "Arpie, wake up!"

King Arpie's eyes opened wide and he drew his sword, putting it to Skreep's throat. "Assassin!" he cried, then saw who it was and put his sword away. "Oh. What is it? Lunchtime already?"

"No, Your Majesty," said Skreep. "A couple of troublemakers have been chained up and brought for your judgement, sire. They were asking questions about *him*." He threw a narrow-eyed glare at Erner, then looked back at the King, probably hoping for some sign of concern.

Instead, the King grinned. "Ah ha! They've got wind of it at last! Sent some spies to check! This is good news, Skreep!"

Skreep gave a huge sigh. "This is *bad* news, Your Majesty. It was only a matter of time, and I'd hoped to talk you round before the Custodians found out, but..."

King Arpie looked at him in horror. "*Talk me round? I'm King Arpie Noss! I make the decisions! I fear nobody!* What's the point of trying to make the Custodians look like fools if they don't know I'm doing it?" He reached to the floor and picked up a tankard, half-full of stale ale. He drank it down and started to bang the tankard against the metalwork that arched over his throne. It was the alarm call everyone in the palace knew well – the King has awoken, and when the King wakes up, all his subjects have to *damn well wake up too*.

"Rise and shine, you lot!" shouted the King. There was a lot of wincing and blinking from the waking revellers, but absolutely no complaining – the heads on spikes were a constant reminder that an unbuttoned mouth was bad for your health. "Seems the Custodians have learned about my little *pet*," he said, smiling at Erner. "And the idiots have sent some spies, who've been so kind as to be captured! I want you all to be on your best form, understand? Lots of sneering and glaring! *Bring in the spies!*"

Everyone in the throne room looked eagerly to the doorway, where, with a burly pirate at the front and another guarding the rear, in came a wretched pair of manacled prisoners, with sackcloth bags over their heads.

Erner felt sorry for them. In all likelihood, they were just two people who'd happened to ask about the King's new trophy because it was *interesting*. The King himself had wanted people *everywhere* to talk about it. To suddenly call someone a spy because they'd done what the King had been desperate for people to do... Well, that made Erner's sense of injustice burn deep inside him.

The two prisoners were led to the only clear area of the throne room floor, right in front of King Arpie and the

17

spiked heads. There was a *reason* that area was left clear –
a reason closely related to a certain *lever* by one arm of the
King's throne.

A lever that, when pulled, opened up a large trapdoor
right where the prisoners now stood.

"Let's have a look at them," said the King. One of the
pirate guards stepped forward and pulled the cloth bag off
the first prisoner's head.

A woman. Erner had seen her before, but for a moment
he couldn't place where. She gave King Arpie a look of
absolute contempt.

Then Erner remembered where he'd seen her, and his
stomach lurched in a way it hadn't lurched since his
horrible sea journey.

Alia, thought Erner. That was her name. She'd
accompanied Patch and Wren back to Marwheel Abbey,
after their trip to see the Witch of Gemspar Mountain. The
trip had been a success – Wren, who had been cursed into
the form of a rat, had been granted the ability to change
back into her human shape, albeit just for short periods.
He'd met Alia only briefly then – she had introduced herself
as some kind of expert in magic, and had seemed very
friendly with Patch and Wren.

He turned his eyes to the second prisoner, who was
quite a bit shorter than Alia, and a terrible feeling washed
over him.

No, he thought. *It can't be.*

The guard gripped the cloth bag covering the second prisoner's head, and yanked.

There, only ten feet from Erner's cage, stood the whole reason that Erner was here at all.

Patch Brightwater. Looking terrified. And Erner could just make out a small shifting bulge in the chest pocket of Patch's coat, which he strongly suspected was a certain rat-shaped friend.

Erner had had plenty of time to wonder how he would feel when he saw Patch again – anger, perhaps, or even hatred. Now that the moment had arrived, he felt no animosity at all. What he felt was *apprehension.*

If they had come to rescue him, they had made a terrible, terrible mistake.

King Arpie cleared his throat. "Pitiful prisoners! You're accused of being spies for the Custodian Elite, on account of you asking questions about my pet Piper." He thwacked Erner's cage with his staff. "Do you confess?" He grinned, and at that moment Erner knew that the King didn't *care* if they were spies, not really. All he cared about was that *other people* would think it.

Alia's eyes narrowed as she spoke. "We don't represent the Custodian Elite, Your Majesty," she said. "We're here to ask you to show mercy and release a friend." She nodded to Erner. "He is a—"

But the King interrupted. "Yes, yes, blah, blah, yakkity yak! You're a spy, admit it! You admit he's a friend, so admit you're a spy and be done with it! We don't have all day."

Erner saw the King's hand move towards the lever. "No!" he cried, and the King gave him a sharp look and another *thwack*.

Alia was also looking at the King's hand, and at the lever it was now touching. "Don't do anything you might regret, sire," she said. Her voice was laced with the direst of warnings, a sound of deep foreboding woven into every word she uttered.

There was sorcery at work here, Erner realized. The woman's voice would make anyone with sense pause for a moment and wonder why it felt like the very stones of the throne room walls were shaking as she spoke. She was obviously powerful; ignoring her would be a very foolish thing indeed.

Unfortunately, King Arpie Noss was a very foolish man.

"This is how King Arpie deals with spies!" said the King. He pulled his lever. The floor under the prisoners swung down, and Erner watched them fall, their cries disappearing into the dark below. Everyone in the room listened, until at last the cries ceased and the trapdoor swung closed again.

Erner was in so much shock he could hardly breathe. He didn't know what awaited his would-be rescuers, but he did know *this*: the trapdoor led to a winding shaft, down which prisoners would tumble until they reached the bottom and found themselves in a place of absolute horror.

A place the pirates called, "The Pit of Screaming Death".

King Arpie clapped his hands together in excitement and jumped out of his throne. "Come on, then," he said. "Everyone to the viewing gallery!" He nodded towards Erner. "Bring him along, Skreep. Let him watch. It'll be fun!"

THE PIT OF
SCREAMING DEATH

When Patch finally hit the ground, his first thought was that he'd crushed Wren.

"No!" he cried. He stood and patted himself down, checking her favourite pocket; finding it empty, he looked around but saw no sign of her.

A few feet away, Alia sat up with a groan. "*That* was annoying," she said. "Are you okay, Patch?"

"I've lost Wren," he said. He called for his friend and listened; there was no reply, not a squeak. "She must have fallen out on the way down." He took in his surroundings: a huge natural cavern, mostly in darkness. A few gaps in the highest part of the rock directly above let in some light. Beside them was the hole they'd hurtled out of, low on the wall. He put his head inside, looking up into the steep tunnel that led from the King's trapdoor. The sides were smooth, giving a human no chance of slowing down, but for a rat everything was different. Wren could easily have found enough grip with her claws.

"Wren?" he called. "If you're in there, stay where you are until we've got this figured out." He listened, but there was no reply. Still, at least that horrible first thought he'd had – of finding her broken body underneath him – hadn't come true.

There was a door further along in the rock wall, but it was heavily armoured, clad in iron. Patch didn't like this one bit.

Alia stood and dusted herself off. They heard a *thunk* from above them, and looked up. There was a large wooden platform near the cavern roof, and onto the platform came King Arpie, followed by several dozen grinning pirates. In among them was Erner – released from his cage, being led along by a chain fastened to his wrists.

So much for rescues, thought Patch. This had not *quite* gone to plan.

The plan had been a simple one. After battling the dreaded Hamelyn Piper at Tiviscan – the home of the Pipers' Council – Patch, Wren and their friend Barver had returned to Marwheel Abbey. There, they found that Rundel Stone remained unconscious, still suffering the effects of the poison that had almost killed him. Rundel was a senior member of the Custodian Elite, one of only a few to hold their highest rank of *Virtus.* He was in good hands – Alia and Brother Tobias were looking after him.

Patch had told Alia and Tobias everything that had happened:

He had told them of the Hamelyn Piper's attempt to take control of the Pipers at Tiviscan, with a vast Organ constructed from obsidiac – the rare and magical substance also known as black diamond.

He had told them of how Barver – half-dragon, half-griffin, and almost indestructible – had flown into the Organ, destroying it, only for the Hamelyn Piper to mysteriously vanish.

He had told them of how Wren had broken the magical bracelet that let her turn back into human form, and might now be a rat for ever.

And he had told them of the prophecy that had warned Patch of *betrayal.* That prophecy had led to him pushing Erner Whitlock off Barver's back, thinking it was *Erner* who would betray them. But then the prophecy had seemed to point suspicion at members of the Pipers' Council instead – at *all* of them, except for the Head of the Council, Lord Drevis.

"Prophecies are sneaky," Alia said. "They can seem to mean one thing, but mean the precise opposite."

"But what about the Pipers' Council?" asked Patch. "Can we trust them or not?"

"I think we should play it safe and assume *not*," said Alia. "For now, at least."

There was one thing Patch *didn't* tell Alia and Tobias, however: that they had discovered where obsidiac came from. They knew how the Hamelyn Piper had come by so much of it, and why he had kidnapped a hundred young dragons all those years ago. Barver's mother had left him a letter after her death that led to this truth, and she had instructed him to tell only Lord Drevis about it.

Once Patch had finished, Alia and Tobias sat in stunned silence.

"We came so close to disaster," said Alia at last. She looked at Patch, Wren and Barver. "The courage and wisdom all three of you showed... I'm so very proud of you!"

"You're heroes!" said Tobias. "All of you!"

They quickly agreed on their next course of action: to find out what had become of Erner. This proved to be much simpler than Patch had expected. Barver sent a letter to some of his old acquaintances in the Islands of the Eastern Sea, the kind of people who tended to *know* things, especially if those things involved very serious wrongdoing. They'd hoped for some information about the mercenaries who'd been at Underath's castle, enough to allow them to begin their search; instead, a reply had come detailing the rumours of a captive Custodian Apprentice, and his purchase by a Pirate King.

They had found Erner!

Tobias had ridden hard by horse to Kenniston, the site of the nearest Custodian Elite outpost. There, he had learned that the Custodians were already aware of the rumours, but had no intention of investigating.

"What do you mean, they're doing *nothing*?" Patch had spluttered when Tobias returned.

"They believe it's made-up," said Tobias. "A bit of boasting by a Pirate King that couldn't possibly be true, because nobody could be that stupid. Most of the Custodian Elite has been tasked with tracking down the Hamelyn Piper, and they can't spare anyone to waste on what they think is a wild goose chase."

Patch was outraged. "But you're one of the Eight, Tobias, surely they'd listen to you?"

Tobias was indeed one of the Eight – the famed group of Custodians who had tracked down the Hamelyn Piper more than a decade ago. So too was Alia. But neither of them would meet his gaze. At last, Patch realized his error – heroes they may be, but they had both left the Custodian Elite and sought anonymity once the Hamelyn Piper was (or so they'd thought) safely imprisoned. The burden of their fame had proved too much; they wanted to live their lives as they chose. Only a select few knew who they really were.

"I'm sorry," said Tobias. "If I'd started claiming to be one of the Eight they'd have thought me a madman. We must wait until Rundel wakes. He'll convince them to act. Every Custodian in the world knows him!"

And so they'd waited.

And waited.

The days passed slowly. Each morning, Patch, Wren and Barver would ask if Rundel Stone had woken. Each morning, Alia and Tobias would tell them that he had not. They had done all they could, and now it was just a matter of time. He would wake soon, they promised.

Soon.

Patch spent the time completing a new Pipe to replace the one that the Hamelyn Piper had broken. He didn't feel *complete* without a Pipe, and finishing it made him feel much better. Guilt burned deep inside him, though – over and over, he would replay in his head the moment that he'd pushed Erner into the lake.

Barver, whose wing had been badly injured when he'd flown into the Obsidiac Organ, was starting to heal. He had help from Brother Duffle, who had designed an elaborate hinged splint for his broken wing.

Wren was quiet, and this worried Patch terribly. Of the three of them, she had lost the most. All hope of ever being human again was gone, it seemed, and she would likely be a rat for the rest of her days. She did little more than eat and sleep, and even the prospect of playing her favourite game of Fox and Owls with Barver held no interest for her.

It was Barver who, seeing his friends suffer so, decided that they'd all had *enough* of waiting. The time for action had come.

"I have a plan," he announced one morning. "A plan that absolutely *cannot fail*."

Of course, having spent the previous seven years working as a Protector – a kind of bodyguard – in the Islands of the Eastern Sea, Barver had plenty of contacts there, and quite a few people who owed him their lives. He would return and see what favours he could cash in. "A week or two in the Islands, and I'll know exactly how to get Erner freed," he told them. "You should all come along, I can show you around!"

Tobias scowled. "The Islands aren't somewhere I'd ever want to go."

Sitting beside him, Alia laughed. "That's because you made a few enemies there, as I recall."

Wren suddenly had a wistful look on her little rat face. She started to sign in Merisax, the hand speech that Patch had taught her. *I've always wanted to see the Islands of the*

Eastern Sea, she signed. *Even before I met you, Barver. Some of the best stories my mother read to me are set there. Pirate adventures were always my favourite!*

"Then you must come!" said Barver. "You too, Patch. I promise you'll never be in any danger."

As far as Patch was concerned, the Islands had always sounded *particularly* dangerous. Still, when he'd escaped the dungeons of Tiviscan, the Islands were the only place he could have made a living as a Piper. Before his pardon by the Pipers' Council, he'd been making plans to go with Barver and see what kind of life he could have there. He'd managed to convince himself that it didn't seem *so* bad.

There was something else, though – something that had already made up his mind. Since they'd returned to Marwheel Abbey, all he'd ever seen in Wren's eyes was a look of utter hopelessness.

Now, he saw *excitement*, and a yearning for adventure. If anything could snap Wren out of the despair she'd been engulfed by, surely a trip to such an exotic location would do it.

"You're sure we'll be safe?" said Patch. "I mean, *really* safe?"

Barver grinned. "There's little to fear in the Islands if you're with someone who knows the ways of the place, trust me. And the *food*… Well, I've told you all about the food, haven't I?"

Patch shared a look with Wren, and they both nodded, smiling. Yes, Barver had told them many times about the glorious grub the Islands boasted. It sounded heavenly.

"Then I'm in," said Patch.

I am too, signed Wren.

"You're most certainly not going alone," said Alia. "Barver, while I have complete faith in you, you'll have to spend time in the company of, shall we say, less *desirable* folk, or visit some of the more dubious parts of the Islands. I'd be much happier if there was an extra pair of hands to keep this young duo safe. I'm coming with you."

"But…" started Tobias, and Alia flapped a hand at him.

"Not a word!" she said. "You're perfectly capable of keeping an eye on Rundel while I'm gone. The poison has cleared from his body. What he needs now is the best Healing Piper in the world to ease him back to waking, and, yes, I do mean *you*."

With Barver's wing still in a splint, there was no possibility of flying to the Islands. Instead, it was a day's walk to Grittleham, then a barge down the Platter River to the port of Trelance, where they bought passage on a merchant ship headed for the most westerly of the Islands – the famous Sunfish Bay.

It was a three-day sail, and Patch loved every second

30

of it. The weather helped – a good warm wind and calm seas made for very pleasant conditions aboard.

What he loved most was seeing Wren's bright smile at every wondrous new sight, her dark miserable cloud gone. She marvelled at the porpoises and dolphins leaping from the water alongside the ship.

The crew were utterly charmed by her, thinking she was merely a highly trained rat rather than a rat-shaped girl. Indeed, Wren and Barver both were the stars of the voyage. Griffins have a special place in the hearts of those who make their living at sea; sighting a griffin was considered one of the luckiest omens on any sea journey. And even though Barver was a dracogriff – half-dragon, half-griffin – having him on board left every sailor in high spirits.

Wren was eager to talk to Alia about magic, but Alia's grasp of Merisax hand speech was rather shaky. Patch spent much of each day helping her improve, and she was just as fast a learner as Wren had been.

Each night, Barver and Wren played Fox and Owls in front of an audience of astonished sailors, while Alia sat sipping rum, and Patch looked on with a glad heart. It hadn't been so long, after all, since he'd watched Wren fall to what seemed like certain death, as he'd stood precariously on the vast Obsidiac Organ, Barver flying hard towards him with murderous intent.

He much preferred *this*.

Even the thought of the Hamelyn Piper, still on the loose, didn't prey on his mind – it was the Custodian Elite's problem now, not his. The biggest knot in his stomach came from his guilt about Erner, but they were on their way to do everything in their power to save him.

The journey was so perfect, indeed, that when Sunfish Bay came into view on the horizon Patch felt an odd sort of disappointment. The following few days were almost as wonderful, though – Sunfish Bay itself was an amazing place. Barver set off to meet various shady characters who might help in his quest to secure Erner's release, while Alia, Patch and Wren made the most of the inns that Barver recommended. The food did not disappoint.

From Sunfish Bay, they headed east to Calamity Sands, then north to Hangman's Cove; a short hop to Dysentery Beach (where the food was much better than they feared) was followed by a longer sailing across to Lanyard Island.

Patch was starting to understand the sheer *scale* of the Islands of the Eastern Sea; he'd known there were over two hundred Pirate Kings and Queens, but not that – as Barver told him – there were over *ten thousand* islands, ranging from half a mile across to several *hundred*.

At last, Barver declared that it was time to head for Pengersick itself, where Erner was being held. "As it turns out, someone I know very well is highly regarded by King Arpie Noss," he said. "I'll go and see how things are.

You three can stop off at The Ungrateful Worm and try their famous roasted natter-clumps, the best shellfish you'll ever taste! *Delicious*."

By evening of the following day, they had reached Pengersick. Barver left them at The Ungrateful Worm, where they found a quiet corner and ordered up some natter-clumps. These had turned out to be probably the strangest thing Patch had ever eaten, odd little fleshy lumps that were fish-like in texture but tasted of juicy pork.

Then, halfway through their meal, Alia went and put her foot in it. When the innkeeper came over to offer her some mead, she asked him a very simple question.

"I heard the King of these parts has a captive Custodian Piper," she said. "Doesn't that worry anyone?"

All conversation died away at once; every pair of eyes was looking right at their little table.

Alia's face fell. "Oh," she said.

In no time at all, they'd been accused of spying for the Custodian Elite, clapped in manacles, had their heads covered, and were being marched off to the King. Alia and Patch had both been searched; Wren had scampered halfway down Patch's trouser leg just in time to avoid being discovered, and Patch had managed not to shriek. Their captors had taken Alia's knapsack; to anyone versed in

33

sorcery, it would have been blindingly obvious that the bag was chock-a-block with magical items. To their captors, it had just been some bits of plants, a few strange stones and some funny-looking lumps of metal.

Patch was immensely glad that he'd left his own bag, with his Pipe inside, tied to Barver's harness packs. If they'd found *that*... Well, finding a Pipe would have been taken as clear proof of guilt, and he really didn't want to think about what their captors might have done. Or *tried* to do, at any rate – Alia certainly wouldn't let them come to any real harm. After all, at Gemspar Mountain he'd seen what kind of power she could conjure up with her bare hands.

"Don't worry," Alia kept whispering to him and Wren, as they were marched along. "When we see the King I'll sort everything out."

And then came the throne room.

And the trapdoor.

And now...

High above, on the wooden platform, King Arpie looked down at them and grinned. Patch could see the despair on Erner's face. He also noticed that everyone on the platform kept turning to stare out into the dark shadows of the cavern beyond, as if expecting something.

"Um, Alia…" said Patch. "What do you think is happening?"

Alia stared at the King. "When we fell, I presumed we'd landed in a dungeon." She started to click her fingers, and Patch had no idea why. "Now, well…it seems we have an audience."

"An audience for what?" said Patch.

"*Exactly*," said Alia, clicking her fingers more frantically.

"Uh, what are you doing?"

"Damn," said Alia. "*Damn*. Not a fizz. Not even the littlest *spark*." She looked out into the dark cavern, and seemed frightened. Patch realized he'd never actually seen her look scared before.

"Spark?" said Patch. "You mean…"

She rubbed her fingers together and frowned. "Nothing's there! *No magic!*" Suddenly she held up her wrists, glaring at the manacles. "Of all the stupid, *stupid* luck… Clag iron! Has to be!"

Behind him, coming from the depths of the cavern, Patch heard a distant noise. It was a *clunk*, little more, but the audience high above them started to chatter, their faces oddly eager. Erner looked sick.

"Clag *what*?" said Patch.

Alia rattled her manacles. "Sometimes cheaply forged iron gets just the right taint of quartz. It weakens the metal, you see, that's why it's cheap, but it just happens to *ground*

35

a Sorcerer, drain their power!" Concentrating hard, she clicked her fingers. A glowing speck floated up and vanished. "See! Almost nothing left! I have to get these manacles off before…"

Before…

There was another noise from the depths of the cavern. This time, it was the echoing sound of a *roar*.

Terror launched Patch into action. He looked around for a moment, then turned to Alia. "Quickly, set your wrists on the ground!" he said. "I have an idea!" He hurried to the cavern wall as Alia kneeled and held out her wrists. Patch ran back, kneeled in front of her, and raised a large rock high above his head. It wasn't easy, given that he was in manacles too. "Now hold very still!"

Alia glared at him and pulled her arms back. "Absolutely not!"

"You said the metal's weak! You said we have to get it off your hands!"

"You're as likely to *break* my wrists as free them, lad."

An odd change came over the audience above them. The chattering stopped, all eyes focused on the shadows.

Alia and Patch stood and slowly turned around. *Something* was out there, but…

They saw a flash of white, rising in the darkness, and watched it go up, up, up, *soaring,* and all the while coming towards them. It started to come down.

With a great *splat*, the object hit the ground ten feet away.

It was the head of a cow. The cow had been dead for a while – the ragged ends of the flesh at the neck were dried, and there was an awful smell of rot coming from it. The nose had been chewed and the eyes were gone.

Patch stared at it. Alia stared at it. The audience gave a cheer of excitement.

Then another noise became clear to Patch's ears: a regular thumping, the sound of great feet galloping towards them.

Fear locked Patch's limbs in place. Alia was still trying to click her fingers, to no avail.

He wondered if he could lip-Pipe something – there were Songs called Shrills that could scare off hungry animals, and certainly a Push Song would come in handy right now. He'd only ever tried those with a Pipe, never with his lips alone, but his lips were too dry; he couldn't get a single note.

And from the dark emerged a vast beast, twice the height of a human. Four-legged, its dark hide was covered in what seemed to be spikes, long and sharp, from almost every inch of skin. Its mouth had two enormous tusks that stuck out to the sides, five feet long at least. The rest of the mouth was a jumbled assortment of horribly jagged teeth; thick gollops of drool poured out as the creature ran towards them.

Above the mouth, the eyes of the monster were huge and black, and sat atop a nose that dripped green mucus.

The monster came at them full speed, but stopped at the cow's head. It sneezed in the cloud of dust that its running had thrown into the air, and for a moment it regarded Alia and Patch with a terrible malevolence.

Alia reached for Patch's hand, and squeezed it. *The end has come*, Patch thought. *After all we've been through.* He thought of Wren, and hoped she was safe, wherever she'd ended up in the fall through the trapdoor.

Then the monster sneezed again and grabbed the cow's head between its teeth, before running back into the dark.

Above them, the crowd whooped and clapped, enjoying the show.

Patch looked back to Alia. She'd kneeled down again, her manacled wrists out in front of her.

"Use the rock," she whispered, not taking her eyes from the dark. "*Use the rock!*"

3

WHAT DUNDER LIKES MOST

Laughter came from the platform above. "Normally this is when people try to run away," cried the King. "Perhaps you think you can defeat the creature with your bare hands?"

Patch ignored him and swung the rock down towards Alia's wrists. He missed completely, the rock thudding into the sandy floor.

Alia winced. "Concentrate, Patch! Take your time!" She threw a quick glance at the shadows that had swallowed the monster. "Also, hurry!"

He nodded and tried again. The manacles consisted of two pieces of metal connected at a hinge; each piece was a thick strip of iron with indentations for the prisoner's wrists. A padlock fastened the other end of the strips, and it was the padlock that Patch was aiming for. This time he connected with it, and cheered.

Alia yelped. He'd grazed her arm and drawn blood. The padlock wasn't even dented.

He caught Alia's eye. "Keep going?" he asked.

Alia glanced feverishly at the shadows. "Yes!" she said. "Absolutely *keep going*."

He swung again, and hit the lock full-square. A chunk of the rock broke away, but the lock itself showed no sign of damage.

"Uh oh," said Alia, and Patch turned to look. There it was: the distant white shape, going up and up. The cow's head was coming their way once more.

Patch turned back and tried again, and again, but the padlock didn't even seem scratched. Then he heard a growl, and the thunder of feet, or hooves, or whatever the creature had on the ends of its legs, because really, when he'd seen it first, he'd been paying *much* more attention to the spikes and the tusks and the teeth and the eyes.

"Please, Patch," said Alia, her gaze locked on the movement behind Patch that he really didn't want to see. "Please. This time."

Patch nodded and tried to ignore the rumbling approach of death. He raised the rock, and just as he was about to bring it down he stopped. He'd been going about this all wrong – the padlock wasn't the weak part, because it wasn't made of clag iron.

He took the chunk of rock that had broken off and placed it under the manacles, at the other side – where the hinge was – then aimed there.

"Hold still," he said. Alia did. He swung the rock with every bit of strength he could dredge up, and he *felt* the hinge give as he hit it. Another quick swing, and the hinge pin fell out. The manacles came apart, and Alia was free!

She rose. The thundering of the monster's approach filled Patch's ears.

"Get behind me," said Alia. Patch moved quickly; he saw just how close the creature was (and *trotters*, he thought, now that he could see its feet again). Alia raised her hands, moving her fingers quickly, shapes being traced out in the light that was coming from them, but it was still terribly weak. "Come on," she muttered. "*Come on…*"

The creature reached the cow's head. It looked at the two of them and bared its teeth in a sneer. It opened its horrible mouth and let out a frighteningly strange noise, somewhere between a bark and a hiss.

The light around Alia's hands was growing, but Patch could sense it wouldn't do much good, not yet – she needed more time. The creature took a step towards them. Alia screwed her face up in frustration and anger, and let out a shriek that made Patch jump.

The creature stepped back. It bent down and gripped the cow's head between its teeth, then ran into the dark again.

Patch let out the breath he'd been holding. "How did you manage that?" he said.

"I'm not sure I did anything much," said Alia. "I suspect that creature does whatever it feels like doing." They both looked around to the wooden platform, as a great shout came from the King.

"*What?*" the King cried. "A *bit* of playing around with them is great fun, but this is taking *far* too long! Hello out there? Mrs Larkweather? Hello? Seriously, get on with it!"

Patch gave Alia a bemused look. *Mrs Larkweather?* he was thinking. *They call that thing Mrs Larkweather?*

And just then, he heard something strange in the distant dark. He stepped away from Alia, towards the noise.

"Where are you…" started Alia, but Patch kept going, and kept listening.

It sounded like: *whojabootyfuldunder*. And: *diddydiddy diddums*. Then: *wasdunderlike*. Then: *tikkytikkytumtums*.

And again: *tikkytikkytumtums*.

Patch took another step, then another, and the sounds in the cavern behind him grew fainter – the King, mostly, shouting complaints to Mrs Larkweather. The sounds in *front* of Patch grew much louder.

"Oogy boogy diddums!" said a voice. "What does Dunder like most? Does Dunder like dat? Yes, he does! Tickly tumtums, tickly tumtums! He likes dat, doesn't he? Yes, he does!"

42

It wasn't the *words* that made Patch's mouth fall open in shock. It was the fact that he thought he recognized the *voice*.

"Barver?" he called. "*Barver?*"

Alia hurried over to him. "You've got to be kidding me," she said. In the darkness far in front of them, in the deep gloom, a head was suddenly visible, popping up from what seemed like a hole in the ground, or a sharp drop in the cavern floor.

Patch heaved a sigh of relief. It *was* Barver.

"Patch?" came the echoing reply. "What are you doing here?"

Patch smiled, but not for long: a moment later, another shape appeared, as the monster leaped from the hole and, snarling, ran right towards him. Alia weaved her hands in the air, and this time they trailed a purple light that had a curious solidity to it. Confidence had returned to her expression, even though the creature was bearing down on them.

"Dunder!" came the voice of a woman, slightly trembly. "Dunder, you stop right there! *Now!*"

The creature halted at once and sat on its haunches, panting. Its great tongue lolled from its terrible mouth.

"It's like a puppy..." said Alia. "But from *Hell*."

Patch nodded. That summed it up very well indeed.

Barver walked slowly towards them; beside him was an old woman, relying on a cane for support.

"Mrs Larkweather, I'm guessing," mumbled Alia. "Presumably the owner of this…creature."

Dunder the Hell-puppy watched Mrs Larkweather and Barver approach, and was certainly very happy as the woman drew near to it and reached out a hand, rubbing its side hard in among the lethal-looking spikes.

"Good boy," said Mrs Larkweather.

Alia started to walk closer, and Patch followed with some reluctance. Even though Alia had recovered her powers, the sight of Dunder was still very unsettling.

Barver was scowling at them, Patch realized.

"I think you two need to explain yourselves!" said the dracogriff.

Alia gave a little cough. "Um, I may have made a *slight* mistake and mentioned Erner to someone while we were in The Ungrateful Worm. We were brought before the King and accused of being Custodian spies. The natter-clumps were delicious, by the way."

"Oh, *don't* try to change the subject," said Barver. "All you had to do was keep Patch and Wren safe, and now look at you! A blink of an eye away from horrible death!" He glanced at Patch and frowned. "Where *is* Wren?"

"I haven't seen her since we fell down the trapdoor into this cavern," said Patch.

"We'll find her," said Barver. "I'm sure she's fine."

Alia nodded towards Mrs Larkweather. "Is she your

44

contact, Barver? The one you said was highly regarded by the King?"

"Ah, yes!" said Barver. "Allow me to introduce Herdy Larkweather. Herdy, my friends Alia and Patch."

Mrs Larkweather bowed her head. "At your service. This here – " she nodded to the creature – "is Dunder. He's a big softy, really, although he *would* have torn you both limb from limb in an instant if he'd felt like it. Not with me here, mind! He's very obedient, is Dunder, so you've nothing to worry about now."

Alia and Patch shared a look. Dunder wasn't *really* what the words "big softy" brought to mind. "Good to meet you," said Alia. "Interesting animal you have there. Any idea what species it is?"

Mrs Larkweather fussed Dunder's chin. "None whatsoever," she said. "But me and him have been together for twenty years! He was a lot smaller when I found him, and had none of them spikes, but he grew. Goodness, he grew!"

"They used to work for the Pirate Queen of Ordin," said Barver. "That's where I know Herdy and Dunder from, you see. Far to the south. I was very surprised to hear that they were in Pengersick."

"We needed to move somewhere cooler," Mrs Larkweather explained. "Dunder started to overheat too easily. Came up here when it was King Popper's rule, only last year. Nice big cavern, they told me, lovely and cosy with plenty of ventilation, and they weren't wrong!"

"Yes," said Alia, not holding back on the sarcasm. "Lovely and *cosy*, for all the executions. That's what you two do for a living, yes? People get dropped down here, and everyone watches as they die?"

Mrs Larkweather seemed quite hurt by Alia's tone. "Well, really," she said. "The *threat* of Dunder is usually plenty by itself. Before King Arpie, an actual execution was a rare thing. But I'm afraid Arpie turned out to be quite keen on them." She stopped and looked at something past Patch. "Oh, heck, speak of the devil…"

Patch and Alia turned to see King Arpie striding towards them from the far wall of the cavern, with a handful of others in his wake. In all the commotion, Patch had forgotten about the Pirate King; he seemed more than a little angry, and was cursing as he walked, using quite a variety of phrases that Patch had never heard before.

At last, the King and his entourage reached them; he paused for a moment, trying to compose himself. "Mrs Larkweather," he managed. "I am *very* disappointed. Do you know how much your…*creature* costs to feed?" Mrs Larkweather opened her mouth to reply, but the King answered his own question: "Three cows a week! *Three!* And what do I expect in return? Just that whenever I send people down here to be executed, they end up dead in as

46

entertaining a fashion as you and your pet can manage, as a lesson to anyone else who dares to betray me, steal from me, or maybe even just get on my nerves! Do you understand?"

This time the King waited for Mrs Larkweather's timid response. "I understand, Your Majesty."

"And do you know what I really do *not* expect?" said the King. "That instead of killing them horribly, you get into a nice little *chat* with them! What next?" He seemed to notice Barver for the first time, and sneered. "Were you and your *friend* going to offer them some tea?"

Mrs Larkweather kept quiet.

"Well, answer me, you idiot!" yelled the King. He stepped towards her and jabbed her in the shoulder with his staff. "Answer your King!"

"Sorry, Your Majesty," said Mrs Larkweather, sounding close to tears.

Up to this point, what had held Patch's attention was the sheer gobsmacking arrogance of the King. Suddenly, though, he became aware of what Alia and Barver were looking at, utterly *fascinated*.

Dunder.

Dunder, who was watching the King with narrowed eyes, as the King made his owner very, very upset.

The man nearest the King had also spotted this, and spoke up with a tremble in his voice. "Um, sire..." said the man. "I think, perhaps..."

"Oh, do shut your face, Skreep," said the King. "I'm King! I'm allowed to lose my temper." He turned back to Mrs Larkweather. "Now," said the King. "I'm going to go back to the viewing gallery, and I expect there to be a nice little show, ending in plenty of blood and guts. Have you got that?" He jabbed her again. Skreep winced and took a step backwards, as did everyone in the King's entourage. There was a barely audible growl coming from Dunder's throat.

"Yes, sire," said Mrs Larkweather.

"Good," said the King, sounding much calmer all of a sudden. "Now that we've sorted out this little misunderstanding, I think we should—"

He didn't get to say anything else.

In one move, Dunder opened his vast mouth and brought his head down, and the King disappeared into the creature's maw. Then Dunder sat back up. There was some muffled screaming.

"Dunder!" said Mrs Larkweather, horrified. "You put the King down right this second! You bad, bad boy!"

Dunder looked ashamed, but he kept his mouth firmly shut.

"I mean it!" said Mrs Larkweather. "Put the King down right now! And don't chew him! Don't you *dare* chew the King!"

Dunder chewed. The King's entourage gasped. Barver and Alia were enjoying every moment.

"*Put him down right now!*" shrieked Mrs Larkweather, wagging a firm finger of disapproval, and at last Dunder obeyed.

He opened his mouth, bent forward, and spat.

Out came the King. Patch looked, but not too closely. King Arpie Noss wasn't going to be doing any more ruling. Or *breathing*, for that matter.

"Oh, Arpie," said Skreep with a sigh. "You daft sod."

Dunder sneezed, then coughed, and out came Arpie's crown, covered in slobber and rather dented. The Hell-puppy whimpered and looked lovingly at Mrs Larkweather.

Mrs Larkweather, though, looked sick. "Oh, Dunder, what've you gone and done?"

"Well, then," said Barver, stepping forward. He gave Dunder a rub under his chin, then picked up the rotting cow's head from the ground nearby. "Go on, boy, fetch it!" he said, and threw the cow's head as far as he could into the dark depths of the cavern. He turned to Skreep. "I reckon you should gather your King's body while you have the chance."

"Reckon so," said Skreep. He nodded to the others who'd come with the King, and reluctantly they picked up Arpie's corpse and started to make their way to the far wall.

"Oh, *heavens*, Barver," said Mrs Larkweather. "Whatever will become of me and Dunder? We killed the King!"

49

"I wouldn't worry," said Barver, looking at Skreep. "I think Arpie Noss brought on his own end, don't you?"

Skreep heaved a sigh and nodded. "I was Arpie's first mate for fifteen years, and when he took the crown he made me his advisor. Then he ignored every word I said." He was watching his friend's body, as its bearers reached the door in the cavern wall. "He enjoyed being King. Worst thing that ever happened to him."

"And now a new ruler must be chosen," said Barver. "Whoever it ends up being, I'll have to have a word with them about my friend Erner, the Custodian Piper your old King decided to keep prisoner. And about my two friends here, who were chucked down into this cavern to die horribly."

Skreep gave him a long appraising look. "Well," he said. "I'd expect a new King or Queen to release all of them. New monarchs tend to be generous like that. Especially when the prisoners have already fled..." He winked, and Barver winked back. "I'll bring your friend down."

"But what about me and Dunder?" said Mrs Larkweather.

Skreep smiled. "Oh, I think you two will keep doing what you do best. Just much less *often,* I hope, if we get a better ruler." He turned and made his way towards the cavern wall.

Barver grinned at Alia and Patch. "Maybe the rescue didn't go according to plan, but we got there in the end.

Now we should find Wren, and get going once Erner's here."

A moment later, Dunder reappeared and dropped the cow's head at Barver's feet; Barver picked it up and threw it once more. Mrs Larkweather watched her pet chase after it, and there was only love in her eyes.

"He'll be sad not to have as many executions," she said wistfully. "I mean, I know it's for the best, but he'll miss it. Dunder does like a tummy tickle, but I think what he likes *most* is eating people. Or *chewing* them, at any rate."

4

MISSION ACCOMPLISHED

While Barver played a little more with Dunder, Alia and Patch walked to the cavern wall, to the hole that led up to the trapdoor. The wooden balcony high above them was deserted now.

"Lift up your hands," Alia told Patch. He did, and she pointed a finger at the manacles that still bound him. A stream of purple sparks corkscrewed out from her fingertip, and the manacles popped open.

Patch rubbed his wrists, grateful. Then he climbed into the hole, onto the steeply inclined smooth rock. "Wren?" he called. "Can you hear me?"

Alia climbed in beside him. "Anything?"

Patch shook his head. "We could do with some light."

Alia created a small bright orb. It floated up, revealing

the tunnel curling out of sight above them. They listened for a moment, and suddenly Patch heard a distant squeaking. He recognized it at once.

"Wren!" he shouted. The squeaking continued. She sounded scared, he thought – lost. "That's her!"

"Keep calling," said Alia. "I'll send up some more light." One after another, she created more orbs, while Patch shouted Wren's name.

The squeaking changed, growing more excited and less fearful. At last, Wren slid down the rock and landed in front of them, covered in cobwebs. Patch picked her up, dusting her off before he and Alia climbed back down to the cavern floor.

"I was so worried!" he told Wren.

She sneezed, and started to sign a reply in Merisax, but she stopped, staring out into the cavern at Dunder running about. She squeaked and pointed, then signed: *A monster!*

"Don't worry about him," said Patch. "He's a friend of Barver. All that matters is this: we're leaving and Erner's coming with us. What happened to you?"

I landed on a ledge near the top, she signed. *It's a bit of a maze up there, and…*

Patch waited for more, but she seemed suddenly distant. "Are you okay?" he asked.

It's nothing, she signed, and although Patch could see that *something* was wrong, it would have to wait.

A loud clang sounded from the armoured door nearby. It opened, and Skreep emerged, Erner leaning heavily on him for support.

Patch hurried over to them, with Wren on his shoulder and Alia beside him, and they all stared at Erner's appearance. From this close, it was shocking how frail he looked.

"Here you go," said Skreep. "He can barely walk, and he needs tending to."

Alia glared. "I should kill you where you stand! Look what state he's in! The poor lad!"

Patch expected some kind of denial, but Skreep nodded. He looked tired. "I tried my best to keep him well," said the advisor. "But there's only so much disobedience a King can put up with, if you get me."

Erner raised his head, and saw them. His smile was broad, though he looked horribly fragile. "Patch…" he said. "Wren…" He took a step forward and almost fell, but Patch caught him, and Alia took his other arm.

"Don't tarry long," said Skreep. "A pirate territory without a King becomes a complicated place very quickly. Complicated, and violent. Safe journey to you all. Especially you, Erner. I wish I could've talked sense into Arpie, and Lord knows I tried, but you're free now."

Erner gave him a weak nod in reply, and Skreep hurried back through the door, locking it again behind him.

With obvious effort, Erner looked up at Patch, struggling to speak. "Why, Patch?" he managed. "*Why?*" And then he sagged, unconscious.

For Patch, the physical weight of Erner was nothing compared to the weight of the guilt he felt at what he'd done to his friend. Soon enough, he would have to explain himself, and hope for some kind of forgiveness. He dreaded it.

They left Pengersick as quickly as they could, and Barver insisted on taking them to Sorkil Island.

The business of Sorkil was fishing, rather than piracy, and the people were renowned for their friendly nature and generosity. This struck Patch as an odd thing, here in the midst of bloodthirsty pirates, but Barver explained: the pirates of the region knew better than to mess with their source of fresh natter-clumps, lobsters and other gifts of the ocean. As a result, Sorkil was a haven for those pirates who suddenly realized that they much preferred a life of fishing to one of, say, *murder*.

That was exactly why Barver had brought them here. They needed a place to hole up for a week or so, to let Erner recover before they set off on the much longer voyage back to Marwheel Abbey.

As soon as they came ashore, Barver made some enquiries. Within the hour, they'd rented a small cottage on the hill overlooking the port, with an outbuilding large enough for Barver. It was a simple enough home, but it had all they needed: beds and warmth. With Erner safely tucked in, Alia sent Barver, Patch and Wren out with a list of needed supplies, giving them more than enough money to cover it.

The folk in the port were eager to meet Barver, of course – they were sailors, after all, and while a dracogriff wasn't quite as big a deal as a *proper* griffin, he was still enough to create plenty of excitement.

When they found a suitable shop, they handed over Alia's list and sought somewhere to have a bite to eat. An inn on the edge of the wharf was perfect; they sat at an outside table, facing the sea, and ordered up some food. Patch and Wren opted for a mutton stew with some bread, Barver a whole smoke-roasted pig. He was hungry.

They ate mostly in silence, save for the crunch of Barver's teeth as he devoured the pig from the head down, bone and all, while Patch and Wren watched him with amusement.

"Sometimes a nice bit of bone just hits the spot," said Barver, a little defensive. "You know what it's like."

"Of course," said Patch. He and Wren shared a smile.

All too soon, the food was gone, save for one last trotter, and their stomachs were pleasantly full. They sipped away at some small ale, and Barver raised his tankard in a toast.

"To being safe again," he said, and the others agreed. "Although…" He shook his head, reluctant to go on.

"What?" said Patch.

Barver looked at Wren, concerned. "You've seemed distracted ever since we left Pengersick. Something's on your mind."

Wren nodded slowly. *You're right*, she signed. *Something happened. When we fell down the trapdoor, I landed on a ledge. There was a small tunnel, maybe an old drain, and I thought it'd be sensible to follow that rather than just hurl myself down after Patch and Alia.*

She paused.

After a while, I reached an opening. A wide chamber of some kind, a sheer drop of a hundred feet or more, but I could see another opening on the other side. And there was something there.

She stopped again, and Patch could tell she was actually *afraid*.

"What was it?" he asked.

A ghost, signed Wren.

Barver's eyes widened. He really didn't like that kind of thing. "A ghost?" he said, sounding nervous.

Wren nodded. *One of the rats from Patterfall,* she signed. *Even from that distance I could tell. She was staring at me. Staring! I couldn't move! I was terrified! And then, suddenly, she was gone.*

Wren was trembling. Patch took her in his hands and tried to comfort her. "You were just seeing things," he said. "You were scared. It's okay."

I know I was just seeing things! she scowled. *But it brought it all back to me. I ended up taking charge of all the rats, and I guided them to Patterfall. To their deaths!*

Patch shook his head. "Wren, I was the one trying to rid the village of the rats, remember? And if I'd managed to Pipe the rats over that waterfall, you would have died too! You can't feel guilty about how things turned out."

It was my fault they were trapped in the village, she signed. *The whole situation was because of me! My plan was to find them a proper home, somewhere safe where food was plentiful, and instead I led them to a frozen village and an awful death!*

Patch thought back to the moment in Patterfall when Rundel Stone, the great Virtus Piper, had played his Song to get rid of the rat plague.

The Dispersal, it was called – a Song that had, in times past, been a Song of Execution. Difficult to perform, its effect was to completely destroy the target, reducing it to its smallest components almost instantly, the fragments scattered over a vast distance, spread so thinly that not even a speck of blood would remain. When Rundel Stone had played the Dispersal that day, its power had been extraordinary. If Patch hadn't helped Wren, she would have died, without any doubt.

"I don't think they suffered," Patch told her. "You know that. They wouldn't even have known what happened."

Wren shook her head. *It was the look in that ghost rat's eyes,* she signed. *It brought it home just how bad I still feel about it. I failed them all.*

"Guilt is a terrible burden," said Barver, frowning. "But you must never forget that it means you're a *good* person, Wren! Do you think the crooked or the evil truly feel it, even for a second? No! They've long cut the guilt out of their hearts. The Hamelyn Piper has never lost a moment's sleep because of what he's done, I promise you that. For the rest of us, it's a hard thing to carry, and we're all burdened with guilt, all three of us."

Patch nodded. "I'm certainly dreading the moment I have to explain myself to Erner," he said. "But what are *you* feeling guilty about, Barver?"

"Bringing you two along on this trip!" said the dracogriff. "Things went very badly back there! If Dunder had eaten you and Alia, that *would* have been my fault." He looked sick at the thought.

Wren gave a squeak of disagreement. *Alia's fault, to be fair,* she signed. *She was the one who put her foot in it, remember?*

"Perhaps," said Barver. "Still, each of us has our share of guilt." He picked up the trotter that was all that remained of his meal, but as he crunched on it, a strange expression formed on his face: a dreamy, far-away look. He swallowed, then raised his eyes to the sky.

Wren frowned. *Is he okay?* she signed to Patch.

Patch shook his head. "I have no idea. Hey, Barver? What's the…"

Suddenly Barver stood tall, his wings stretching out beside him. He called out with a great tuneful cry that neither Patch nor Wren had heard from him before. *Kikikaa*, it sounded like, over and over; then there was a rush of air as a huge shadow passed low overhead, Barver's call being returned.

For a moment, Patch felt terrified, thinking back to Tiviscan Castle as the dragons attacked, but then he smiled as he saw what had made the shadow.

A griffin! Flying just above the rooftops of the port, it continued to call, making two wide circles above, before heading west and disappearing over a low rise.

Everyone in the port was cheering.

Where did it go? signed Wren.

"Back to his ship, I suspect," said Barver. "He's almost certainly a pilot."

What's a pilot? asked Wren.

This, at least, was something Patch knew about from his studies as a trainee Piper in Tiviscan. "That's what you call a ship's navigator," he said. "Especially through the most dangerous seas. And griffins make the best pilots of all!

60

It's why sailors count them as good luck. *Griffin* pilots can fly high and signal to the ship how to pass through the most terrifying Treacheries!"

Treacheries were the greatest threat to shipping in many places of the world – deadly rock formations that lurked just out of sight, ready to rip open the keel and drown all on board.

"There it is!" cried Barver, pointing out to sea. A large ship had just appeared around a headland, and the people in the port started cheering again when they saw it. A few seconds later, the griffin was visible once more as it swooped down and landed on the vessel.

Just as the ship was tying up at the docks, the shopkeeper's lad arrived with a sackful of items, explaining that the heavier goods were still waiting for them at the shop.

"I suppose we should get back," said Barver. "We've been out long enough, Alia will be wondering where we got to."

Wren could see a wistful look in Barver's eyes, as he watched the pilot griffin. *Don't you want to say hello to that pilot?* she signed. *I mean, it would be rude not to, surely? We can pick up the rest of the shopping on the way home.*

Barver seemed agitated. "I don't know," he said. "I'm… Well, I'm a bit shy when it comes to other griffins. I mean, a greeting call is one thing, but actually *meeting* them…?"

Patch and Wren stared at him. "You?" said Patch. "*Shy*? Now I've heard everything."

"I lived all my life among dragons before I left the Dragon Territories," said Barver. "My father was the only griffin I'd ever met, until I came to the Islands."

"You *should* go and say hello," said Patch.

Absolutely, added Wren.

Barver weighed things up for a moment, before nodding. "I suppose you're right, it would seem rude not to introduce myself." And then, as if it was an afterthought and of absolutely no importance, he said: "My father was a pilot too, you know."

Patch and Wren looked at each other, dumbfounded. Barver had only ever mentioned his father once, not long after they'd returned to Marwheel Abbey; they'd been speaking of their families, and Patch had told them about how his parents had died. When he asked Barver about his father, Barver's reply was short. "He was lost at sea," was all he said, and his tone made it rather clear it was a topic to avoid in future. So they had.

Now here he was, trying to sound indifferent while he told them more than he'd ever done before.

"A pilot?" said Patch, as casually as he could manage. "We didn't know that. Come on, let's go and say hello."

5

AWKWARD...

The ship was called the *Heaven's Reach*.

Patch, Wren and Barver stood on the edge of the dock by the stern of the ship, watching the forty or so crew unloading their vessel; the crew sang while one of their number played shanties on a tin whistle. Patch yearned to join in – the musician had a decent enough way with rhythm, and the melodies were solid, but Patch reckoned he could have raised things to a much higher standard, even on a tin whistle.

And with his *Pipe*, well... He thought of the Songs that could boost the energy of a flagging labourer – all of them had joyous melodies, and he couldn't help but smile.

Barrel after barrel was hoisted up from the bowels of the vessel, their salt-packed catch carried down the boarding ramps to the dockside, and even though the crew looked tired, they were all high-spirited now that their expedition was at an end.

"I wonder how long a rest they get," said Patch. "Before they have to set out again."

"Two days is all," boomed a voice from behind them. "Then it's back to sea for the lot of us!"

They turned to see the griffin, leaning against the ship and smiling slyly at them. He was much bigger than Barver, his feathers brown and black. "The name's Shanny Pledger," said the griffin. He stepped closer and offered his hands to Barver. "And yours, my dracogriff friend? I heard you call!"

Barver shook his hands – both hands at once, which was the griffin way. "Barver Knopferkerkle," he said. "This is Patch, and the rat is called Wren." Patch and Barver always felt slightly uncomfortable introducing Wren as if she was just an ordinary rat, but Wren had a simple rule – if she wanted people to be told that she was actually a girl who'd been cursed, she would wave to them and take a bow, then let Patch or Barver explain. Most of the time, she preferred to go unnoticed.

"Good to meet you all," said Shanny. Suddenly he turned to the crew on the deck and yelled: "Watch the yaw on the barrels, you fools, you'll tip the lot!" He turned back and smiled. "I have to shout at them now and again, to remind

them I'm watching. Now tell me, and tell me honestly…
what do you think of my ship?" He strode to the hull and
patted it with affection.

"*Your* ship?" said Barver. "You're the captain?"

"Aye," said Shanny. "The *Heaven's Reach* is mine.
Captain and pilot, all in one! We work the Outlying
Treacheries, the most dangerous waters in the whole of the
Eastern Sea! Weeks at a time, we spend there, finding the
rarest things the sea can offer. Pearls the size of apples, and
that's not the half of it! Angry storms, waves as high as
mountains, and I wouldn't live any other way! Ever thought
of piloting yourself, Barver?"

Barver shook his head. "It does sound like a good life,
but I've not got the loft for piloting. Being a Protector has
proved much more my thing."

"A Protector!" said Shanny. "An exciting life, by all
accounts! I have to admit, it appealed to me as a youngster,
although it likely goes against a Griffin's Covenant – or so
my father told me. I suppose that as a dracogriff, you have
more options open to you."

"My dad was a pilot," said Barver. After a pause, he
added: "You didn't know him, by any chance? His name
was Gaverry Tenso."

It was strange to Patch, hearing the name of Barver's
father for the first time.

"Now it's a funny thing," said Shanny. "It's said that

humans outnumber dragons by a thousand to one, and dragons outnumber griffins by the same, so people *always* think every griffin knows every other. That's not true, of course, not by a long way, but your father, I *did* know. Gaverry Tenso was one of the best pilots I ever worked with! I spent a year as a pilot in the Southern Churns, off the southernmost point of the Dragon Territories. Thirty years ago, this was! There was good fishing down there. Humans crewed the ships, of course – I mean, dragons love their fish, but they're *terrible* seafarers."

Barver nodded, a distant look in his eyes. "Dad told me about the Churns," he said. "Rocks would tear the bottom out of any vessel without a pilot! All kinds of ships would hire him. That was how my parents met – a dragon settlement on one of the large islands had an outbreak of disease and needed medicine, but storms were raging and the conditions were impossible for a direct flight. Only a piloted ship stood any chance of making it through in time. But none would risk it!" He took a long breath, nodding. "My mother was an advisor to the Triumvirate, and they sent her to deal with it." The Triumvirate were the monarchs of the Dragon Territories – three dragons who ruled as one. "My dad was the only pilot willing to help."

"A Triumvirate advisor!" said Shanny. "I'm impressed! I'd come up north by then, but I imagine your parents made a fine couple."

Barver smiled. "They did."

"Well, it doesn't surprise me that Gaverry was the one to volunteer," said Shanny. "Your father was brimful with courage."

Wren caught Patch's eye and signed: *Ask him if he's got stories, Barver would love that!*

Patch nodded. "I'm sure you've got plenty of stories about him, Shanny," he said.

"I do indeed!" said Shanny, and Wren was very pleased with her idea, although Barver's next words made things take a rather dark turn.

"Do you know how he died?" said Barver, his eyes sadder than Patch or Wren could ever recall seeing. "The details of it, I mean... My mother only told me he was lost at sea. She couldn't talk about it without crying, and I never heard more than that."

For a moment Shanny seemed taken aback, but at last he gave a slow nod and began: "Of course, lad. It's a tale familiar to all pilots, and you deserve to know. The port of Darnass Wenning has the greatest fishing fleet in the world, and two pilots are needed to keep it safe in the far reaches of the Great Grey Ocean. There are such Treacheries there, one griffin alone couldn't hope to spot them all. Your father was one of their pilots; him, and another griffin called Tundin Wrass. They hit a storm, the kind you get once in a lifetime, while they were out deep among Treacheries.

Rocks everywhere, and lightning raging, but the pilot griffins both kept flying, guiding the ships between the rocks. Lightning brought your father's end, hit him full-square and down he went, under the waves. The last the fleet saw of Tundin Wrass, he was searching the water in vain. But the fleet made it home. They lost four vessels out of twenty, sixty human lives gone and both pilots, but it could have been hundreds! Your father and Tundin Wrass were heroes, Barver. You should always be proud of him."

Barver nodded, silent.

Patch stepped closer to Shanny, and whispered: "Um, do you have any *pleasant* stories about his dad?"

Shanny nodded, and whispered back, "My thoughts exactly, don't worry."

Patch clapped his hands theatrically. "Well," he said, nice and loud, "I think me and Wren should get back to Alia with what supplies I can carry. Barver, why don't you stay with Shanny a while longer, then collect the heavy stuff on your way home?"

"Uh, okay…if you're sure?" said Barver. There was a definite emotional sheen to his eyes. "And if that's fine with you, Shanny?"

"Oh, it'll be my honour, lad!" said Shanny. There was a loud *thump* from on deck, and a huge barrel swung out from the ship, dangling from the hoist, spilling seawater from the top as it went. Shanny scowled. "Secure that grandel!" he cried. "Keep it where it is, you buffoons, I'll guide it down myself!"

He strode across the dock, and stretched up – the great barrel was easily within his reach, and he steadied it, ignoring the water splashing onto him, then did as he'd promised, guiding it safely down.

Patch, Wren and Barver joined him. Patch was fascinated by the huge barrel, and Shanny could see how impressed he was.

"These grandels are the biggest barrels we carry," said Shanny. "For one of our most prized cargoes!"

The top of the barrel wasn't sealed. Instead, it was covered by a mesh of wire, and water was visible underneath. Patch reached out, but Shanny grabbed his arm. "Careful, lad!" he said. "If you were fool enough to put a hand in that barrel, three seconds later it'd just be bone and gristle!"

Patch stared at the barrel. "What…what's in there?"

With a mischievous grin, Shanny reached down and found a stray fish that had fallen from one of the salted barrels. He tossed it onto the wire mesh; the water seemed to boil up, and a flurry of small black shapes began to push through the mesh, jabbing at the fish, so rapidly that it took Patch a moment to work out what he was seeing.

They were like small crab claws, he realized, but more elongated and sharp-ended. In no time at all, not a trace of the fish remained, and the water surface settled.

Patch, Wren and Barver were wide-eyed.

"Natter-clumps!" said Shanny, his expression dark. "Dangerous and terrible little beasts! I don't know of a more vicious and ugly creature in this whole world, above sea or below." He patted the barrel and smiled. "But they are *very* tasty."

When Patch and Wren reached the cottage, Alia ushered them through into the small kitchen, where she unloaded the bag of supplies. Wren hopped down from Patch's shoulder.

"Oh, good, the ten-jack thistle is fresh," said Alia, pulling out a small string-tied bunch of spiky weeds. "Dried is never as good."

"Barver's bringing the rest soon," said Patch. "He's staying in the port for a bit, because…"

"I heard the griffin, Patch. Couldn't really miss it screeching overhead, could I? Friend of Barver, then?"

"Barver didn't know him. He was a bit nervous, to be honest. I don't think he's ever had that much to do with griffins, really."

Wren sniffed at the ten-jack thistle. *What are you going to make with all this?* she signed. *Medicines or potions?*

Alia smiled. "Both!" she said. "I remember promising to take you on as an apprentice one day, Wren Cobble! Let's see if you're an attentive learner, shall we?"

Wren clapped her paws together and grinned. *I've nothing else planned,* she signed. *How is Erner doing, anyway?*

"He still has a fever," said Alia. "There are open sores on his legs, and he's underfed, but once I can get food in him he'll quickly improve." She looked at Patch. "You wouldn't sit and watch him, would you?" she said. "While me and Wren get cooking? Let me know if he wakes."

"Of course," said Patch, but it was with real reluctance that he made his way into the bedroom, closing the door behind him. Alia had lit a fire, and the room was very warm. Patch sat on a wooden stool beside the bed. Erner was tucked in under a sheet and a thick woollen blanket.

After an hour or so, Erner started to talk in his sleep – garbled little sounds that Patch couldn't make out.

"It's okay," Patch told him. "You're safe here."

More garbled sounds came, but suddenly there was a word: *"Patch..."*

Patch ignored his first instinct – to simply run and fetch Alia. In all likelihood, Erner would drift back under again in a moment. Better to leave Alia and Wren to get on with their work.

He leaned over. "You're not with King Arpie any more, Erner," he said. "You're..."

Erner sat up suddenly, eyes wide; seeing Patch, he leaped from the bed and put his hands around Patch's throat, squeezing, squeezing, and they both fell to the floor, Patch

71

struggling for breath. Suddenly Erner's expression changed, from rage to horror. He took his hands from Patch, staring at them. "I…" he said. "I…"

Then he collapsed beside Patch, out cold.

Patch stood and backed away, coughing.

A voice from behind made him jump.

"I'll get him back into bed," said Alia. She was at the door, with Wren on her shoulder. "He'll be fine. You, on the other hand, look like you need some air."

Patch went through to the kitchen. Alia and Wren joined him a few moments later.

Wren jumped down from Alia's shoulder to the table, and watched him with real concern; beside her was a cup, and she tapped it twice with her paw. *Drink this*, she signed.

Patch picked it up and sniffed. There was a strong smell of honey, and something a little like mint. "What is it?" he said.

"Ten-jack thistle tea," said Alia. "It'll settle your nerves. Take it all in one gulp, though."

"Didn't you make this for Erner?" he said.

Alia nodded. "We'll make more. Go ahead."

Patch looked at Alia, then at Wren, before he plucked up the courage. The tea had a peppery edge to it, but it was sweet. He sat down.

Wren hopped onto his shoulder. *Erner meant no harm*, she signed. *He's having nightmares, that's all.*

Patch shook his head. "We got him out," he said. "That's what counts. I never expected him to forgive me for what I did, Wren."

Of course he'll forgive you, she signed. *You two are friends, aren't you?*

"I've known Erner since I first came to Tiviscan," said Patch. He could feel a heavy sorrow wrap itself around him. "He treated me with kindness. Not all of the older trainees did, you know, when novices arrived to begin learning the Piping Arts. Yet without hesitating, I pushed him off Barver and into the water. I thought about being put back in the dungeons, and I pushed him. I think I should keep out of Erner's sight as much as possible."

Don't be silly, signed Wren. *This can be fixed!* She turned and looked at Alia. *Can't it?*

Alia said nothing.

"Sometimes there's no going back," said Patch. "Sometimes if you cause someone hurt, the best you can do is take away the reminders of it. Even if that's you. *Especially* if that's you."

Wren shook her head. *You're wrong,* she signed.

"Think about it," he said. "Imagine if it had been *you* I'd thrown off. Imagine how you would feel."

She stared at him. Long seconds passed, and tears

73

welled up in her eyes. Even the thought of it was unbearable.

"Go and watch the patient," Alia told her. "I left the door open just a crack. Keep an eye on him."

Wren nodded. She scampered down to the floor and left the kitchen.

Once she was gone, Alia took a seat next to Patch and put a comforting hand on his shoulder. "You wouldn't have thrown her off Barver," she said.

Patch shook his head. "No. And I think Erner would realize that. I'd known her for a few weeks, yet I'd known Erner for years. If Wren had been the one to say the words of the prophecy, I'd have told myself it was nonsense, that there was some kind of trick to it. But Erner..." He looked at Alia. "The best I can do is keep out of his way, isn't it?"

Alia gave his shoulder a squeeze. There was real pain on her face. "Erner is a good lad, and he'll want to get to a point where he forgives you. Let him go at his own pace."

It was almost dark when Barver returned, the rest of their supplies strapped to the sides of his harness.

"Hello there!" called Patch. "How did it go?"

"Very well indeed," said Barver. "Give me a hand with this lot first, would you?"

He and Patch unloaded the shopping – several large sacks and a medium-sized cauldron, lashed to Barver's harness with a considerable amount of rope.

Alia came out to check it over. "Welcome back," she said. "Did they have everything on my list?"

"Not quite," said Barver. "A few items proved tricky." He fished out a piece of paper from a pocket on his harness, and squinted at it. "You wanted some unwashed wool straight from a sheep, which they'll have tomorrow, but it was a definite no on the Kanda Bat droppings."

Alia shrugged and took the paper. "It was a long shot, really. I'll just have to make do." She lifted her cauldron with surprising ease and headed back inside. A moment later, Wren emerged and scampered up onto Patch's shoulder.

How was it? she signed to Barver.

Barver smiled. "It was good," he said. "Thanks for encouraging me to say hello."

Our pleasure, signed Wren.

"I told Shanny how shy I felt around griffins," said Barver. "He told me I wasn't to think ill of myself, as he often feels the same way. Griffins don't tend to seek out the company of other griffins, if they don't have to."

Is it true what Shanny said? signed Wren. *Do dragons really outnumber griffins by a thousand to one?*

"Nobody really knows how many griffins there are in the world," said Barver. "A thousand to one is probably an exaggeration, but they're few and far between." He looked thoughtful for a moment, then smiled. "There's an old joke sailors play on inexperienced new shipmates. You point at the sky and say, 'Oh, a flock of griffins,' and when they look, you just say, 'Too late, they vanished behind a cloud,' and the whole crew would burst out laughing."

"Is there a special word for that?" asked Patch. "A flock of griffins?"

Barver laughed. "Of course not! Seeing *two* griffins flying together is rare enough. Why would there be a word for a *flock*?"

But why are there so few griffins? asked Wren.

"It's just the nature of things," said Barver. "Griffins are very closely related to birds, and there are plenty of birds who are similar in their solitude – falcons, say, who spread out over large areas, so their numbers never grow by much. Dragons are happy to live in large communities, so they're far greater in number. And *humans*…well…" He coughed. "Let's just say there are a *lot* of them."

Did Shanny have some good tales to tell? signed Wren.

"Absolutely!" said Barver. "And to hear stories about my dad, other than the ones my mum would tell me, was wonderful."

Wren squeaked with joy. *I'm so glad*, she signed.

"I've never heard you talk about your father before," said Patch.

76

"I don't suppose I have," said Barver. "When my mother died, it brought back how hard I'd found it to lose him. In the year before his death I didn't get to see him much. I was already missing him badly, and then the terrible news came…" For a second, he looked distraught. "When me and my mum drifted apart, I felt absolutely alone. Dragons didn't really accept me as one of them, and as for griffins… You heard Shanny mention the Griffin Covenant, yes?"

"We did," said Patch. "What's that about?"

"It's a promise a griffin makes when they come of age," said Barver. "A code of honour, really. Griffins vow to only do certain kinds of work. Anything involving violence is frowned on, which is why there aren't many griffin Protectors – they have to be careful that everything they do is in self-defence, or in the defence of others under attack. And anything related to *war* is completely forbidden."

What happens to a griffin who breaks their vow? signed Wren.

"They'd be in disgrace," he said. "*Rejected.* And because the Covenant is only for griffins, not for dracogriffs, I always thought other griffins would know I'd not taken it. I suppose I always avoided them, in case they'd reject me too."

Well, Shanny didn't reject you, did he? signed Wren, getting slightly cross at the thought of somebody being mean to Barver. *And anyone who did…they'd have me to deal with, for a start!*

Barver smiled at her. "You're a good friend," he said. "And don't think for a moment that I forgot about you! I plucked up the courage to ask Shanny for a favour."

Wren looked puzzled. *What favour?* she signed.

"I asked him about Underath's griffin, Alkeran."

Wren felt herself scowl at the mention of Underath – the Sorcerer who had turned her into a rat. But Underath's griffin had been kidnapped, and he'd promised that, if his griffin was returned, he would undo his curse.

"Shanny had never heard the name before," continued Barver. "It's possible that Alkeran is not his true name. You recall the metal collar and chain we found in Alkeran's home?"

Patch nodded. "A reminder, we assumed, that he'd escaped from captivity somewhere."

"Indeed," said Barver. "A new name would make sense, if he feared that someone might have been looking for him."

Wren's paws flew to her mouth in horror. *The woman who kidnapped Alkeran!* she signed. *You think she was taking him back to captivity?*

"It's possible," said Barver. "When you and Erner spoke to Underath, he told you it was the griffin that she'd been after all along. And Alkeran didn't go with her willingly…"
That was certainly the case – the woman was a Sorcerer, and had torn out Underath's heart to use in a spell to

78

bewitch the griffin. Underath himself had barely survived, using all the magic at his disposal to replace his heart – somewhat unconventionally – with a shoe.

"Anyway," said Barver. "Shanny promised that the Echoes would hear of it."

"The Echoes?" asked Patch.

"It's another griffin thing," said Barver. "News is passed from one griffin to another. Most of the time it's the only reason griffins meet, and they like to keep it as brief as they can. Anyway, Shanny will make sure to get word to us, either here or at Marwheel Abbey, if anything comes up." He reached out a hand to Wren, and Wren hopped onto his huge palm. "We'll find the griffin, little one. We'll get Underath back his heart, and his powers shall return, enough for him to keep his promise and make you human again."

Wren wiped away a tear. *Thank you,* she signed. *But what if it's too late?*

"Nonsense," said Patch. "Alia says it's not too late, and she should know." He met Barver's eyes and had to look away – for while Alia had always been optimistic about it when talking to Wren, there had been times in Marwheel when she'd been open to both Patch and Barver about her fears: fears that Wren might be a rat for ever.

6

ALL ABOARD
THE DUBIOUS PLUM!

Over the coming days, Erner's fever reduced and his leg sores healed. Wren told him everything about their adventures, and made sure that Patch sounded suitably heroic in her telling – especially the part where he donned the Iron Mask, inside out, and went to face the Hamelyn Piper.

Erner never brought up his ejection from Barver's back, and said very little about his own "adventure" that had brought him to Pengersick, and the court of King Arpie. This was for the best, Alia explained – talking about it too soon could set back his recovery.

Patch, doing everything he could to avoid Erner, spent much of his time in the outbuilding where Barver slept. When alone, he took out his Pipe and got some practice in, doing the familiar exercises he'd been taught at Tiviscan. At dusk, little swarms of midges would gather under the bows of a large beech tree next to the cottage, and Patch would play his Pipe; the midges would ripple and shift like the murmurations of starlings.

Part of him wanted to start practising the Push Songs of the Battle Pipers, the kind he'd used in his confrontation with the Hamelyn Piper. He had a real knack for it, he knew, but it was also something that scared him. Whenever he thought of that evil Piper still being free, he imagined taking up his Pipe and not stopping until the villain lay broken and still.

But that was not the future he wanted for himself. He needed to find a different path.

One morning Alia announced she had news. "I sent a letter to Marwheel Abbey when we arrived in Sorkil, telling Tobias how things had gone. I just received his reply. Rundel Stone has woken from his illness!"

You should tell Erner! signed Wren.

"I already did," Alia told her. "Hearing that piece of good news has buoyed him up even more than my ten-jack thistle tea does!" She frowned a little. "Tobias was slightly vague about how *fully* Rundel has recovered, which worries me. The moon-rot he was poisoned with can leave a mark, causing damage that lasts years. Rundel is well enough to travel, though – they've left Marwheel Abbey and relocated quite some distance south."

"Relocated?" said Patch. "Why?"

"Oh, you'll find out in good time," said Alia. "Barver, can you arrange passage for us? A little port called Welderby is our best landing point. I'll give you what silver I have left. The fastest ship you can find! A long sea voyage is the last thing Erner needs. He has no sea legs whatsoever, that boy."

"Leave it with me!" said Barver.

By early afternoon, arrangements had been made. They went to the harbour, and Barver led them down a wooden pier. In front of them, on either side of a single jetty, were two ships. One was a simple three-masted fluit, a speedy vessel that had plenty of room for cargo. It was clean and solid, and looked almost new. The crew seemed like decent people, tidily dressed in identical white cotton clothing and getting about their business in a professional manner.

The *other* ship was a battered old sloop, bedecked with weapons and roughly tied barrels. Most of the crew were playing cards and drinking rum, or sleeping. Some were stitching rips in sailcloth that seemed to already carry the scars of older damage.

The name of the first ship was the *Steadfast Voyager*.

The second was called the *Dubious Plum*.

Alia looked from one ship to the other, then turned to Barver, her eyes narrowing. "Which is ours?" she said. "The good one...or the pirate ship?"

"That is *not* a pirate ship," said Barver. His tone was rather defensive, and answered Alia's question immediately. "It'll get us where we need to go in three days, while everyone else would take a week or more. I did make a tiny compromise on where we'd be dropped off, but they'll be fast, I guarantee it!"

"It does *look* like a pirate ship," said Patch, nervous.

"These people are traders," said Barver. "Yes, they're well-armed and used to fighting. They have to be, in the seas they sail. They were highly recommended."

Alia nodded, but she didn't look convinced. "They'd better not cause us any trouble, that's all I'll say."

It wasn't long before they set off. The ship cut smoothly through the water, and even Alia's sceptical frowning lessened as they made rapid progress. It was a good thing too – Erner's seasickness was so bad that by the time evening drew in, Alia grew worried. She gave him a sleeping potion that knocked him flat out, and then had him bunked down below.

As night fell, Patch listened to the sea shanties the crew sang, intrigued by how similar they were to several Songs he'd studied at Tiviscan, Songs for the control of air and liquids. Trying to join in with his Pipe, he managed to create a little whirlpool in a tankard of water. Wren was delighted.

Ooh, water magic! she signed. *I saw something like that in Underath's books. I didn't have long enough to memorize it, though.*

Alia leaned forward, keeping her voice low. "I imagine you came away from Underath's books with a few other tricks up your sleeve," she said. "What *did* you memorize?"

Wren was coy. *Oh, this and that*, was all she would give as an answer.

On the third day of sailing, Barver announced that it was time to disembark.

Erner didn't pay any attention, being too busy leaning over the side and being sick. Alia, Patch and Wren, however, looked around. Something very important was missing.

"Um, Barver?" asked Patch. "Where's the, um, *land*?" He scanned the horizon, but there was only sea.

"I *did* mention that I made a bit of a compromise on where we'd be dropped off," said Barver. "This is as close as we get to shore."

Wren's face fell. *You have to be kidding*, she signed. She noticed that some of the crew were shifting cargo around on the deck, clearing a path that ran all the way back to the stern of the ship. *Are they doing what I think they're doing?*

Barver looked sheepish. "I need to get up some speed before take-off," he said. "I'm not quite ready for a standing start."

"And how is your *wing* today?" said Patch. "Only I do remember Brother Duffle insisting that you kept that splint on for at least a few months…" Barver said nothing, but Patch saw an evasive look in his eye. "You've been flying already, haven't you?"

"Well…" said Barver. "Of *course* I have. It's fine, I've been practising! I'd sneak off sometimes in the early hours of the morning. The splint doesn't even get in the way, not really. Come to think of it…"

To Patch's horror, Barver reached up to the splint on his wing and snapped it off.

"All good," said Barver. He flexed his wings, as if to prove the point. "It's only a few miles! There are some great thermals around. I can probably glide much of the way once I get some height." The crew finished shifting cargo and gave him a thumbs up, which he returned. "All ready! Oh, if we do go straight into the water, this lot promised they'd fish you out quick smart! Just don't splash about too much. You don't want to attract the attention of anything that might be…you know, in the water."

A few minutes later, Barver was at the ship's stern,

all his passengers on his back: Erner at the front, looking green around the gills, with Alia behind him, then Patch. Wren was on Patch's shoulder, but she soon scampered down into his pocket.

The crew cheered mightily as Barver started his run, and the cheer became a huge roar of well-wishing as he took off into the air. He plummeted towards the surface of the sea, and pulled back just in time, flapping hard.

Patch wondered if there were any disappointed sharks looking up at them.

COLD STONE

Barver managed to gain good speed and height. Soon they could see the coast, and a small port town.

"Head west of the port," Alia called to Barver. "Two miles beyond you'll see a hill overlooking a village. The mansion at the top of the hill is where we'll find Rundel and Tobias."

Barver turned his head back. "Why did they come here?"

Erner, seated in front of Alia, began to respond: "Because this is the home of—"

Alia interrupted. "Don't spoil the surprise, Erner. I promise it'll be explained soon enough!"

They flew on, leaving the coast behind. The hill Alia had spoken of was forested; as they drew nearer, they saw a huge mansion on the summit, surrounded by ornate gardens.

And somewhere in that mansion, thought Patch, was Rundel Stone, one of the most famous Pipers of the Custodian Elite, woken at last from his poison-induced sleep. The man who had rescued Patch from the villagers of Patterfall, only to see him imprisoned in the dungeons of Tiviscan, with a sentence of five hundred and ten years! The thought suddenly made Patch very nervous indeed. Instinctively, his hand went to his pocket, where he kept the pardon given to him by the Pipers' Council as reward for his heroics against the Hamelyn Piper. In the pocket below that, he could feel the warm bulge of a snuggling rat. "We're about to land, Wren," he said. Wren stuck her head out, eyes squinting against the fast-flowing air.

Barver veered down, clearly enjoying himself. He skimmed unnervingly close to the treetops on the edge of the forest, and approached the centre of the garden at some speed. Then, just in time, he tilted up and caught the air in his wings as a brake, so that when his feet reached the ground he was at walking pace.

Wren caught Patch's eye and shook her head. *Show-off,* she signed.

They dismounted. As they reached the mansion, the large front doors opened, and there stood Brother Tobias, waving at them and grinning. "Welcome!" he said. "Come in, come in! Your timing couldn't be better – I was just putting the finishing touches to some stew. Barver, the doorway might be a squeeze but it's roomy inside!"

Soon enough they were standing in an opulent entrance hall, the air full of the smell of cooking. A vast wooden staircase was in front of them, and enormous portraits of serious-looking men and women filled the walls. As Tobias had promised, Barver had plenty of space – enough to spread his wings and have a good flap if he'd wanted.

The dracogriff peered closely at one of the portraits, which depicted a young woman, stern yet beautiful, standing beside a large and ferocious-looking boar which seemed to be on a lead. Barver squinted at the inscription on the frame. "Posna de Frenn," he said. He gave Alia a pointed look. "Where are we, and why are we here? I mean, you did promise to explain."

"I did," she said. "This, Barver, is the estate of Lady Posna de Frenn, the woman in that picture. She was sole heir to the de Frenn fortune, and died thirty-five years ago alongside her husband Gregor, leaving a son, Yemas de Frenn, to inherit everything." Alia pointed to another portrait on the furthest wall, which depicted mother, father and son; the boar was there too, looking much older and slightly frail. "Yemas was fifteen at the time and wanted nothing of wealth. Instead, having natural skill at Piping, he took on a false identity and went to Tiviscan to train as a Piper. He excelled, and also grew fascinated with sorcery; he devoted his life to the study of how the two magics of sorcery and music overlapped. Eventually, he became a celebrated hero, but the thought of *fame* horrified him. Instead, becoming Yemas de Frenn once more, he used his family's fortune to secretly continue his studies, here in his childhood home." Barver was frowning, and looked like he was about to speak, but then the penny dropped. He smiled, as did Wren. Alia smiled back. "Now you understand," she said.

Patch scowled, none the wiser. "Not *entirely*," he grumbled.

"This," said Alia, gesturing around the room in which they stood, "is the family home of Yemas de Frenn. Better known to you as Ural Casimir, the Sorcerer Engineer, one of the Eight."

"Oh, I *see*," said Patch, suddenly very excited. He nodded at Wren.

You got there in the end, she signed.

"But hang on," said Patch. "I thought Casimir lived in a run-down shack in the far reaches of Turniss! And under his shack was his greatest secret, the Caves of Casimir, a treasure trove of mysterious magical artefacts hidden deep underground! I mean, that's what it said in *The Adventures of the Eight*. I read it until the pages were worn thin!" He looked to Wren. "I'm right, aren't I?"

Wren nodded. *I know the story as well as you do*, she signed. *But just because it said it in the story, doesn't mean it was all true—*

"Not…not all *true*?" said Patch, appalled; Alia and Tobias shared a smile.

A voice came to them from above: "There were certainly some tweaks." They all looked up. At the top of the staircase stood Rundel Stone. "Ural most definitely did *not* live in a shack, as you can see," he said. He descended the stairs, and as he did, Patch noticed the anxious expression on Alia's face, and on Erner's. The reason was obvious: Rundel was moving slowly, his left hand holding a cane, his right keeping a tight grip of the bannisters. Now and again, a hint of a grimace crossed his face, as if he was in pain but trying to hide it.

Alia's fears had been well founded. The poison had indeed left its mark.

When Rundel reached the bottom of the staircase, he stepped over to Erner and embraced him, much to Erner's surprise.

Everyone else was surprised too. Alia turned her head to Patch, who was standing beside her. "Not something you see every day…" she whispered, before adding: "Nor *that*."

For a moment Patch didn't know what she meant, but then he saw the tears in Rundel Stone's eyes. Here was the man widely known as the Cold Heart of Justice, famed for his emotionless enforcement of the law. Tears were not expected.

Rundel released Erner and wiped his eyes, seeming perplexed at his own display of emotion. "Apprentice Whitlock," he said, his voice uneven. He cleared his throat, then added: "Good to have you back."

"So now we know *where* we are," said Barver. "But why have we come here?"

"We stand in a crime scene," said Rundel. "It was here that Ural Casimir was killed." He clenched his fist, clearly enraged by the thought of his old friend's death. "Bludgeoned from behind, his life's blood pouring over the very floor he'd played on as a child!"

Horrified, Patch looked to the floorboards beneath his feet. He shifted position a little, half-expecting a squelch.

"No, Brightwater," said Rundel, sounding rather impatient. "*Not* where you stand. Ural was murdered in his library. Through there." He pointed to a small oak door that led from the entrance hall. "I have come here to complete the task that my poisoning interrupted. The investigation of Ural Casimir's murder!"

Everyone stood in absolute silence as Rundel Stone's words settled in their minds. The atmosphere was one of total solemnity, and was only broken by a long and extremely loud rumble from Barver's stomach.

"I'm sorry," said Barver. "But that food does smell *amazing*."

"Thank you," said Tobias, smiling. "Indeed, there's

plenty of time for murder-solving later! If you would all take a seat in the dining room, I'll serve up shortly."

To Barver's great relief, the dining room was through a large double doorway next to the stairs, which he could fit through with ease. The dining room itself was enormous, big enough to have a slight echo. The table was vast too, made from a very dark wood and finely carved, as were the chairs.

Barver moved three of the chairs away from one side to give himself plenty of space. Patch sat next to him, and Wren scampered down from Patch's shoulder onto the table. Soon enough Tobias came through another doorway, pushing a huge blackened cooking pot that perched precariously on top of a wooden trolley, beside a stack of bowls. He pushed his trolley around, filling each person's bowl in turn.

"Forgive the simple fodder," said Tobias, taking a seat as they all tucked in. "Mutton stew with plenty of onion! A Palafox family speciality, one which the monks of Marwheel never seem to get bored of." He smiled at Wren, who was already stuffing her little face with delicious onion shreds as if she'd never eaten in her life. She gave a thumbs up and kept eating. "I'm glad to see you all enjoying it," said Tobias. "It's well deserved."

"It is indeed," said Rundel. "And I am the most grateful of all to be sitting here with those to whom I owe a great debt. I must thank all of you. Erner, for getting me to the Abbey so quickly when I was poisoned; Tobias, for keeping me alive while you sought the poison's remedy from the Witch of Gemspar; and Alia, of course, whose remedy proved so effective."

At this, Erner's eyes widened. He looked at Alia with awe. "You…?" he said. "You're the Witch of Gemspar?"

Alia smiled and clicked her fingers, creating a shower of purple sparks. "Guilty as charged," she said.

Rundel continued. "Alia, I thank you not only for your cure, but also for seeking out Erner and bringing him back. You have my eternal gratitude. As do the three of you – Barver, Wren and Brightwater – both for Erner's safe return and for destroying the Obsidiac Organ when all looked lost. You are heroes! Although the Council didn't mention any of you by name in the official report of what happened, and described you only in the vaguest of terms."

"That's for the best," said Alia. "Trust me. Your lives would never be your own again if people knew who you were."

"Perhaps," said Rundel. "Now, to other matters." He reached to a pocket and produced several sheets of folded paper. "Once I woke, I contacted the Custodian Elite and requested news from Tiviscan. It will interest you all, I think."

Alia scowled at him. "You'd better not have told the Council where we are," she said.

"Of course not," said Rundel. "Tobias explained to me about the prophecy: of how it warned of a betrayal, and led to Erner's capture." He looked at Patch, and Patch felt his blood chill. "He told me how the Pipers' Council then seemed to fulfil the prophecy instead, suggesting that it's the Council itself who'll betray Brightwater. To whatever you fear most, I understand?"

Patch nodded.

"Rest assured that I was cautious, Alia," said Rundel. "My contact at Tiviscan will not inform the Council without my express order. The question must be answered eventually, though – what kind of betrayal is predicted? What does Brightwater fear most?"

"I hate prophecies," said Alia. "I especially hate it when it was *me* doing the prophesying. I honestly don't know what to expect. There's every chance that it's not just Patch who would be betrayed. It could be *all* of us. That's why we should play it safe, and assume the Council isn't to be trusted. And as to what Patch fears most? There's an obvious candidate for that, of course, but prophecies are rarely obvious. There's no guarantee that it refers to the Hamelyn Piper."

Rundel grimaced. "Even the mention of that name riles me," he said. "What terrible news to wake up to – that the Hamelyn Piper, a vile criminal I thought dead by dragon fire was not only *alive*, but had been free all these years. And to learn that we'd imprisoned an innocent man in his place…" He shook his head, and opened the pages in his hand. "As I said, I requested news from Tiviscan." Everyone pricked up their ears. "Across the world, people know that the Hamelyn Piper still lives, and they're afraid. So, the Pipers' Council is putting *everything* into finding him. They're calling it 'The Great Pursuit'."

"I like the sound of that!" said Alia. "Now that Erner's safe, I rather fancy the idea of tracking down the villain myself."

"You've changed your mind about the Council, then?" said Tobias.

"I certainly have not!" she said. "There are many ways they could betray us, but at least their Great Pursuit means they're not in league with the scoundrel."

"Can we be certain of that?" asked Tobias. "Does this hunt seem genuine, Rundel?"

"My contact at Tiviscan, Harston Wynne, is one of the Custodian Elite scribes," said Rundel, looking through the pages as he spoke. "He said that ten expeditions of Custodians have been sent hunting for the Hamelyn Piper. Lord Drevis embarked on the first of these, and has not been back to Tiviscan since."

"How many Pipers were in each expedition?" asked Tobias.

"The smallest group was twenty," said Rundel. "The largest was fifty."

Tobias looked horrified. "That must be half of the Custodian Elite! When we were on the case, we only had eight in total!"

"What happened to the remains of the Obsidiac Organ, Rundel?" asked Alia. "If there's one thing the Hamelyn Piper would like to get his hands on, it must be that!"

"I asked Harston about it in my letter," said Rundel. "The Council have stored the remains in Tiviscan Castle."

Alia shook her head in dismay. "I'd hoped Lord Drevis would see sense and destroy it all. It's too dangerous to keep."

"Lord Cobb convinced him otherwise," said Rundel. "Harston assures me that it's absolutely secure, though. If anything, they'd *prefer* the Hamelyn Piper to attempt to steal it. At least then they would know where he is!"

"They must have *some* information about his location?" said Tobias. "Surely the Council doesn't have the Custodians chasing shadows?"

Rundel frowned. "Sadly, that may be the case," he said. "These expeditions have been sent to far-flung places based on little more than rumour and speculation. The Council is desperate to show the world that it has everything under control. They're putting so many resources into this hunt that the normal duties of the Custodian Elite are being neglected. I fear the Council has made a terrible error."

Tobias nodded. "Removing Custodians from their normal duties could have a severe impact. The world doesn't stop squabbling just because the Hamelyn Piper is at large."

"Precisely," said Rundel. "In the great forests of the Ortings, for example, there are ludicrous tales of ghostly armies attacking traders, based on some old legend about a knight in black armour – all nonsense, but it's stirring up bad-feeling between countries who have always hated each other. Exactly the kind of situation the Custodians should step into, and calm down, but none can be spared from the *Great Pursuit*, apparently. I have half a mind to go there myself and deal with it." He shook his head. "The Council takes a great risk, if it thinks the world is sensible enough to do without the wisdom of Custodians, even for a short while."

Silence fell for a time, except for the sounds of eating, as they concentrated on the important task of filling their bellies.

"So, then," said Barver, after what Patch reckoned was his tenth bowl of stew. "We're going to have the honour of witnessing the eminent Rundel Stone solving a crime!"

"Oh, please, Barver," said Alia. "He has a big enough head already without your flattery."

"It will be *my* honour," said Rundel. "Ural was a friend, and a good man. He deserves justice. The local authorities investigated, but found no culprit. They gave up easily, but we will not."

"Why didn't the Custodians investigate his death?" said Barver. "It seems odd, given how famous Casimir was."

"The Custodians did not *know*," said Rundel. "And Ural wished his identity to remain secret even after his death. All of the Eight knew, naturally. He had two housekeeping staff – a husband and wife, Hest and Tipa Raqan, who'd been with the family since before he was born. *They* also knew, of course, and it was they who discovered Ural's body that dreadful morning. The Raqans are old now, and live in Yarmingly, the village at the base of the hill. They visited Ural twice a week. Had they been here when he was attacked, they probably would have been killed too. Ural had instructed them that should anything ever happen to him, they were to send word to me that Yemas de Frenn had been killed. Erner and myself rushed here at once when word reached us. Mere minutes after our arrival I found that damnable puzzle box on the floor, a curious metal cube. No sooner had I picked it up than I felt the sting of a treacherous needle, and the poison entered my veins!" His gaze fell on his right hand, which he clenched and

99

unclenched, the effort and pain of the action written clearly on his face. "I told Erner that we had to reach Brother Tobias in Marwheel Abbey as soon as possible, and that the Raqans were to report the death to the local authorities, with no mention of our visit. Ural's body was placed in the family mausoleum, and I vowed to return as soon as I could. I instructed the Raqans to keep the scene of the crime unchanged, beyond dealing with the body and..." He paused. "And the immediate *implications* of the attack."

"He means the blood," muttered Barver to Patch, earning a sharp glare in return.

Rundel continued: "And now I *have* come back, and the investigation can truly begin. There is a murder to solve, yes. But I will need help from all of *you* to solve it."

It wasn't long before all at the table had eaten more than their bellies could comfortably fit – Barver being the exception, of course, as his belly could fit several whole sheep and a barrowful of onions. With the meal done, Tobias loaded his trolley with the empty bowls and took them back to the kitchen.

"And now, I would like to talk to my apprentice," said Rundel. "In private, Erner."

"Of course, Virtus Stone," said Erner, addressing him by his rank. Rundel stood slowly, in clear discomfort, but with an air of stubborn determination. Patch could see on Erner's face how much he wanted to help, yet there was no way Rundel Stone would welcome any assistance. Rundel set off, leaning heavily on his cane, with Erner just behind.

Once the door had shut, Alia let rip with a long and echoing belch that could have won awards. Wren chirruped with glee, while Alia grinned with satisfaction. "That was a good meal," she said. "And a good meal deserves the respect of a good burp."

To his great disappointment, Patch found that he didn't have much of a store of gas in his gullet. Any attempt to outdo Alia's effort would be pitiful, so he opted to hold back entirely.

Barver, on the other hand, rose to the challenge. He raised his head, and a terrific gurgling came from his stomach; he opened his mouth, and out came a rumbling, bubbling belch that seemed to last for ever, growing into what was almost a roar.

A look of astonishment was on Alia's face, mingled (Patch reckoned) with a degree of admiration. The victory was deservedly Barver's. Patch and Wren, meanwhile, were reduced to hysterical laughter as the burp kept going.

Then, just as it started to falter, the sound changed and a sudden burst of fire shot out from Barver's snout. With a shriek, Alia ducked under the table, but she was well out of range. Barver clamped his mouth shut, looking absolutely mortified.

Patch checked that Wren was okay, then glanced at the table and ceiling, neither of which showed signs of damage. He stared at Barver, shocked.

Barver coughed. "That caught me off guard," he said, in an unusually subdued voice. "Must have been the onions." He rubbed at his throat, concerned. "Forgive me! That's never happened before."

"No chance of it being anything serious?" asked Alia. "I'm sure Ural has books that cover dragon ailments, if you think it could be."

"I don't think so," said Barver. "All the worst dragon illnesses have the opposite effect, really – sick dragons lose their fire completely. Besides, it's often been the case that ailments that affect me are unusual. Being half-dragon and half-griffin has complications. Every dracogriff is one of a kind. You really don't know how you're going to turn out."

Alia raised an eyebrow. She made a point of looking at her own hands, then at Patch, and finally Wren. "Well, Barver," said Alia, with a smile. "I don't think you're alone in *that*."

Patch knew exactly what she meant. Here was Alia Corrigan, a famous Piper turned legendary Witch; here was Patch Brightwater, imprisoned for life, an escaped convict turned hero; and here was Wren Cobble, just as much a hero as Patch, but ten times braver and a hundred times smarter, all packaged up in a rat's skin.

As Barver had said, you really don't know how you're going to turn out.

8

WORD FROM HOME

Tobias came back from the kitchen waving some pieces of paper in his hand. He set them on the table, and Patch could see what they were: letters, three of them.

Tobias grinned. "You've all had replies from the ones you sent out when you left Marwheel!"

Before setting off on their adventure in the Islands of the Eastern Sea, they had each written a letter – Wren to her parents, Patch to his grandparents, and Barver to his aunt and uncle – to try and reassure their loved ones that they were safe and well. Patch and Wren, not wanting to worry anyone, had pretty much made everything up. Patch's letter described how well his training at Tiviscan was going, while Wren's letter explained how successful her maid's job was. Wren had dictated it for Patch to write;

she'd tried doing it herself but kept getting ink on her paws and leaving little prints on the paper.

Tobias handed the replies out.

Patch broke open the little wax seal on Wren's letter and folded it out for her, before opening his own and reading it as hungrily as he'd eaten the stew.

It was wonderfully boring. The handwriting was the small, pristine script of his grandmother. They assured him that they were fine, and said how much they missed him and how proud of him they were. To hear from his grandparents was a great relief. They weren't ill, and they weren't having sleepless nights worrying about him.

He realized that Wren was watching him. "Did you read yours already?" he asked.

She nodded. They both glanced at Barver, who had by far the longest letter. He seemed to be on the third page, and it wasn't easy to tell how many more pages remained. *It's good to hear from home*, signed Wren.

"How are things with your parents?" said Patch.

A few little dramas, but nothing bad, she signed. *Our dog fell ill, that was about the worst, but he's okay now. Apart from that, just gossip from the village and wishing me well in my job as a maid.* She paused, and shook her head. *Maid! If only they knew! What about your grandparents?*

"Nothing much to report," he said. "I wish *our* lives could be that uneventful, at least for a while."

They looked at Barver again, just as he set the last page down and let out a breath. "Blimey," he said.

"It was your aunt and uncle you wrote to, wasn't it?" asked Patch.

Barver nodded. "I've not been in touch since I fell out with my mum and left for the Eastern Sea," he said. "I tried to keep my distance from them too. It seemed easier. They were really pleased to hear from me, though."

Wren smiled. "Well, if your letter is like ours, hardly anything happened but they told you about it in mind-numbing detail. Am I right?"

"Quite the opposite," said Barver. "For a start, they've moved. My aunt is now the Triumvirate's Delegate in the city of Skamos, no less!"

Alia and Tobias both sat up at that. Skamos was the only city in the Dragon Territories where humans lived, a place that had led to problems between dragons and humans more than once. Not that the residents of the city were the problem – one in twenty of the inhabitants were dragons, yet the citizens got along with each other perfectly well. In spite of this, or perhaps *because* of it, Skamos was a focus for all those humans who hated dragons, and for all those dragons who hated humans. The Custodian Elite had a permanent delegation in the city, and so did the Dragon Triumvirate – the three rulers of the Dragon Territories. Together they had helped steer a path of peace

106

in Skamos for over a century.

"Impressive," said Alia. "A Triumvirate representative. Any other interesting news?"

Barver picked up the first few pages of his letter again. "There's rather a lot about politics in the Dragon Territories. The dragon army attacking Tiviscan has proved very controversial."

Tobias nodded. "We'd caught some whispers. Most dragons thought it was going too far, as I understand."

"Not quite," said Barver. "*Some* thought it was going too far, but on the other extreme, there are plenty of dragons who think the attack didn't go far enough!"

Tobias looked at Alia, his expression serious. "What do you mean, not far enough?"

Barver checked his letter again. "Some dragons think the army should have wiped Tiviscan off the map when they had the chance."

"There have always been dragons who'd like to see Tiviscan destroyed," said Alia. "They usually keep their opinions rather quieter. Thankfully the Triumvirate has never gone down that path."

Patch didn't like all this talk of politics. "But what about your aunt and uncle?" he said. "Are they well?"

At this, Barver grinned his widest grin. "Ah, yes! Good news! My aunt laid an egg, and the egg hatched six months ago!"

Patch could feel tears prick at his eyes. "A cousin!" he said. Barver didn't look very far from tears himself.

A *cousin*.

Patch thought, then, of the hot desert – the Dragon Wastes, where the three of them had flown to satisfy the dying wish of Barver's mother. And there, uncovered the terrible secret of the origin of obsidiac.

Also called black diamond, obsidiac was the most powerful magical substance in existence, and the terrible secret was this: obsidiac was formed from the bones of dead dragons, and it was dragon *children* that made black diamond of the purest kind.

Barver had had a cousin, once, a younger cousin he had doted on. A girl, called Genasha, who had died of an illness. Barver's mother had stolen her body and buried it secretly in the Dragon Wastes, seven years before. It was Genasha's skeleton that the three of them found that day, blackening, proving the theory that Barver's mother had hoped was wrong.

Genasha's darkened bones had answered at last why the Hamelyn Piper had done what he'd done, at least when it came to the hundred dragon children he'd stolen: he had killed them so that he could plant their bones, and harvest obsidiac when the time came, giving him the means to create his terrible Obsidiac Organ and attempt to take over the world.

It was a secret so appalling that they had told no one the truth – not even Alia or Tobias. In the letter from Barver's mother, she had been quite specific about who they could tell: only Lord Drevis, the leader of the Pipers' Council.

All this was in the tears that fell now, down the cheeks of Patch, and Wren, and Barver – sorrow at what had gone before, mixed with the joy of the news that had come.

"Yes," said Barver, once he'd settled his emotions enough to speak. "A cousin! The news is not all dark, not by a long way."

Erner returned to the dining room alone. "The Virtus would like to talk to you upstairs, Patch," he said.

Patch felt all the blood drain from his face. Without a word, he made his way out of the room, moving as slowly as he possibly could without actually stopping. As he reached the halfway point on the stairs, Rundel Stone's voice came from above, startling him.

"Don't be all day," said Rundel, standing at the top step. "Have your feet been weighed down with rocks?"

Patch hurried upstairs, following Rundel as he went into a small room with a desk and two chairs.

"Take a seat and close the door," instructed Rundel, and Patch silently did as asked, his gaze downward. Rundel let out a long sigh, and shook his head. "Do you think I'm going to shout at you, boy?"

Patch didn't look up. "Yes," he said.

"Why? Because of what you did to Erner?"

Patch nodded.

"Perhaps I *should* shout," said Rundel. "Do you have your pardon from the Pipers' Council? Tobias told me you carry it at all times."

Patch felt uneasy giving his pardon to Rundel Stone, almost as if he expected the man to tear it up and laugh.

Rundel read it and gave it back. "I took no pleasure in seeing you taken to the dungeons, Brightwater. I did what had to be done."

Patch said nothing. If Rundel Stone wanted his conscience eased, Patch wasn't going to help him.

"I spoke with Erner," said Rundel. "He bears you no malice, but is understandably pained by your *betrayal*."

The word, and the way Rundel Stone said it, almost made Patch jump.

"That's how the prophecy referred to it, yes?" said Rundel. "A betrayal?"

"No!" said Patch. "The prophecy was talking about someone who would betray *me*. Or us, or… Anyway, Erner spoke the words in the prophecy, and that was why I pushed him off Barver's back. Then the Pipers' Council spoke the words, and…"

110

"Yes, yes," said Rundel. "I've yet to decide what the prophecy tells us about the Council. A worrying thought, I have to admit, but my focus at this very moment is you, and what you did to Erner. Did you think he would betray you? Send you back to the dungeons, perhaps?"

"I didn't think, not really," said Patch. "I was just scared."

"Scared…" said Rundel. "And so you condemned someone – supposedly a *friend* – to an uncertain fate." He stopped talking, and looked at the various papers that lay across the desk, deep in thought. "Oh, did Tobias remember to give you the letter that came from your parents?" He frowned. "No, not your parents. My apologies. From your *grandparents*. Your parents died when you were very young, yes? I recall hearing the sorry tale when you first came to study in Tiviscan. What was it again?"

"My family made a living crafting with wood and leather," said Patch. "My parents sometimes travelled far to get the best prices on finer work. They were in Southern Praze when…" He stopped, unable to say the rest of it.

"Ah, yes, I remember now. They were caught up in the Great Rains, and perished in one of the many landslides that followed."

Patch nodded.

"So you have craft running through the family, then?" said Rundel. "You made the Pipe you used when you fought the Hamelyn Piper, Tobias said. Can I see it?"

"It was broken. I made another. It's in my satchel, tied to Barver's harness."

"I'll be sure to examine it. In your trial, Lord Pewter was very much taken by your skill at Pipe-making." Rundel looked at his own right hand, and flexed the curled fingers. "I cannot Pipe, not any more. My hand is in constant pain. The poison has twisted and slowed my fingers. Even if they straighten, they will never regain their speed." He seemed distant for a moment, then shook his head and looked back at Patch. "To business. You are here, Brightwater, so that we may discuss your actions against Apprentice Erner Whitlock, and your actions in Tiviscan that led to the defeat of the Hamelyn Piper."

"I expected as much," said Patch.

"Tobias has told me your account of events. Erner has confirmed those events he witnessed, and has told me of his experiences in the court of the Pirate King, Noss. I understand that before now, he's spoken very little about what he suffered?"

"Hardly a word," said Patch. His mouth felt terribly dry as he spoke. He knew there was much he would eventually learn about what had happened to Erner – a deep pit of dreadful tales was waiting for him, and he wasn't sure if he could bear falling into it.

Rundel shook his head in sorrow. "Erner's training as an Apprentice Custodian was intended to prepare him for many of the horrors the world can inflict, but I can't think of another Apprentice given such a trial by fire. Now listen carefully, Brightwater. I know you're in anguish about your betrayal of Erner. But I have a way to rid you of that."

Patch was puzzled, but said nothing.

Rundel continued. "Tobias told me you returned to Tiviscan because your dracogriff friend, Barver, had a message for Lord Drevis. Couldn't he simply have sent a letter?"

"Barver reckoned it had to be done in person," said Patch. "It was the dying wish of Barver's mother that the message was only for Lord Drevis. A letter could have been read by *anyone*."

Rundel nodded. "So, given that Barver would have caused a very considerable degree of alarm had he approached the castle, and you yourself would have been sent back to the dungeons for the rest of your life, you decided that your rat friend, Wren, would locate Lord Drevis. She was in human form at the time, as I understand it?"

Patch nodded. "Me and Barver stayed in the forest. Wren went to the castle and came back with the news that Drevis was in Monash Hollow, at the festival."

"Indeed," said Rundel. "And there, the Hamelyn Piper had constructed his terrible Obsidiac Organ, and you were able to protect yourself from its effects by wearing the Iron Mask, turned inside out. Very clever, by the way."

"Thank you," said Patch. "The Hamelyn Piper said the same."

Rundel paused, clearly not appreciating the comment. "Events progressed, the Organ was destroyed, and the evil Hamelyn Piper defeated, at least for now. That much we know. But suppose you had not pushed Erner into that lake. What then?"

Patch frowned, not liking where this was leading. "What do you mean?"

"If Erner had still been with you, surely *he* could have been trusted to take a message to Lord Drevis? Then you wouldn't have placed yourself at such risk. Erner would have insisted on that, there's no doubt."

"Maybe," said Patch.

"In fact, you wouldn't have had to return to Tiviscan at *all*," said Rundel. "You, the only one with the Iron Mask to protect yourself. Without you there, events would have progressed very differently indeed! The Hamelyn Piper would surely have triumphed! And think of the courage you showed! Would you have *had* that courage, without the guilt you felt for what you did to Erner?"

Patch didn't say a word or move a muscle. He could feel a little nugget of anger building deep within him.

"Do you understand me?" said Rundel. "You betrayed Erner. You betrayed a *friend*. But if you hadn't? Disaster would have befallen us! The Hamelyn Piper would have won! So, why should you feel any guilt now? Instead, you should be *proud!* Your decision to push Erner into the lake was *necessary.* Your decision led to *saving the whole world!*" Rundel Stone smiled, he actually *smiled.*

Patch stared in disbelief. He couldn't recall ever being quite as angry as he felt right now, like a kettle left on the fire until the scalding water started to slop out of the top. "I betrayed my friend!" he said, his voice almost trembling with the rage he felt. "I was scared, and I was panicking, and if I'd thought about it for even a second more I very much hope I *wouldn't* have pushed him into the water!" He squirmed in his chair, trying not to let his voice build into a shout. Never in his life could he have imagined talking like this to a Custodian Piper, let alone Rundel Stone himself. "Let me tell you, *Virtus,*" he said. "Just because things worked out, doesn't mean what I did was right! You make a decision with what you know at the time, nothing else! Doing the right thing doesn't depend on the toss of a coin or the roll of a dice!" He stood from his chair and pointed at the Virtus Piper, jabbing his finger at him as he spoke. "A stupid decision isn't suddenly *good* because of some lucky outcome! And a courageous choice isn't made wrong because luck turned against you! And...and..." Patch's anger was overwhelming, making it hard to find the words. "And the betrayal of a friend is *not* something to be proud of, Rundel Stone. *Even if it did lead to saving the whole world!*"

Rundel said nothing. One eyebrow was raised, but his expression was unreadable.

Patch gradually caught his breath, and then noticed he was still pointing an accusing finger. He lowered his hand and sat back down, shaking.

Rundel Stone, at last, nodded. "And that is the correct answer," he said. The look on his face was an odd one, thought Patch, and not something he'd ever seen on the Virtus Piper's face before – certainly not while that face was looking right at Patch's own.

It was… Well, it was almost *approving*.

"Now," said Rundel. "I would ask that you return to the others. I shall join you shortly."

"Yes, Virtus," said Patch. As he was about to close the door behind him, Rundel spoke again.

"And Patch? The betrayal wasn't what saved the world. Nor was it luck. It was courage, and friendship, that won the day. Never forget that."

9

THE CAVES OF CASIMIR

Patch went downstairs in a state of bewilderment. In part, it was because of how Rundel Stone had looked at him, but the main reason was that he'd called him by his first name.

Not Brightwater. Not *boy*.

He'd called him *Patch*, and it would take him a while to get his head around that.

The others had left the dining room, and were now seated in front of the enormous hearth in the entrance hall, under the de Frenn family portrait. Barver was lying on the floor, with Wren sitting on top of his head. They looked up at Patch warily.

"Virtus Stone will be down in a moment," said Patch. Wren squeaked at him, and he reached his arm out so she could scamper up to his shoulder.

We couldn't make out what he said, she signed. *Are you okay? He seemed to raise his voice an awful lot!*

"I'm fine," said Patch. For some reason he was reluctant to explain that *he* had been the one raising his voice.

It wasn't long before Rundel made his way downstairs, each step taken with immense care. He walked over to a closed door under the stairway. "This is the library, where Ural Casimir met his end," he said. "Come and look, please."

They gathered in front of the door as Rundel opened it.

The room was circular, about thirty feet across, and shelves covered every part of the curving walls. A desk was in the middle of the room, alongside two plush reading chairs. It was carpeted, and on the floor beside the desk was a very obvious bloodstain, browned with the passing weeks.

The most startling thing was this: the shelves were empty, while the books were in a heap in one half of the room. Each book was damaged – torn in half, or the cover ripped away from the spine.

From the titles Patch could make out, the books all seemed curiously *ordinary.* Adventure novels, classic myths and legends, poetry and plays. He presumed all the ones on magic were out of sight at the bottom of the pile.

"When I came here with Erner, this is as we discovered it," said Rundel. "Ural's body lay there, where the Raqans had found him. When I finally woke from my poisoned sleep and returned with Tobias, we met with the Raqans. They'd remembered something important. Several months before his death, Ural had received a rare and unusual book, after years of trying to find a copy. The Raqans thought nothing more about it until the days after his death. But Ural's killer had clearly been searching for a book, so could this 'rare and unusual' one be what the killer was seeking? Finding that book is the first step in finding the murderer!"

"Whoever killed Ural, the timing is suspicious," said Alia. "Days before the Hamelyn Piper intends to use the Obsidiac Organ, and Ural Casimir is murdered? I tested the box that poisoned you, Rundel. Only myself and Tobias made it react. What if it was designed to poison the Eight? What if the murderer knew who Ural was, and that was why they killed him?"

Rundel shook his head. "I don't think so," he said. "For a start, Ural was bludgeoned from behind. Why do that, if the box would simply poison him? But I do agree with you about the suspicious timing. My instinct tells me that Ural's murder was linked to the plans of the Hamelyn Piper, which means the *book* is linked. Find the book that his murderer sought, and it may do more than lead us to the killer – it could even bring us closer to the Hamelyn Piper himself!"

Patch gestured to the pile on the floor of the library.

"But they *must* have found it," he said. "They went through every single book!"

"Say that again!" said Rundel.

"They went through every single book, so…"

"Yes!" said Rundel. "*Every single book!* Think about that! If you're looking for something, and you find it, what do you do?"

Patch was lost for an answer.

"You stop looking!" said Rundel. "*Every* book has been taken and discarded. If they'd found what they sought, they would have stopped! There would still be books on the shelves. *Therefore they did not find it!*"

"What about the rest of the house?" said Barver. "Perhaps it was hidden elsewhere, but they discovered it?"

Rundel smiled. "If this book was important to Ural, there is only one place it could be. And that place is *not* in the house. Perhaps you could fetch a lantern, Tobias? We must go to the Remembrance Lawn!"

Alia and Tobias smiled and nodded. "It's about time!" said Tobias.

Barver, Patch and Wren looked at each other in bemusement.

Rundel and Tobias led the way outside, following a gravel path around the mansion. It seemed strange to Patch that

Tobias had been told to bring a lantern – it would be hours yet before darkness fell. They emerged at the rear of the house, in a well-tended garden area which had a grey stone building at the far side.

As they walked across the grass towards the building, Barver suddenly stopped in his tracks. He was at the back of the line, and Wren, holding fast to Patch's shoulder as usual, was the only one who noticed. She prodded Patch's neck.

Something's up, she signed to Patch, then pointed at Barver.

Patch walked back to his large friend, who was staring around nervously. The others were almost at the stone building.

"What's the matter?" Patch asked him.

"What did Rundel Stone call this place?" whispered Barver, looking like he expected some kind of ambush.

"The Remembrance Lawn," said Patch.

Barver glared at him. "Exactly! Have you seen? *Have you seen?*" He pointed around rapidly, and Patch noticed small rectangles of stone laid into the grass around the edges of the garden.

Leaving Barver where he was, Patch strode to the nearest stone rectangle. There were words carved into it, and he read aloud: "Larsian, Faithful Hound and Companion." He moved to the next: "Brandywine, Expert Mouser, Much

121

Missed." He looked at Wren. "It's a pet graveyard," he said, but Wren shook her head, pointing at the next stone.

Not just pets, she signed.

Patch read it out: "Enniver Watts, Gardener, Who Wished To Be Buried With His Work."

"This is a graveyard!" hissed Barver right into Patch's ear, making him jump.

"Don't sneak up like that!" said Patch.

Barver's eyes darted around in near-terror. "We're in a graveyard!" he said. "With graves! *Graves!*"

"You really are easily spooked, Barver," said Patch. They made their way to the stone building to join the others, but when they reached it Barver's look of dread seemed to worsen.

Patch could see why. The building was ornately decorated, and had the name "de Frenn" carved in large letters above the wide doors.

It was a crypt.

Barver did not look at *all* happy. "Why are we in a *graveyard*?" he said. "Beside a *crypt*?"

Rundel unlocked the crypt doors with a large key. They swung open, the horrible creaking from the hinges not helping Barver's nerves one bit.

Around the sides of the crypt were three sealed coffins, one visibly newer than the others; in the centre was a large sarcophagus, on the top of which was a stone figure of an armour-clad man, clutching a broadsword to his chest.

"Get inside the crypt, please," said Rundel. "All of you."

"I am *not* going in there," muttered Barver.

"Oh, don't be daft," said Patch. "Of course *you're* not going inside. You're far too big."

"I said all of you, and I meant it," said Rundel. He gestured to Barver, who managed – barely – to squeeze his wings inside the doorway and stand by the wall, absolutely still in case he knocked one of the coffins.

Patch shared another look with Wren, both of them baffled. With Barver inside there was hardly any room to *breathe*, let alone move. Worse was to come: Rundel reached out to the doors and closed them.

"If you would, Tobias," said Rundel, and Tobias held his lantern aloft. Rundel started to examine the stone knight, pushing and prodding at various parts of it. There was a gentle *click,* and the hilt of the carved sword opened, revealing a circular recess. Rundel pushed the centre of the circle. There was another *click*, and he stood back, satisfied. But nothing else happened.

"It will take a few moments," said Rundel. "A little history while we wait! The de Frenn fortune came from the mining of tin and other metals. This mansion was built three hundred years ago, on the site of one of their mines, long emptied of all it had to offer. The entrance to the mine was hidden, and within the deep caverns the owners could hoard their precious gold and jewels. The most *recent* owner hoarded a different kind of wealth. He also added a layer of magical protection, which takes a little time to work. This gateway will only open to those Ural would have trusted. Those of good heart, courage and honour." He looked at Patch and raised an eyebrow. "Let's see what the protective spells make of you all…"

The seconds passed. Patch wondered if he'd be asked to wait outside, but then a much deeper *clunk* sounded.

"Ah!" said Rundel. "It seems you have been approved. Now, please keep clear!"

The sarcophagus started to sink, along with a sizeable part of the stone floor, to reveal a wide stairwell carved in rock, leading down a sharply descending tunnel.

"Behold," said Rundel Stone. "The Caves of Casimir!"

There certainly were a *lot* of steps.

Tobias was at the front with Erner, followed by Alia and Rundel. Alia was helping support Rundel as he took each step – the kind of help he would have refused from anyone else. Patch, Wren and Barver were at the rear, and had already fallen behind by quite some way; Barver was going even more slowly than Rundel, wincing as he descended.

"Are you okay?" asked Patch.

"You go ahead," said Barver. "These tiny steps were made for humans, and they are *not* comfortable. The edges keep cutting right into the tender parts of my feet. Ow!"

Wren looked at Patch. *Tender parts of his feet?* she signed.

"I suppose some part of him had to be," said Patch. He sped up, passing Alia and Rundel to join Tobias and Erner a little further ahead.

"Is Barver having trouble?" asked Tobias, glancing back.

"The steps are awkward for him," said Patch. "He'll be fine."

"At this rate he'll be left in the dark," said Tobias.

"He has his own way to light things," said Patch, grinning. "If he needs to."

Further down the tunnel, he could see there was a corner coming up, but there was something unusual that he couldn't quite figure out. Only as they drew nearer could he tell what was strange.

"Something's glowing!" he cried, pointing.

Tobias stopped his descent and put his lantern behind him so it was darker up front, and there it was – a mysterious glow.

Alia smiled. "The walls of the Caves self-illuminate. You didn't think Ural would have missed an opportunity for spectacle, did you?"

Patch grew more and more excited, and couldn't help

speeding up, even as he felt Wren's claws dig into his shoulder. She squeaked a complaint, but nothing was going to slow him down.

And then they were at the corner. Two more steps, and the Caves of Casimir were revealed.

What a sight!

They emerged at the base of a large elliptical cavern. Around the circumference of the cavern, shelves were laden with leather-bound volumes; bottles contained fluids of every colour imaginable. Ladders and stairs led up to additional levels of construction, where the maws of further tunnels gaped wide, promising yet more marvels in the spaces beyond.

In the middle of the cavern floor, a great globe of the world was surrounded by curving desks and a tall cabinet filled with bizarre contraptions. All of this was lit by a glow that came from the actual *rock* of the cavern roof.

Patch was lost to the sight as he walked towards the centre, and the huge globe. Wren was the same – eyes glistening, enrapt. Erner, too, was standing with mouth agape.

Barver was the last to arrive. The entrance narrowed a bit and he had to wriggle to get inside, but the moment his eyes caught the majesty of his surroundings, he let loose with a series of dramatic and very rude phrases that made it clear he was just as flabbergasted as the rest of them.

"Feel free to explore this main cavern for a while," said Rundel. "Don't enter any others, or ascend to higher levels – those are off limits. Please disturb as little as possible. And in your case, Barver…take care not to *destroy* anything."

Barver gave him a playful salute. "I'll endeavour to do minimal damage," he said.

Patch found himself being bossed about by Wren, who seemed eager to see absolutely every book, artefact, bottle and jar in the whole cavern.

Those shelves with the red books, she'd sign, and no sooner had they reached them than she'd point somewhere else, at something different that she was *even more desperate* to see up close. Patch grew quietly infuriated, as he kept spotting things that *he* wanted to spend some time gawping at, like a four-foot-high specimen jar filled with a murky liquid, in which he was sure he could see *tentacles*. Still, he kept his annoyance to himself, as he knew that all of this magical bric-a-brac was absolute heaven for Wren. The sheer joy on her little face was a wondrous thing of its own, in these caves *filled* with wondrous things.

At last, Rundel called them back to the centre of the cavern. He stood before the globe. "Now it's time to begin the real work," he said. "Somewhere in here is the rare and unusual book that Ural's killer was looking for. And we must find it!"

There had to be *thousands* of books. Yet somewhere among them was a clue that might explain the murder of Ural Casimir, and possibly lead them to the Hamelyn Piper.

"You see why I need your help," said Rundel.

10

UNEXPECTED GUESTS

Rundel divided the cavern into sections, marking the floor with chalk. In each section were large tables piled high with a mixture of printed books and handwritten notebooks. "I shall assign each of you to one of these areas," he said. "We know almost nothing about the book we seek, only that it is rare and unusual. It could be any size, and about any subject."

"So how are we supposed to know we've found it?" asked Alia.

"A fair question," said Rundel. "Given that Ural had been seeking a copy of this book for years, he's likely to have included some references to it in his notebooks. With luck, he's been studying it – the chances are good that it's among the books on the tables."

"Admit it, Rundel," said Alia. "You're just hoping that it'll be obvious when we see it."

"Of course I am," said Rundel. "But there's no guarantee of that, which is why we must be methodical. Books on the tables should be examined first, before searching those on the shelves. And as I said, pay close attention to notebooks, and to loose pages too. We can't afford to miss any clues." He looked at Patch, and pointed to the section nearest him. "You and Wren will work together in this area."

And so the search began.

Wren sat on one of the tables, with several notebooks open around her, reading hungrily. Every minute or two she scampered across a page and used her hind legs to push it over.

"I can turn the pages for you, if you like," said Patch.

I'm fine, signed Wren. *Found anything interesting yet?*

"Not really," said Patch. "Lots of books about the history of sorcery, but all rather dull so far. How about you?"

These notebooks are packed with spells, signed Wren. *All kinds of stuff!*

"You're supposed to look for clues," he said. "Not read every word."

Try and stop me, she signed, grinning. Patch couldn't help smiling back.

For the next few hours, the Caves of Casimir were silent save for the gentle rustle of turned pages, the thump of books dropped on tables, the small clap of covers being closed.

But at no time was there a shout of discovery. Eventually, Rundel Stone waved for them to approach. "We must return to the house," he said. "We've made a start, and that was all that could be expected. A night's sleep is needed, so we'll be fresh for more searching tomorrow."

The climb back up the steps seemed to take for ever, but at least Barver wasn't suffering as he'd done on the way down. He'd found blank sheets of paper, and had strapped two thick piles to his feet with some twine – a pair of makeshift shoes to protect his soles from the steps' cruel edges.

Near the top of the tunnel, a wooden lever sat in a recess in the stone wall. Rundel pulled it, and the crypt entryway opened up again in front of them.

There were plenty of bedrooms in the mansion, but Barver, being too large to get upstairs without causing serious structural damage, was to sleep in the entrance hall itself.

Patch and Wren opted to stay with him. The ornate couch in front of the fireplace was far more comfortable than it looked, or perhaps it was simply that Patch was so tired; either way, he was asleep in an instant.

131

They were woken the next morning by the smell of baking bread, which, with the addition of some carrots in beef fat, made for a simple breakfast. This time the descent down the tunnel seemed nowhere near as long, and with his paper shoes Barver found it no trouble.

The morning went much the same way as the previous visit. Wren spent her time engrossed in the contents of Casimir's notes, and Patch carefully checked the books. He'd managed to get through about a fifth of the total in their section the day before, so it still seemed like a massive task – several more days of drudgery, most likely. Wren, on the other hand, was clearly enjoying herself. When Patch had a sneak look at a notebook she was reading he saw various tips on creating fireballs, but as he leaned in closer she waved him away.

Keep your nose out, she signed. *I'm learning!*

By the time they stopped for lunch, Patch was desperate for a break. Tobias cleared a table next to Barver for the food they'd brought down with them. Patch buttered a few crackers, took a chunk of cheese, and went for a closer look at the great globe, and the cabinet at the centre of the cavern. Wren came with him, nibbling the cheese on his shoulder.

He started by looking for Tiviscan on the globe, and even though his sense of geography wasn't great, he found it quickly; the globe turned with ease. He traced their journey – his, Wren's and Barver's – as best he could, to Marwheel Abbey, Gemspar Mountain, Axlebury, the Dragon Wastes... Some of it he had to guess, as smaller places like Axlebury and Patterfall weren't marked on the globe. "We've come a long way," he said, and Wren nodded. He put his finger on Southern Praze, where his parents had died, then moved it west to Praze-by-Desten, where he'd grown up in the home of his grandparents. He wondered when he'd see them again.

Leaving the globe, he stepped over to the cabinet, six tiers of wood and glass filled with curious items. He and Wren studied them in silence.

There was a blue gem necklace made with delicate gold filigree; a pair of sea-glass pendants, the cloudy glass seeming to swirl as he looked closer; a copper box, with gearing visible through slits in the metal; a dark-green glass sphere that made him feel very uneasy; a pyramid of grey rock, carved with eyes on each side. And that was just the first tier.

Alia appeared next to him. "Ural made quite a collection of magical artefacts over the years," she said. "But these were his pride and joy. Devices created by Sorcerers, to help focus their magic. I particularly love the ones that are part-mechanical. See the tiny mechanisms? So intricate!" She smiled. "Some of these came from Imminus Rock. When we dug them up, they just looked like bits of rust held together by mud, but when Ural cleaned them there was no rust at all."

"Imminus Rock!" said Patch. "That's my favourite chapter!"

"The Terror of Imminus Rock" was the second chapter in the official account of *The Adventures of the Eight* – in it, the heroes sought the help of a great Sorcerer, but only found an island full of monsters. Patch first heard it when he was *very* young, and it had scared him half to death with descriptions of manticores and basilisks and other terrifying beasts, but as he got older he relished the story.

Tobias joined them, while Alia continued: "Ural was especially fascinated by one of the ancient Sorcerers, a man called Lar-Sennen. He was the Sorcerer whose help we sought at Imminus Rock. Not *him* as such, mind, he was long dead – a thousand years ago! Instead, we sought things he'd left behind. Lar-Sennen, legend has it, created magical devices of such *power* that when he died, he buried them in secret locations all over the world, for fear that his greatest enemy would misuse his work. The Hidden Places of Lar-Sennen, they were known as."

"Oh, Lord, Ural wasn't just fascinated, he was *obsessed*!" said Tobias. He sounded oddly annoyed by the whole topic. "One thing about travelling with Ural Casimir, he never missed an opportunity to bang on about good old Lar-Sennen. He'd go on for *hours*."

"I liked to hear him talk," said Alia, wistful in spite of Tobias's grumpiness. "Wait a second, I'm sure there's a—" She walked off mid-sentence, and the others followed as she crossed to a table in Rundel's section. There, she pulled a huge book over to her and opened the cover. Inside were drawings. Some were simple sketches; others were coloured in vibrant hues.

"Ural drew these himself," said Alia. "He was quite an artist, although he wouldn't have agreed. Ah! Here we go…"

She'd reached a full-page title, with the words "The Hidden Places of Lar-Sennen".

And then, page after page came of fantastical landscapes. There were dragons in some ("Deep in the Territories" was written at the bottom of one page); another, titled "Solantis", seemed to be entirely underwater. Patch noted one that showed a vast army of ghosts – "Battlefields of Blood in the Ortings".

The next picture showed an island, with a craggy hill at its heart, on top of which was a small hut; in the hut stood a man, holding what seemed to be a ship's wheel. Nothing was drawn to scale – the hut, and the man inside, were huge compared to the trees around the hill. At the shoreline, ominous tentacles protruded from the water, hidden terrors from the deep.

"Is that Imminus Rock?" said Patch.

"No," said Alia. "See the title? This depicts the mythical

'Massarken', the mysterious moving fortress of the great Sorcerer himself! An island that can sail the seas! Some of the old legends say it was on the back of a giant crab." She pointed to the figure on the mountain. "The wheelhouse, Lar-Sennen himself steering it." She pointed now to the trees dotted around the base of the hill. "There, a forest filled with devil birds. And around the island, vast whirlpools suck vessels to their doom, and any that make it through are destroyed by great beasts of the sea." She shook her head, and her eyes glistened. "Lar-Sennen was Ural's hero," she said, with a sad smile. "According to the legends, Lar-Sennen thought that one day, someone worthy of continuing his legacy would find the devices he'd hidden. I think Ural hoped *he* would be the one to fulfil that legacy. When the hunt for the Hamelyn Piper began, he'd already spent years seeking the Hidden Places – well, the ones he thought weren't just fanciful myths. He was convinced we'd find something that would help us."

"Yes," said Tobias. "And so Ural led us on a merry chase, didn't he?" He looked at Patch. "The devices we dug up on Imminus Rock proved entirely useless."

"Ural was overjoyed to find them," said Alia, looking back to the cabinet. "The devices from Imminus Rock were among those he treasured most in his collection."

"Not worth a sparrow's spit, though, were they?" said Tobias. "Junk, nothing more."

Alia was rather defensive. "Ural believed they were genuine. A thousand years old, imagine it, yet with hardly a trace of corrosion! It's true that he never made any headway understanding them, but it wasn't for lack of trying. Their secrets were lost to time."

Tobias raised an eyebrow but said nothing more.

The rest of that day passed without further discovery. Then, on the third day of their search, something happened that would change everything.

As usual, Barver, Wren and Patch had slept in front of the fireplace. For breakfast they had oats and bacon, and once they'd assembled their lunch they set off towards the crypt once more.

"I don't know about you two," muttered Barver as they started their descent, the others ahead of them. "But I hope this doesn't go on for much longer. Looking through all those books is starting to give me eyestrain."

Speak for yourself, signed Wren. *I'm enjoying every second!*

"Well, you would say that," whispered Patch. "You're just reading whatever takes your fancy, not helping the search at all."

That's not fair! signed Wren. *I'm doing my bit!*

Patch looked her square in the eye. "What, by finding

interesting spells?" She folded her arms and looked away. "Exactly," said Patch.

When they were halfway down the steps, Barver suddenly stopped.

"Are your feet giving you trouble?" asked Patch.

Barver was wide-eyed, and had an odd expression on his face. "What was that noise?" he said.

Patch looked to Wren, who shook her head. "We didn't hear anything," said Patch.

The three of them stood in silence for a few seconds, then Barver's eyes widened further. "There it is again!" he said. Without another word, he turned and started to run back up the steps. This was a sight in itself, given the careful pace he'd maintained before – now he was absolutely hurtling up them.

"What's wrong?" called Rundel.

"I don't know," said Patch. "But I've seen that expression on his face before." He chased after Barver; Wren, squeaking in anger, was only just managing to hang on.

He caught up with Barver at the top of the tunnel; the entrance was opening in its slow, grinding way, Barver's agitation to get outside clear. Patch was thankful for the chance to catch his breath.

Wren let out a very cross squeak. *Will you please tell me what's happening?* she signed.

"Shanny," said Patch, still breathless. "He had the same

138

look on his face when we heard Shanny Pledger's call. I'm right, aren't I, Barver?"

Barver nodded, watching the crypt floor slide down, finally locking into position.

Wren was staring at Patch. *You mean…?*

Barver was already up through the hole, opening the crypt door.

"He heard a griffin," said Patch. He didn't want to raise Wren's hopes, but there was only one reason Patch could think of for a griffin to be here: Shanny had promised to get the message out about Alkeran, using the Echoes – the griffin way of sending news.

Up he went, through the crypt, out onto the Remembrance Lawn, and then to the front of the house. Barver was standing at the edge of the gardens, looking over the tops of the forest. As Patch reached his side, they heard a distant high-pitched screech; Barver answered it, then thrust his arm forward, pointing. "There!" he said, but he had the eyes of a predatory bird, and it was a long thirty seconds before Patch saw it too.

Griffins!

Three of them.

The first was black with white mottling on its wings, and was the largest of the three; the second was predominantly blue, with black wingtips; the third, and smallest, was brown and cream, with streaks of shimmering purple, which suddenly caught the morning light and drew a gasp of appreciation from Barver.

They touched down on the grass a short distance away, and began to walk towards them.

"Wait," whispered Patch. "I don't know anything about griffin etiquette! How do I address them?"

"Just be polite," said Barver. "Follow my lead."

"But what's considered polite? Is there anything that's a real no-no I might do by mistake?"

Barver looked thoughtful. "The greatest insult one griffin can give another is to poo in front of them," he said. "If you can avoid that, we'll be fine."

The griffins reached them, and the largest stepped forward.

"My name is Merta Strife," said the griffin – Patch suspected this was a *she*, as the voice was softer than Shanny's had been. "We seek Brother Tobias of Marwheel Abbey. We went to the Abbey first, and they directed us here, but until we heard your call the place seemed deserted."

Patch turned and saw Tobias hurrying to join them. Alia was just emerging from the hedge-lined path, and she started running too.

Barver jabbed a thumb towards them. "That's Tobias coming now," he said. "Can I ask if you're here because of Shanny Pledger?"

Patch felt Wren's claws dig into his shoulder a little – she was as tense as a drum skin.

140

Merta Strife shook her head. "The Echoes said to speak to Brother Tobias, so we speak to no other." She eyed Barver over. "You're a dracogriff?"

"The name's Barver," he said with a nod. "It was me who gave the message to Shanny. He said he'd make sure it reached the right ears. A message about a griffin, under a spell, with a box around his neck? A box containing a human heart?"

"We speak to Tobias only," replied Merta, but she'd paused for the briefest of moments, and her eyes had widened just enough for there to be no doubt: they had brought news of Alkeran!

Barver looked at Wren. "Sorry," he said. "Shanny wanted a reliable point of contact, and Tobias seemed the obvious choice."

Tobias reached them at last, his face reddened with effort, Alia only moments behind. Alia gave Wren an urgent look; she clearly knew what this might mean.

"You are Brother Tobias of Marwheel Abbey?" said Merta Strife.

"I am," said Tobias.

"We seek your help," said Merta. "A griffin has been found, in a strange condition."

Barver was close to exasperation. "Yes, yes, under a spell with a box around his neck," he said. "Can we get to the important stuff, please? Is the griffin alive?"

Merta gave Barver a long, hard look before answering.

"Those who found him thought he was dead, at first. He was pulled up in the nets of a fishing fleet in Pardissan, a town in the far south. Lashed to his saddle was the body of a woman, drowned." She gestured to the blue griffin. "This is Cramber Hoon, the pilot of that fishing fleet. He was there, and witnessed everything."

Alia raised a hand. "No one tried to remove the box, I hope?"

"No," said Cramber Hoon. "I'd heard the Echoes, which had said it was a magical device, and its removal would be very dangerous."

Barver nodded. "I'd been very clear about that," he said.

Alia patted his arm. "Well done for remembering what I'd told you," she said. "We have no time to waste! Although we do have to go north first."

Merta Strife scowled. "Absolutely not! We go south at once, to Pardissan! My only interest is in saving the life of that griffin."

"We've no choice, I'm afraid," said Alia. "I know some things about the magic that's keeping the griffin alive, but nowhere near enough." She looked at Wren, with a hopeful smile. "Underath must still be alive, if the griffin lives." She turned back to Merta Strife. "We must go north, to Axlebury. We have another passenger to collect!"

THE FISHERMAN

The third griffin was called Wintel Dree; she bowed her head in greeting as Merta introduced her.

Tobias handled their side of the introductions, describing Alia as an expert in magical affairs. The griffins were more interested in Wren, however, when they learned of her curse and the possibility that finding Alkeran could be her salvation.

Rundel and Erner opted to remain behind at the mansion, to continue their search through Casimir's books and papers.

It was time to go. Merta Strife looked the passengers up and down. "You'd better dress more warmly," she told them. "The low windways aren't favourable – a two-day journey, but half a day if we take the high windways.

They're cold, I warn you!"

Wintel nodded. "Speed is key," she said. "But not if your passengers freeze to death."

Patch waited for Wintel to admit she was kidding, but no admission came. "You're serious," he said, and then he looked at Barver. "She's serious!"

"Yep," said Barver. "Dragons don't tend to use the high windways – they don't fly well in the cold."

"Will you be okay?" asked Patch.

Barver shrugged. "I've not had much experience that high up, but the cold doesn't really bother me."

"Well, if you struggle you can always turn back," Merta told him.

"Come on, then!" said Alia. "Coats! Gloves! Scarves! Extra pairs of socks! I'm sure there'll be some in the house!"

And so there were. Patch felt rather uneasy about taking things that didn't belong to him, but Alia waved his concerns away. "Ural would want you to have them," she said. "Trust me."

His coat was still serving him well, so he'd taken a long scarf, a pair of gloves, extra socks and a warm woollen tunic. He spotted a cushion that had burst its seams and teased out some stuffing to put into one of his coat pockets. "A little extra warmth for you," he told Wren.

The passengers were shared out: Patch and Wren on Barver, Alia on Wintel, and Tobias on Cramber. Soon

144

enough they were airborne, Merta Strife at the lead, the others spread out behind her.

"You know the way to Axlebury," Patch said into Barver's ear. "Shouldn't you lead?" They were far enough from the rest that even with his voice raised there was no risk of being overheard.

"Show some respect!" said Barver. "Merta is obviously a Pila."

"A what?"

"It's like an Elder," said Barver. "That's why Cramber went to her when he found Alkeran. It's also why Wintel is here – a Pila always has an assistant, like an apprentice, who lives nearby."

"I didn't think griffins had rulers."

"That's not what I mean. A Pila is an old and highly respected griffin, who'll give advice and help when it's needed. And as for her taking the lead, you can bet she knows more about the high windways than I ever will! When we get close to our destination, she'll let me take over."

And she did. First, though, came five hours of high-level flight. The air was bitter, yet thankfully dry. Barver had no trouble at all in the cold. Wren made use of the stuffing-lined pocket almost at once, and Patch wrapped his long scarf around his head, fully encasing it. Even with the extra socks his feet quickly went numb in the chill, but when

Merta at last asked Barver to guide them, they were able to drop down to warmer air. By the time they saw Fendscouth Tor in the distance, Patch's toes had woken up again.

On the far side of the Tor sat the castle of Underath the Sorcerer; below it lay the forest, and within the forest was the shimmering surface of the lake he'd pushed Erner into. He tried hard not to look at it, glad that Erner had stayed back in the mansion.

Barver took them down close to the castle entrance. The passengers dismounted, and removed their extra clothing before they overheated.

Merta Strife sniffed the air. "The person we've come for lives in this castle, I presume," she said.

Alia nodded. "The griffin that was found is called Alkeran. He lived here, with a Sorcerer by the name of Underath. It's Underath we've come to get."

"Another Sorcerer kidnapped Alkeran," said Barver. "Presumably the woman you found strapped to his back. The box around Alkeran's neck is dark magic that allowed the kidnapper to control him. It contains Underath's heart, cut from his chest."

Merta blinked in surprise. "His heart?" she said. "So we're here to collect a *body*?"

"Actually, no," said Alia. "He had just enough magic left in him to survive."

Patch shuddered. Wren and Erner had been the only

146

ones who had actually *met* Underath and seen the hurried replacement he'd used – a shoe, pulsating horribly in the blackened hole in his chest. But Wren had described it in such gleeful detail, the image was very real in Patch's memory.

Alia continued. "The fact that Alkeran is alive means that Underath must be alive too. They are paired." There was an ancient magic between griffins and humans; a *pairing*, which could only be formed if each would give their life to save the other. If one was injured, the life force of the other would help them recover – or at least stop them succumbing to death. This was the only reason Underath had had enough time to save his own life, and the only reason Alkeran hadn't drowned. "Time to get on with it," said Alia. "Everyone stay here, I'll see if there are any magical protections in place before I knock." She walked towards the castle doors and stood, arms folded, deep in thought. After a few minutes she shrugged and took hold of an iron-chain bellring and pulled it. A single, deep tone rang out.

They waited.

Alia tried the bell again; and again. She pulled at the door, but it was locked. At last, she walked back to them. She gave the griffins a reassuring smile, then with a tilt of her head drew Barver to one side. Patch and Wren, naturally, stayed close enough to hear.

"Barver, you couldn't just fly up and see if there are signs of life?" she said, her voice low.

Wren squeaked. *Oh, no,* she signed. She looked utterly desolate.

"What?" said Barver. "What is it?"

"Alkeran is a whisker away from death," said Alia. "He's only alive because he borrows from Underath, yet Underath was only just alive himself. His shoe-heart was using up all his magic."

Barver frowned. "So Underath could be inside somewhere, unconscious like Alkeran."

"Exactly," said Alia. "Just go over the wall into the courtyard. Have a quick look around and report straight back."

Barver nodded. Up he went, but just as he was about to go over the castle wall he changed direction and flew towards the forest.

"Where is he going?" said Alia, shaking her head in agitation. It wasn't long before he reappeared, and landed beside them.

"Sorry," he said. "I spotted someone fishing at the lakeside. Sleeping, actually. I got close enough to be sure: it's him."

It can't be him, signed Wren. She, Patch and Tobias were walking through the forest towards the lake. Barver and Alia had stayed at the castle, Tobias having successfully

148

argued that Underath might react badly if a fearsome dracogriff and a Sorcerer (which Underath would surely be able to recognize Alia as) approached him.

Wren had to go, since she was the only one Underath actually knew, and there was no way Patch was letting her go without him. Tobias, in his simple monk's habit, hoped to come across as unthreatening.

Wren, meanwhile, was convinced that Barver had misidentified the fisherman. *I mean, fishing?* she signed. *The very idea of catching his own food would give Underath a rash!*

When they reached the lake, Patch felt slightly sick. This was where Erner would have been captured by the mercenaries, he thought.

"Well?" whispered Tobias. "Is it him or not?"

At the edge of the water, a man slept, his back propped against a tree trunk. He wore a long tunic, belted at the waist and rather grimy. A simple rod was propped up beside him, the line in the water, a bell at the top of the rod. Nearby was a small fire, burned down to hot embers. A pan lay beside it, together with a bundle of foraged greens.

Wren was open-mouthed with shock. Patch had only seen Underath's face briefly in the visions conjured up by Alia in the bonfire at Gemspar, but it was definitely him – much grubbier, it had to be said, and his face had a touch of sunburn, but Barver hadn't been mistaken.

149

"It's him all right," said Patch. Wren nodded, staring. The three of them walked closer, reaching the fire.

Tobias cleared his throat loudly. "Hello, sir!" he called.

Underath opened his eyes, blinking away the sleep. He looked briefly at Tobias, then closed his eyes again. "Don't often get folk here," he said. "Don't you know that castle is owned by a terrifying Sorcerer?"

"You don't seem all that terrifying," said Tobias.

This time, the Sorcerer's eyes snapped open and stayed wide. A sneer spread across his face. He started to stand, something that was clearly difficult for him. At last, he noticed the rat on Patch's shoulder, and a curious thing happened.

His sneer vanished, replaced by a smile. Not for long, it has to be said – the smile seemed to realize it didn't have permission to be there, and ran off as quickly as it had arrived. "You!" he said. "Um…um…" He snapped his fingers, concentrating.

"Wren," suggested Patch.

"Yes! Wren!" said Underath. "I've often wondered how you were getting on."

He's gone weird, signed Wren. *I think he's broken.*

The thought drew Patch's eyes to Underath's chest. Hidden under the tunic was a beating shoe; he couldn't take his eyes away, picturing it from Wren's very vivid descriptions.

Underath noticed his stare, and brought an arm up over his chest. "Your friend could do with some manners," said Underath to Wren, and Patch suddenly felt very small indeed. Underath went to the lake's edge, pulling a catch-net from the water. In it was a single small fish. He shook it from the net, back into the lake. "Slim pickings," he said. "Doesn't seem worth the cooking time. I'll just fry up the greens and call it a day." He came to the fire and put the pan onto the hot embers, then added his bundle of greens and a little oil from a bottle he took from his pocket.

As the greens simmered, he stood; again, Patch noted how slow his movement was.

Underath frowned, looking at Wren. He reached out, and ran a finger along the black ring around her midriff. "You've broken your morphic deflector," he said, a hint of sorrow in his voice. "That's why you came, to find out if I had news of Alkeran. Sadly there is none. As you see, I'm surviving, but without the magic to preserve it, the food in the castle is rotten. My wealth is gone too. The mercenaries left soon after you came, stripping the castle of everything valuable. So I fish! I've even trapped my own game, once or twice. There are greens to be foraged at the lake-shore." He sounded exhausted.

"Underath," said Tobias. "There is news of…"

But Underath's attention was taken by the smell of burning. In the pan on the fire was a sorry mass of charred green leaves. He crouched and stirred it, forlorn, and looked up with tears in his eyes. "You see what I've become," he said. "In recent days I've been worse than ever. Too weak to do anything more than survive, and my only true friend is out there, enslaved by the woman who made me think she was my wife, then attempted to murder me."

Tobias tried again. "But the—"

"If only I'd hidden my wealth better!" wailed Underath. "Perhaps I could have paid some mercenaries to help me, like she did! Oh, Alkeran, *Alkeran*, forgive me!"

"Oh, please shut up!" cried Tobias, his patience at an end. Underath, too tired for rage, looked timid, as Tobias counted things off one by one on his fingers: "First, Alkeran's been found alive in a fishing village in the far south. Second, there are griffins waiting at your castle who will take us there. Third, Alkeran urgently needs your help if he's to survive. Now are you coming or not?"

Underath looked at Tobias, and there was hope in his tear-reddened eyes. With aching slowness, he stood, and Patch wondered if Underath would even be able to walk, or if Tobias would have to carry the man.

And then, without warning, Underath started running back to the castle, calling out for Alkeran as he went.

Wow, signed Wren. *He can really move fast when he wants to.*

152

12

HEART OF
A SORCERER

Patch easily kept up with Underath, leaving Tobias wheezing in his wake. When the Sorcerer broke through the edge of the forest to find a group of griffins, a dracogriff and Alia, he was entirely unfazed. "Tell me everything!" he cried.

"My name is Cramber Hoon," said Cramber. "I am a pilot for the fishing fleet in Pardissan, a town in the southern reaches of the country of Ginwiddian. It was a clear and sunny morning when the fleet, expecting a good haul of leaping redfin, left harbour and—"

"Tell me *not quite* everything!" cried Underath. "Start with finding Alkeran, and if I wave my hand like *this*, skip to the next important part!"

And so the details were passed on. In the middle of it,

Tobias reached them at last, panting and muttering under his breath about running up a tunnel already that morning.

"I must gather equipment," said Underath. "You there!" He pointed to Tobias. "Come with me! I cannot carry everything."

Underath went to the castle entrance, which he unlocked with a surprisingly small key. He vanished inside, and Tobias grudgingly followed him. A great deal of clattering and banging echoed out of the doorway, and when they emerged again, Underath had a small pouch in one hand, while Tobias was struggling with a heavy sack.

Alia, who'd been keeping a low profile since Underath had reached them, stepped forward. "What do you have there?" she asked.

"Everything I might need!" said Underath. He gave her a long uneasy stare. "You have a touch of sorcery about you," he said.

Alia almost laughed. "Yes, you could say that," she said. "A *touch*."

Underath's eyes widened. "Are you the one who tried to break Wren's curse with that morphic deflector?"

"Morphic deflector?" she said. It took her a moment to realize what he was talking about. "Ah, her bracelet! I am. What of it?"

Underath shook his head. "Just, well, it was…clever." Alia didn't really know what to say, while Underath seemed almost taken aback, as if complimenting someone else's skill was entirely alien to him.

Which it was.

Barver gave Tobias instructions for tying the heavy sack of equipment to his harness, so that it rested just behind where Patch would sit. Tobias heaved it up, and it clinked and rattled as he fastened ropes around it.

"Try to be gentle with that," called Underath. "It's not *very* explosive, but best be on the safe side, eh?"

Tobias paused, then tied with a degree more care.

Patch stared at it. Barver, though, seemed entirely unconcerned. "Don't worry," he told Patch, with a mischievous smile. "I'll fly *really smoothly*."

The townsfolk of Pardissan cheered as the group approached over the water. "Four griffins!" some cried out, astonished, although as they flew closer there was a good deal of arguing over what the fourth shape in the sky actually was, before they settled on, "Three griffins, and possibly a dragon!" Even after landing at the docks, the crowd still weren't quite certain, but Barver was used to that and didn't take it to heart.

Cramber Hoon was clearly much loved by the people. Children who'd been anxious when he'd left gave him hugs; adults welcomed him home. He waited for the clamour to subside, then spread his arms and addressed them.

"My friends," he said. "I promised I would hurry back with help, and I have! There is nothing to fear now. Tend to your nets, and mend your sails, for tomorrow our boats will be back at sea!"

They gave a loud cheer in return. Cramber led the group away from the townsfolk, onto a rock-and-sand beach at the edge of the docks, then towards a large rickety-looking building at the far end of the beach. The townsfolk, anxious faces all, watched them go.

"They're scared," said Cramber, sorrow in his voice – he clearly felt deeply about his people. "Pulling a stranger's corpse from the sea is dreaded by all fisherfolk. A terrible omen. But two corpses? Unimaginable! And then to find that the griffin was still alive, against all natural order? They put a brave face on it, but they're more afraid than they have ever been. Until this situation is resolved, they won't dare sail again."

The ramshackle wooden building had large doors that took up the whole of the front; an old man stood there, and greeted Cramber with a nod. "Good to have you back, Cramber!" said the man.

"Good to be back, Ned!" said Cramber. "Anything from our guest?"

The man shook his head. "No change," he said.

"We'll take things from here," said Cramber, and the man hurried off, a quick nod to each of the new arrivals.

Cramber stepped over to the doors. "We put them in here when we found them," he said. "It was a boatwright's shed, many years ago, before the new docks were built." He pushed the doors inwards. Underath let out a gasp.

There was Alkeran, flat on his back, wings spread. The griffin was dark grey; many of his feathers stuck out at angles, broken. His eyes were closed. Barver stared, as did Merta and Wintel, and Patch could understand why – Alkeran was horribly still. From where they stood, he didn't seem to be breathing at all.

"Stay here for a moment," Underath said, his voice faltering with the shock of seeing his friend in such an awful state. He walked into the building.

Cramber looked at Merta. "What should we do?" he said.

Merta took a deep breath. "The hardest part comes now, Cramber," she said. "We must stand aside, and wait." She nodded to Alia. "The griffin's fate is in the hands of your friend," she said.

"*Friend* is a bit strong," said Alia. "But, yes. Where is the woman's body?"

"Over there," said Cramber in a low voice, pointing. In the far corner of the building lay a shape with white canvas draped over it.

Alia scratched at her chin, thinking. "She can wait for the time being," she said. "I'll speak to Underath and see what he makes of the situation. I don't know how long this could take, or how dangerous it will be. This is dark magic, so the risks are very high indeed. All of you should keep some distance. If I need you, I'll call. Or scream, if it's really urgent. Tobias, bring that sack and follow me."

She walked into the building. With an anxious glance to Patch, Tobias untied the sack from Barver's harness and followed her.

As the doors behind them closed, Alia and Tobias stood quietly. There was plenty of light; the roof was a patchwork of rotting timber and sky. Ahead of them, Underath stood by Alkeran, studying the wooden box that was tied around the griffin's neck. Eventually he noticed them watching, and left Alkeran's side to join them.

He took the sack from Tobias and began to rummage inside, taking items out one at a time and setting them on the floor next to the wall: a variety of metal and earthenware containers, several small wooden cases, and tied bundles of sticks that Alia recognized at once – among them tansy, burdock and lavender. He opened up each of the cases, revealing a tight-packed collection of glass phials. He selected some of the little bottles, each a vivid colour. Then he turned to Alia, speaking with some reluctance: "I could use your help."

"Gladly," said Alia. She nodded to Tobias. "Wait outside,"

she told him. "Stay ready. We might need your Healing Songs at any time."

"I'll be at the door," said Tobias. "Be careful."

Alia gave him a reassuring smile. Once he was gone, though, the smile dropped from her lips. She was worried. "Tell me you have a plan," she said to Underath, looking at the heart-box around the griffin's neck. "I can feel the dark currents of that spell from here, and I don't like it."

"Strong, isn't it?" said Underath. "A challenge! What little magic I have is taken up by staying alive, but with your help, we can break the bonds of the spell." He paused. "The danger is great, though. I think I might be able to manage the final part alone. Why risk both our lives?"

Alia smiled again. "If you don't mind me saying, I think the loss of magic has done you some good."

"How so?"

"You seem to actually care about people other than yourself. From how Wren described you, that's a welcome change."

"It's not the loss of magic that's changed me," said Underath, looking at Alkeran. "I'd taken my friend for granted. Losing him…it hurt more than I could have imagined."

"Wren told me he'd been a prisoner before you met him," said Alia. "You freed him, then? From some awful captivity?"

"I didn't free him," said Underath. "I found him, yes,

years ago, in circumstances very similar to this – on a shoreline, exhausted, his feathers sand-caked. He'd been trapped on a sandbar in the Great Grey Ocean for days, his flight to the mainland a last desperate act, weighed down by his chain. For the first time in my life, I realized I could help someone. Yes, I saved his life, but if anything, it was Alkeran who saved me. Darker sorcery had always called to me, but Alkeran steered me away from that path. No matter what I did, he didn't give up on me. He always believed I was better than I thought. With him gone…" He shook his head, miserable. "Perhaps you wouldn't understand."

"I can sympathize," said Alia, and her eyes drifted to the door, where Tobias waited on the other side. "Right, enough of this. Show me the box with your heart, and explain how you plan to untangle the spell!"

The box had a beat of its own. That was the most unnerving thing, for Alia.

It was carved from a single piece of hard, dark wood – probably red birch, she thought, a tree whose blood-like sap gave it its name and made it a favourite among a certain kind of Sorcerer. A silver clasp on the top kept a hinged lid in place; Underath told her not to look inside, yet, and she was happy to oblige. The box was slightly larger than her hand, tightly bound to Alkeran's neck with leather straps.

Underath asked her to place a hand on either end of it, and tell him what she thought. That's when she felt it beat, a regular pulse.

"The heart *itself* doesn't beat," said Underath. "I already looked. It is the wood of the *box* that beats. Fascinating, isn't it?"

She let go of the box, glad to be free of its pulsing rhythm. "You've had plenty of time to plan for this," she said. "Do you know what ritual she used?"

"No," said Underath. "But I've studied many dark Sorcerers in my time. Some of this feels…familiar." He looked to the canvas-covered shape in the corner. "Alkeran's bond to her keeps him close to death; his bond to *me* stops him from succumbing. Even so, it's lucky for us that she's dead. Without her, the spell is ready to collapse. All it needs is a little encouragement." He unfastened the silver clasp and opened the box. "Take a look at what's left."

Alia looked. The heart inside was shrivelled and black. "She may have set traps for us."

Underath shook his head. "To do that, she would have had to plan for defeat! She didn't expect this outcome."

"So what do you intend to do?"

"We will prepare a fire," he said. "I will take the heart. I will burn it."

Alia's eyes widened. "Bold move," she said. "I expected you to reclaim your heart somehow, not destroy it. What about…" She gestured towards his chest. "Well, what about that?"

Underath unbuttoned his shirt and showed what lay beneath: scarring encircled the middle of his chest, the skin dark red, and in the centre the flesh was uneven, forming an outline that was unmistakably shoe-like. "It's doing quite nicely," he said. "Part of me is trapped in my old heart. Burning the heart will release it, and it should find its way back home. Once I am whole, my powers will return in full. My shoe-heart will be complete, and Alkeran will be free from the spell." He closed the box lid again. "We must prepare," he said.

Alia's task was to create a Volsan Flame, a magical fire hot enough to melt copper or, as was needed here, to destroy an object that was the foundation for a powerful spell. It was a risk, certainly – destroying the main component of a hex or curse could have unexpected consequences.

Among Underath's equipment was a thick clay bowl – a crucible – into which Alia arranged clippings of the stick bundles. The preparation was painstakingly precise, as the weave pattern of the sticks had to be exactly right. Into that went the contents of the phials Underath had selected. Finally, Underath carefully removed the dried-out heart from the red-birch box and placed it in the centre. The Flame itself would be triggered by Alia, requiring a tightly focused outpouring of magical energy that Underath couldn't manage in his weakened state.

With everything ready, Alia flexed both hands, generating purple flecks of light that wove around her fingers. She looked at Underath. "Are you sure about this?" she said.

"Oh, my dear lady…" he replied. "You're a Sorcerer, just as I am. We pretend we're wise, but are we ever truly sure about anything?"

"Then here goes," she said, and she released a stream of power at the contents of the crucible. The air around it began to shimmer, forming a column that climbed six feet high. The first signs of fire appeared among rich blue smoke within the crucible, and with a sudden *whoosh* the Volsan Flame appeared: a swirling vortex of heat that filled the column perfectly.

Underath began to chant, and the heart started to glow: green first, then white, so bright that Alia had to look away. The heat coming from it was astonishing – both Sorcerers stepped back, as the fire roared even higher, then suddenly faded to nothing.

The only sound now was a regular *clink* as the crucible cooled down. Underath took a wary step closer, and used a brass rod to poke around in the ashes. "Nothing of the heart remains," he said. "The task is done."

"Do you feel any different?" asked Alia.

He shook his head. "I thought it would be immediate," he said. "Nothing yet, though." He frowned suddenly. "No, wait, I can feel something… It's working." The frown deepened and became a look of alarm. "Oh," he said. "Oh dear. I was afraid of this. All a bit much, not sure I can keep it contained…" He grabbed Alia's shoulder, urgency and fear in his voice. "Alkeran is free of the spell, but he is still on the very edge of death." He stepped back: away from Alia, and away from Alkeran. "Save him, whatever happens to me."

"Of course," said Alia. "But there's no need to…" *Panic*, she'd been about to add, but then she fell silent, staring. She'd noticed Underath's hair.

It had started to *glow*.

At the shoreline, the waves were breaking in a way that should have been relaxing, but Patch had never felt more tense in his life.

Barver was also nervous; he was biting his nails, which was new for him, and very distracting. His nails were huge and incredibly strong, as were his teeth. Each chomp sounded like an iron door being hit by a cannonball.

Wren was the worst, naturally. With the path of her entire life depending on the outcome, she was perched on

Patch's shoulder, trembling slightly, not taking her eyes off the doors of the boatwright's building. All Patch could do was give her the occasional reassuring stroke.

Outside the building, Tobias paced back and forth. From time to time he would stop and turn to the doorway as if he'd heard something absolutely crucial, but then he would simply start pacing again.

The griffins were largely silent, watching with patience.

This had gone on for almost an hour, when the roaring sound of the Volsan Flame reached them. They all looked to the building, expectant. What they did *not* expect was a Sorcerer suddenly hurtling out of one of the many gaps in the roof, leaving a trail of green-and-red sparks in his wake.

Wren squeaked in terror. Patch stared.

Barver crunched on one last nail. "Uh oh," he said.

Cramber pointed up at Underath. "Oooh!" he said. "He can fly!"

"No, Cramber," said Merta. "I really don't think that's *good*."

Wintel, though, seemed to have snapped into a different gear altogether. "He must be unconscious, going at that speed!" she said. "And look at how he's flopping around. That is *not* controlled flight!"

Alia ran out of the building and came towards them, screaming: "Do something! Please *do something!*"

Merta looked to Wintel; Wintel nodded, and launched herself into the air.

Cramber readied to leap after her.

"No," Merta told him. "Let her work! She's the most agile of us all. She knows what she can do."

"She's going to catch him?" cried Patch.

"Yes," said Merta, and they watched as Wintel gathered height and speed. Far above, the ascent of Underath, the human firework, began to slow; the bright trail of sparks subsided, then failed completely. He started to fall.

Wren dug her claws into Patch's shoulder.

Wintel flew higher and higher, and even from this distance they could see how much effort she was putting in to gain height. She was closing on Underath with every moment that passed, and then…

"She missed him!" yelled Patch, horrified.

Merta shook her head. "Wintel has to get above him, then swoop down. She must match his speed if she wants to avoid injuring him. Humans are so fragile, you see."

They watched as Wintel turned and dived, hurtling down after the falling Sorcerer: closer, closer, and then – yes! She seized the wizard!

But the ground was coming up quickly.

"She's too low," cried Cramber.

She *did* look low, to Patch.

"Fly, Wintel!" shouted Merta. "*Fly!*"

Barver said nothing, his hands over his mouth.

And then, impact seeming a certainty, Wintel managed to catch the air, flaring the feathers on her wings and pulling out of her dive – flying over their heads and out to sea as all of them cheered with relief.

Merta looked at them with a sly smile. "You see?" she said. "She knows what she can do!"

Wintel made a slow turn and brought Underath back to shore, laying him gently on the sand. He opened his eyes and looked around at the faces above him, settling on Alia. "I...I didn't explode?"

"It seems not," said Alia, smiling. "Although it *was* rather spectacular."

Underath looked at his hands as green sparks danced around his fingers. "It worked," he said, then sat up suddenly, his face filled with worry. "Alkeran!" He tried to stand, but was still too weak and fell back to his knees.

"Don't worry," said Alia. "Alkeran is in good hands. Listen!"

And from the building, the sound of gentle Piping drifted out to them. Patch smiled. In the commotion, he'd not noticed that Tobias had gone into the building to be with Alkeran.

It was a Healing Song. Tobias had started his work.

13

The Cure.
Again.

At first, they left Tobias to get on with it, as they listened outside. Later, when Underath was steady on his feet, he and Alia went into the building to join him.

Cramber left to tell the people of Pardissan that everything was well, in spite of the spectacle of a Sorcerer exploding through the roof.

The early evening sun had kept the day pleasantly warm. Patch was sitting on the sand; Wren was on his shoulder, keeping a close eye on the building behind them. The Song Tobias was playing had a soothing effect, and Patch could have happily slept right where he was. Wren, though, was understandably agitated, desperate to find out if Underath could undo the curse that had made her a rat. Underath had created the curse in the first place – if *he* couldn't reverse it, that would surely mean she was condemned for ever.

Patch wanted to reassure her, though telling her not to worry, or that everything would be okay, seemed wrong – easy things for him to say, but meaningless to her. "Not long now," he said. "We'll ask Underath soon."

Eventually, Wren lost patience and insisted that Patch take her inside the building. There in the middle of the floor lay Alkeran, a very different griffin to the one they'd seen when they'd first arrived. Instead of the shallow, imperceptible breaths, the griffin was breathing deeply now.

Near Alkeran's head, Tobias played, sitting on an empty old pitch barrel, several of which had been dragged over from a stack of them in the corner. He looked up as Patch approached.

"We wanted to see how things were going," said Patch. "We'll not get in the way, I promise."

"You're welcome to sit," said Alia. She put a hand on Underath's shoulder. "It would do you good to stretch your legs, after all that whizzing about. Let's take a walk."

"I'd rather stay," said Underath, but Alia wasn't having it.

"Tish and tush!" she said, pulling him to his feet. "Your friend is resting, and no amount of worried gawping is going to speed things up." She led him outside.

Tobias patted the barrel next to him. "You two can keep me company," he said. Even though he'd stopped playing, the music kept coming, the Pipe sustaining the Song. It would need attention soon, of course, to stop it fading, but short breaks were perfectly safe.

Patch sat. "How's the patient?" he asked.

Tobias held up a hand. "In a moment," he said. "Let me bolster the Song first." He played, focusing on an underlying rhythmic sequence that Patch couldn't identify, then switching to a more familiar high melody. Soon enough, Tobias was satisfied with the Song once more. "Alkeran is responding well to my playing," he said. "I've tweaked the basic form of the Curative Sleep – did you recognize it?"

Patch nodded, realizing that was the name of the part he'd found familiar. "I did, but my Healing Songs could do with a little work."

"Healing is a speciality," said Tobias, with a sigh. "At Tiviscan, they teach the students Battle Songs long before they teach Healing. Erner did an excellent job with Rundel when he was poisoned, but that was only because of his Custodian training. If you watch me work, I think you'll get a feel for the method. The Curative Sleep is at the heart of all the best Healing Songs."

Wren was just as interested as Patch. *Have you done much Healing on griffins?* she signed.

Tobias smiled. "My experience on non-human patients

is limited. I've helped livestock at the Abbey now and again, but this is my first griffin. There are important changes needed in the Healing Song, depending on the species." He played again, building up a deep and complex counterpoint that Patch hadn't really noticed before, long notes that changed very slowly. Done, Tobias looked at Wren again. "It's good that you take an interest in Alkeran, Wren, but I think your real interest lies elsewhere, yes? With Underath?"

Wren chittered. *I'm scared to ask*, she signed.

"Alia has already asked him," said Tobias. Wren was almost rigid with nerves. "Underath is confident that it can be done. He plans to unweave the curse once night has fallen."

Wren's paws went to her mouth. A tear formed in one eye, and she trembled. Patch gently stroked her head, but said nothing.

When Alia and Underath returned, Wren wasted no time: *Tobias told us about the cure*, she signed.

"Good," said Alia. "We can begin soon, but there are things to discuss before you can decide."

Decide? signed Wren. *My decision's already made!*

"There are possible dangers," said Alia. "I'll explain them to you in a moment, but you must promise to listen

171

carefully." She held out her arm; Wren scampered onto it, and sat on Alia's shoulder, giving Patch a nervous glance as she went. "You're ready, Underath?" said Alia. "Your griffin is safe, as you can see. Your power is restored. Do you have all you need?"

Underath reluctantly took his eyes from his beloved griffin and turned to Wren. "I made a promise, and I always keep my promises. I'll gather the necessary items, and once the sun has set we shall start."

Thank you, signed Wren.

Underath smiled. "Ah, yes, the hand speech! I can see that would be useful. The mercenaries who took my castle used it often. I saw them, from my hiding places, but I was at a loss to understand. I've studied many ancient languages, but did I have a book on hand speech? No, I did not!"

Did you see what happened when we left your castle that day? signed Wren; Patch translated.

"I know they caught the young Custodian, while the rest of you escaped," said Underath. "They plundered the castle and went on their way. Alia told me the lad survived his ordeal, which is pleasing. They were a nasty bunch, and I didn't much like his chances. I expect, as a Custodian, he had sacrificed his own freedom so that you could get away?"

"Something like that," said Alia quickly, putting a gentle hand on Patch's arm. "Now, Patch, I have to ask you to leave Wren with us."

"But…" started Patch.

Alia shook her head sternly. "Once we're ready, we need to go inland and find a clearing in the woods. We must concentrate completely, in a place free of distractions. You and Barver would be distractions!"

Patch looked at Wren, and Wren looked at Patch. It didn't need saying. Wren would much rather have her friends there; Patch didn't want her to do it alone.

But the last time a cure for Wren's curse had been attempted, Patch had tried to intervene when he'd thought it was going wrong, and all he'd managed to do was prompt Alia's prophecy.

"I understand," said Patch. He gave one last sign of *good luck* to Wren, and she nodded in return. Then Patch walked outside. The low orange sun reflected off the sea. Cramber and Wintel were circling above the water. Merta was curled on the sand, apparently asleep. Barver was at the shore, watching the flying griffins.

"They're going to begin Wren's cure soon," Patch said to him as he reached his side. "When the sun sets."

Barver said nothing, instead taking in a huge breath and letting it out very slowly. "How is she?" he said at last.

"Scared," said Patch. "Excited, of course, but mainly scared."

"Me too," said Barver. "Well, at least we'll be there to help her get through!"

Patch shook his head. "We're banned," he said. "Too much of a distraction. And there was something else Alia said, about possible *dangers*."

"What dangers?" said Barver.

"I don't know," said Patch. "Alia wanted to explain them to Wren before she decided whether to go ahead or not. Although I can't imagine how bad they would have to be, to put Wren off."

The doors of the boatwright's shed opened. Out came Alia and Underath, Wren on Alia's shoulder. Underath carried his sack, far less bulky than it had been when they'd first arrived, presumably now containing only those things he needed to undo Wren's curse.

Patch and Barver could only watch as they walked towards woodland a short distance from the beach, disappearing into the trees.

Patch looked back out to sea, where the last of the sun would soon disappear behind the horizon. "Now we wait," he said, overcome with the burden of worry.

"Do we, though?" said Barver, a twinkle of mischief in his eyes. "I mean, I'm sure we can find *somewhere* to watch from?"

It wasn't hard to keep track of Alia and Underath. Once the sun had set, the two Sorcerers used magic to light their way

– a bright green orb moving in the air ahead of them. The green orb faded and a purple one replaced it.

"That purple one is Alia's," said Barver. They were too far away for Patch to be able to see more than the general glow, but Barver's pinpoint vision was easily up to the task.

Barver, with Patch on his back, was flying just above the treetops of a hill as they watched, not wanting to risk being spotted against the darkening sky. At times he would hover; mostly he kept circling at a slow pace.

Eventually, with darkness complete, it seemed that the Sorcerers had chosen their spot. Deep in the woods, a wide circle of orbs appeared one by one – alternating green and purple – illuminating a clearing.

"I think I've spotted somewhere closer to set down," said Barver. "A hillock that may give us a good view. What do you say?"

"You can see from much further away," said Patch. "Better that you tell me what's happening, rather than risk them seeing us."

"Don't worry," said Barver. "I'll keep out of sight on the approach, and as long as we're quiet we'll be fine."

Slowly, they got closer to the lights, and Barver set down on a rocky hillock directly overlooking the clearing.

Below, the two Sorcerers were ready to begin.

THE UNWEAVING

Barver and Patch watched nervously as Alia walked to the centre of the clearing and set something down, a shape too small for Patch to make out. He glanced at Barver, who nodded: *Wren.*

Alia stepped back to the edge of the clearing, joining Underath under one of the purple orbs. Underath took something from his sack, then went to Wren and waved his hands above her. A coloured cloud formed, and he returned to the sack to take something new. Back and forth he went, and each time he waved what he held before returning, leaving coloured dust in the air. There was a light wind, but instead of dispersing, the dust cloud thickened, until neither the tiny shape of Wren nor the ground she was on were visible. The cloud began to swirl slowly. Multicoloured sparks formed within it, then brighter flashes, as if it was a miniature thunderstorm.

Underath took position a little way from the cloud. He stood, head bowed, and his arms rose up either side of him. For a time, nothing happened: seconds became minutes, but Patch could sense *something,* like a high-pitched whistle getting ever higher, yet there was no sound. Just a feeling of tension building, until at last...

Underath flung both arms to the sky, and with that motion, chaos erupted in the clearing. Thick tendrils burst out from the cloud, dozens of them unfurling, of every colour. They shot from the centre of the clearing to fill it, some rolling on the ground, others reaching thirty feet high – like tentacles of coloured dust, writhing in silence.

Patch and Barver looked at each other, stunned.

"What is that?" whispered Barver. "Is Wren safe?"

"Does Alia seem worried?" said Patch.

Barver looked to the clearing's edge, where Alia stood. "She looks interested, nothing more," he said.

"Then Wren's safe," said Patch.

Underath began to gesture with his arms, and the tendrils seemed to follow his commands, moving over one another, turning and curling, straightening, and suddenly Patch could see it:

Some of them were knotted together, and Underath's movements were undoing those knots. Then, as the tendrils separated, he would tie them together again in a slightly different way.

Unweaving. That was how Tobias had put it: unweaving the curse.

And that was exactly what Underath was doing.

Slowly at first, yes, but the Sorcerer's movements sped up gradually, flinging an orange tendril out to the right, a red one straight up, yellow to the left, then curling over, around, down. Then multiple tendrils moved with each gesture, five, ten folding over one another, ever more rapidly, until it was too difficult to follow the individual knots being unformed and formed. All of this was silent, but Patch realized that it was almost *musical,* a dance of colour, like a Song made for the eye rather than the ear. He had a jolting vision of the Hamelyn Piper, playing the Obsidiac Organ with the same kind of crazed fervour.

Faster, it went, *faster.* Patch grew dizzy at the spectacle. It was *madness*, almost, but with an underlying pattern, a marching, driving, frenzy of motion and hue that overwhelmed everything else.

At last the tendrils pulled back, disappearing into the cloud; then the cloud itself – with a rapid sequence of sparks – began to drift and thin.

Underath sank to his knees. Alia ran out to him, supporting him just as he began to slump to the side, exhausted.

Then she turned to the hillock and looked straight at

Barver and Patch, giving them a wave.

"Rumbled!" said Barver.

"You may as well come down now," called Alia. "The work is done."

"Done?" Patch said. "Does she mean…"

She did.

The pair looked to the cloud in the clearing, as it dispersed to reveal a standing figure. It was Wren, human once more, in the red-and-white striped dress she'd been wearing on the day they faced the Hamelyn Piper.

What was left of the cloud of coloured dust billowed around Barver's wings as he landed, and as soon as his feet hit the ground Wren wrapped her arms around his neck and hugged him. Patch leaped off Barver's back and hugged her too, grins all round, the three of them scarcely able to believe that finally – finally! – her curse had gone.

"We were so worried!" said Patch.

"Did it hurt?" asked Barver. "Watching Underath do all the…" He waved his arms around. "You were underneath that, and I didn't know what to think!"

"It didn't hurt," said Wren. "It did feel very strange, but there wasn't any pain."

"It's such a relief!" said Patch. "I mean, when Alia mentioned *dangers*…"

At that, Underath and Alia reached them. "Nothing to worry about!" said Underath. "I knew I had it all under control!"

"So it worked?" asked Wren. "Just as you said?"

Patch frowned, and so did Barver, because it had *obviously* worked, given that Wren was human. Unless… unless there was something else.

"What are you talking about?" said Barver. He said it with his sternest expression, his eyes boring into Wren's conscience until she looked away.

"Um," she said.

"Out with it!" said Barver.

Wren cracked under the pressure. "Well, I had a choice of a simple cure, or something a little more risky and interesting. And I chose *interesting*."

Barver and Patch turned to Alia.

"Don't blame me!" said Alia. "It had to be Wren's decision."

"I repeat, nothing to worry about!" said Underath. "I'd merely noticed that Wren's morphic countenance had become untethered when her deflector had broken, so we had the option of either fixing it back in place, or allowing it to bilocate at will! There was a degree of danger, yes, but I was always on top of things!"

Barver frowned. "Well, that's as clear as mud," he muttered.

Patch looked at Wren. "Tell us what he meant," he said. "Wren, did you do something stupid?"

Wren's eyes widened with indignation. "I can still change into a rat!" she snapped. "Okay? Happy now? That's all! I've got a chance to learn to change at will, and if I'm lucky I might be able to choose *other* forms too. It seemed worth the tiny little risks!"

"Hold on," said Patch. "What risks, exactly?"

Wren shrugged, as if it was no big deal. "That the cure would fail. Permanently. But Underath was very sure that—"

"Wait," said Patch, looking from Alia to Underath and back. "You let her take a risk that the cure might fail and she'd be stuck as a rat, just so she'd be able to turn into a rat *if she wanted*?" They said nothing. "How could you let her?"

"How could they *let* me?" said Wren. "To be able to shape-shift? How could I turn that down? And as Alia said, *it was my choice*." She folded her arms and glared at both of them.

Patch hung his head, looking at the ground. She did have a point. "Sorry," he muttered.

Barver, still agitated, scratched at the earth with a claw. "I'm sorry as well," he said. "It's just…you know."

"I do know," said Wren. "I love you both too."

Underath clapped his hands together, satisfied at a job

well done. "Good!" he said. "Now that's all sorted, how about giving us a lift back to the beach?"

"So you'll be able to turn into a rat?" asked Barver. "Whenever you want?"

They were sitting around a large fire that the griffins had built above the high-tide line. Underath was inside the boatwright's shed with Alia and Tobias, examining the sleeping Alkeran. The other griffins were curled up close to the flames, basking in the fire's heat.

"That's the plan," said Wren. "I mean, it's not guaranteed. Natural shape-shifters are born differently, and everything I've been through has left me with the same condition."

"With an untethered morphy thingummy," said Barver, nodding.

"How does it work, then?" said Patch.

"I'm a bit vague on that myself," she said. "There are lots of things I have to try, but apparently it's different for everyone and takes years of practice." She frowned.

"I'd have thought you were fed up being a rat," said Patch. "Wasn't it agony every time you changed?"

"It's not supposed to hurt if you do it right, and a rat would just be the start!" She beamed with excitement. "You see, if I manage it, I can try other animals too! The curse

182

imprinted a rat into my morphic countenance, but it's possible to imprint a few other forms as well. For the most talented shape-shifters, that is." Her smile stayed right where it was, leaving Patch in no doubt that she planned to be one of those.

"But why doesn't every Sorcerer put themselves through the same process?" he said. "Surely they'd all be turning into dragons and bears and sharks if they could? I mean, *I* would if I was a Sorcerer."

"Of course they *want* to," she said. "Underath told me the chances of it working are so slim that hardly anyone wastes their time trying."

Barver grinned. "So it really could be sharks and dragons?"

She shook her head. "Even if I mastered it, I could only turn into things that are smaller than me."

"*Tiny* sharks and dragons?" said Patch, getting a chuckle from Barver.

"Please," said Wren. "This is serious."

"Sorry," said Patch. "And I'm sorry for earlier."

"You don't have to keep apologizing," she said. "I understand."

"I really would have tried to talk you out of it," he said. "I mean, I know Underath said the chance of it going wrong was small, but he *would* say that, wouldn't he? He wasn't the one taking the risk."

Patch woke in the soft sand without even realizing he'd fallen asleep. He could remember dreams, of his mother looking down at him, smiling – as always – and also of his grandmother, tucking him into bed. He opened his eyes and saw that Barver's wing was covering both him and Wren, like a tent.

He shuffled out on his front, into bright sunlight. The griffins were nowhere to be seen.

Barver stirred, and opened a sleepy eye. He lifted his outstretched wing and folded it back to his side.

Wren sat up and started to wash her face with the backs of her hands, which she then rubbed behind her ears. She froze, and looked at her fingers. After a moment, she grinned. "It might be a while before I get used to being human again," she said.

"Good morning," said Tobias. Patch turned to see that he was on the other side of Barver. "The townsfolk have promised us a good breakfast. We should eat before we set off."

"We're leaving?" said Barver.

"I've done all I need to for Alkeran," said Tobias. "He's clearly out of danger. He may not wake for a day or more, I think, but that's simple exhaustion. He swallows the water we give him, and beyond that Underath will take care of his friend. There's no need for us to stay."

Wren frowned. "I was hoping to talk to Alkeran," she said. "I wanted to know who the woman who kidnapped him was."

"What will they do with the body?" asked Barver. "I can't imagine the townsfolk want her buried here."

"There's a place called Sella Doren," said Tobias. "It's a graveyard for the lost. The unknown dead. Merta has agreed to take the body there for burial."

"And did the woman have anything?" said Wren. "Any clues to what she was up to?"

"Come and look," said Tobias. "But be prepared for disappointment."

They went to the boatwright's shed. Merta and Wintel were there, silently watching the sleeping form of Alkeran. Alia was sitting on one of the pitch barrels; Underath was asleep on the floor by Alkeran's side.

Tobias led Patch, Wren and Barver to the far corner. There, an old piece of sailcloth covered a shape that had to be the body of the unknown woman. Next to the sailcloth was a leather harness, similar to Barver's, with half a dozen large packs attached. The straps on each pack had been undone.

Tobias spoke softly. "This is Alkeran's harness," he said. "The packs mostly contained supplies for a long journey. Here, we have the only unusual item we found." He reached down and lifted a small brass disc, which opened into two sections when a clasp was pressed.

"A compass?" said Wren, but if that's what it was, it was the strangest compass they'd ever laid eyes on. There were no markings on the face, and as Wren rotated the device, the needle didn't turn.

"Water damage, I thought," said Tobias. "Alia thinks there may be more to it. But look at the cover again." He closed the disc, and showed them: engraved on the surface was a simple drawing, a circle containing several lines. "And now look at her wrist…" he said, and he moved back the canvas to reveal the dead woman's arm. On the wrist was a tattoo, of precisely the same shape.

"A bird's foot, maybe?" suggested Wren.

"Is it a tree root?" said Barver.

"Your guess is as good as mine," said Tobias. "I told you to be ready for disappointment. The lady is a mystery, for now."

Then a call from Alia got everyone's attention: "Quickly!" she cried. "I think Alkeran is waking!"

"Get back!" ordered Underath. "Give him room!"

The griffin's eyes opened, taking in the faces gathered around. Alkeran flinched.

"Step back a little more," said Alia. "You're crowding him. You too, Barver."

Alkeran tried to speak, but started coughing instead. Underath held a bucket of fresh water for him, and he drank. Sated, he looked up again.

"The boy…" said Alkeran. "The boy needs to know…"

Alia, Tobias and Underath all turned and looked at Patch, absolute confusion on their faces, but Patch could tell that Alkeran wasn't looking at *him*.

Alkeran was looking above Patch's head. He was looking at *Barver*.

Barver stared back. "Needs to know what?" he said.

"That I wish it had been your father who survived, and not me." Alkeran had another fit of coughing, and took another drink.

"How do you know who I am?" Barver asked.

"You are called Barver, and you are obviously a dracogriff," said Alkeran. "I think that narrows it down! Your father spoke of you often, lad." He coughed again. "You see, before I called myself Alkeran, I had another name. I was called Tundin Wrass."

Barver's eyes widened. "You were the other pilot in the fleet."

"Yes," said Alkeran. "I was with your father when he died. A storm came from nowhere, and a wave caught me unawares. Vast and merciless, it threw me into the hull of the pride of our fleet. The crew managed to drag me aboard, dazed. For an hour, Gaverry piloted the fleet alone. He…" Alkeran began to cough again, more violently this time.

"Enough talking, my friend," said Underath. "You must rest."

187

"I've heard the story," said Barver. "Lightning hit him. He vanished beneath the waves…"

"Yes," said Alkeran, ignoring Underath's protests. "I left the safety of the ship and flew to where he'd vanished. I tried, in that awful tempest, to find him. But I could not. He was gone. By then I'd lost sight of the fleet. The next I knew, I woke at the entrance to a cave with a collar around my neck, *chained*. Food was plentiful, within the reach of the chain. Rabbits, unnaturally slow and easy to catch. Fish, that appeared for me each morning. But no warden, no jailer. No one to ask the reason for my imprisonment. I was there alone for two years, until the ground shook with such violence that the roof of my cave collapsed. Badly injured, I managed to crawl from the debris, and found that the falling rocks had sheared through my chain. I flung myself from the clifftop into the sea, desperate to escape my prison – alive or dead! Yet I was found, and saved, and a new life began, a *good* life." He turned to Underath and took his hand, smiling. "Yet it was a life I felt I did not deserve. I had no loves, no children. Gaverry had a wife and a son. He had *you*. That is why I wish it had been your father who survived, and not me."

Underath shook his head. "You did all that could be asked of you, and more," he said.

With great effort, Alkeran raised his head from the floor, and caught sight of the sad spectacle in the corner –

188

the woman's body, her arm still visible. "She's dead, then," he said.

"She deserves no sympathy, my friend," said Underath. "She almost killed us both."

Alkeran looked sorrowful nonetheless. "She was lost, Underath. Driven towards darkness, like you once were."

"Why did she take you?" asked Wren, eager for answers.

"To find the place where I'd been held prisoner. She sought an object hidden there, some *treasure* that was everything to her. She had a device, like a compass, to help her. I was under her control, utterly, but she talked to me even so. The device, she explained, could find the places I had been, at any time in my past. And so I held it, and together we searched, but the compass led us only to empty sea. She would alter the device and we would try again. Day after day. Week after week. She kept pushing, until we were both exhausted. After a day of solid flying my wings gave way. We fell from the sky, far out to sea. I remember hitting the water, but nothing more until now. Whatever drove her, it drove her to madness. Her belief in the compass was unbreakable."

"And did she have a name for the place she sought?" asked Alia. Visibly weak, Alkeran's head dropped back to the floor and he started to cough again. Alia was about to repeat her question, but Underath's glare stopped her.

Yet Alkeran had one last thing to say: "She called it the Bestiary," he managed, and then his breathing grew slow and steady, as he fell into a deep sleep once more.

The townsfolk, as promised, delivered an excellent breakfast of rice and fish, together with a large kettle of dardy-root tea. It would set them up for the journey back to Ural Casimir's mansion.

As they ate, Barver seemed distant.

"Are you okay?" Wren asked him.

"Hardly," muttered Barver. "For so long after my father's death, I knew almost nothing about what happened to him. Yet in the space of weeks, I've learned the truth and now met an eyewitness." He looked at Patch and Wren. "It worries me," he said. "As if…"

Alia had overheard them, and approached. "As if there's magic at work?" she said. "Perhaps there is." She looked over to the boatwright's building. "Dark magic, at that. Pulling us towards…something." She shook her head and walked off.

"I'm so glad she was here to ease our fears," said Patch, and that at least earned a smile from Wren and Barver.

Merta and Wintel would stay in Pardissan for a few more days, to help Underath should he need it, allowing Cramber to set off with the fishing fleet. The townsfolk had lost enough good fishing weather, and were eager to get back to the sea.

Farewells were said.

"It was an honour to work with you," Underath said to Alia, and the compliment didn't seem to stick in his throat at all. He did seem changed, Patch thought. He whispered as much to Wren, and she agreed.

"A little humbling can work wonders for a sense of empathy," she whispered. "Let's hope his head doesn't swell up to its old size, now that his powers have come back."

Alia, in return, thanked Underath. "You know," she said, "I expected to completely dislike you. You sounded like a horrible man. Instead, you've actually been tolerable company."

Barver shook the hands of each of the griffins. "I wish we had longer," he said. "I've hardly spent any time with griffins, not since my dad died."

Merta smiled. "Once we're done here, perhaps I'll drop in and see you. Will you be in the same place long?"

"On the hill above Yarmingly?" said Barver. "For a while, at least. I'll keep my eye on the horizon."

"And you are welcome to visit my home in Sullimer Forest," she told him. "The forest is vast, but you can spot Sullimer Knife easily enough. A mountain ridge near the coast. Find that, and you'll find me."

15

TROUBLE IN
THE ORTINGS

The high windways were kind to them. The skies were clear, and it was only a few hours before the coastline near Yarmingly came into view.

Erner and Rundel emerged from the mansion entrance as Barver touched down. Erner hurried out to them, so keen for news that he'd already called out, "How did it go?" before he'd noticed the most important fact:

There was one more human passenger than they'd left with.

The moment Erner saw Wren, he let out a great cheer.

"Things went well," said Alia, smiling. "As you can see."

"The Sorcerer undid his mischief, then?" called Rundel, limping slowly towards them.

"He did," said Alia. "And without complaint or resistance. His griffin is recovering, his power is restored, and Wren is cured. A more successful trip is hard to imagine."

Tobias peered rather closely at Rundel's face. "You look pale," he said. "Have you been eating well?" He turned to Erner immediately, as if he didn't expect honesty from his old friend. "Did he eat well, Erner?"

"Mainly cheese," said Erner.

Tobias frowned. "Oh, Rundel, how do you expect your condition to improve if you don't eat properly? I said before we left, there's plenty of dried beef and turnips, easy to boil up for a delicious soup."

"We had no time to cook," said Rundel, irritable. "My contact at Tiviscan sent us an extensive update on the activities of the Council and events elsewhere. We've spent our time studying what was sent."

Alia shared a worried look with Tobias. "Has something happened?" she said, and everyone knew what she meant: has the Hamelyn Piper attempted some new horror?

Rundel shook his head. "Not in the way you mean, but the news is not encouraging."

In the dining room, the surface of the huge table was covered in papers and scrolls.

Rundel selected a few of the papers and began to speak. "The Great Pursuit of the Hamelyn Piper continues, but with no sign of actual progress. They are hunting shadows, as we feared. And there's still been no word from Lord Drevis." He looked to Barver. "I'm aware that there's a message you wish to pass on to him, but at the moment his whereabouts are a mystery. The Pipers' Council is much in need of his leadership...it's not like him to be out of contact."

"Drevis may have picked up a trail," said Alia. "If he's close to finding the Hamelyn Piper, it might explain the lack of word."

"It might," said Rundel. "But the Council continues to pull Custodians out of their normal activities to aid in their quest. And now all Custodian Delegates have been called back to Tiviscan!"

This brought a gasp of shock from Alia and Tobias, and Patch knew why: there were Custodian Delegates in many nations of the world, especially those prone to wars, famine or disease. The wisdom and guidance of the Delegates had saved countless lives through the years.

"Are they fools?" said Tobias.

"Perhaps," said Rundel. "The Council claims that any disruption will be limited. Wait, I have it here..." He opened out a scroll and read from it: "*The people of all nations are behind us, as one. The Hamelyn Piper is the greatest threat we face, and only with the efforts of all the rulers of these lands can we ensure that peace holds and evil is vanquished.*" He rolled the scroll up again.

"The sooner Lord Drevis returns, the better," said Alia. "If the rest of the Council think that some kind of *spirit of togetherness* is going to make up for the loss of the Custodian Delegates, they certainly *are* fools."

Rundel nodded, and his expression was dark. "The Delegates work hard to talk leaders out of stupid and selfish decisions, choices that could lead to disaster. Without the Delegates, without anyone to *stop* those mistakes…I dread to think what may happen." He shook his head, exasperated, and threw the papers back to the table. The action uncovered another document, a wide sheet of paper with a map drawn on it. Rundel saw it and picked it up. "Hah! A good example of the chaos that may come – the squabbles in the Ortings have worsened!"

"The ghostly army nonsense?" said Tobias.

"The same," said Rundel. "More attacks against travellers and traders, day after day across the central region, all blamed on a small group of supposedly *ghostly* soldiers."

"It's probably just smugglers," said Alia. "Using legends as cover, like the bandits of Gemspar. Having some supernatural tales to scare folk off comes in very handy if you don't want them poking around. I'm sure it's nothing very serious."

"But it *is* serious," said Rundel. "People have died in those attacks, and the countries of the Ortings are close to threatening war with each other. The report is here somewhere..." He hunted through the scrolls again. "Ah ha!" he said, opening one and reading directly from it: "The Ortings is a huge area of woodland that overlaps two countries, Gastyl and Pard, who have been at war on and off throughout history. For a century the region has been calm, but peace is now under threat. The Ortings is rife with superstition and legend; the most famous is of ghostly armies that haunt the forests. In recent weeks, there have been many attacks on traders; survivors have spoken of ghostly soldiers, led by a general in black armour. This figure has become known as the Black Knight. Law enforcement officers have also been attacked: ten of the Gastyl Royal Guard and eight of the Pard Watch were killed. The enforcers of both countries have pulled their patrols back from the borders. Both Gastyl and Pard called on the Custodian Elite to assist them; the Custodians said they would only help when the Great Pursuit of the Hamelyn Piper is concluded." Rundel set the scroll down, shaking his head in despair. "It may be too late by then. Gastyl thinks the ghostly attackers are really Pard soldiers; Pard thinks they are soldiers of Gastyl. Both countries are wealthy enough to buy extra soldiers and prepare for war – there are rumours of mercenaries heading for the region in large numbers."

"And all because of the Great Pursuit," said Tobias. "I'm sure the Hamelyn Piper would be very pleased with that. Even in hiding, he's still causing chaos."

Rundel and Erner summarized the rest of what they'd heard from Tiviscan – a long roster of countries where Custodian Delegates had already been removed from service, as well as details of the various expeditions that had been sent out.

Barver curled up on the floor, tired and aching from all his recent flying. From time to time he started to snore, and Patch nudged him with his foot to get him to stop.

When Rundel and Erner finished, Tobias insisted on cooking a proper meal before they resumed their work in the Caves. "There's a sack of dried dermy beans in the kitchen," he said. "Dermy bean and onion stew, on its way within the hour!"

Patch had an image of Barver's fiery belch incinerating all the papers on the table. "No onions!" he said.

Tobias frowned. "What? The onions are the best part!"

"Trust me," said Patch. "The onions don't agree with Barver."

"I can vouch for that," said Alia. "Are they unusual onions, Tobias?"

"Pickled in hedge-beet vinegar," said Tobias. "Gives them a real *oomph*."

"Ah!" said Barver, rising and having a stretch. "Hedge-beet! That explains things. Causes uncontrollable flatulence in dragons. The kind that causes widespread *burning*. And explosions." He leaned down to Wren. "*Both ends!*" he whispered.

Tobias gave it some thought, then nodded. "Very well," he said. "Dermy bean and...um...*turnip* stew?"

"Sounds good," said Barver. He yawned, settled back down, and closed his eyes again.

"I'll give you a hand, Tobias," said Alia.

"Call us when the food is ready," said Rundel. "We haven't quite gone through everything yet, we'll take these upstairs and get it finished." He and Erner gathered up the papers and scrolls.

Once they'd all gone, Wren wandered around the room, looking at the tapestries on the walls.

"How is it, Wren?" asked Patch. "Being human again, I mean."

She smiled, thoughtful. "I keep wanting to run up to your shoulder," she said. "Everything is much more colourful. And detailed! A rat's eyesight isn't much to boast about, I have to say." She looked down at herself, and tutted. "Still wearing the same clothes I left home in too!" She spun where she stood, her red-and-white striped dress billowing out a little. "Time for a change," she said. "When you were hunting warm garments for the journey, I spotted boxes of clothes. I think I'll go and see what I can find."

It didn't take her long. "How's this?" she said when she returned. "Much better than my old dress!" She'd chosen a style of patchwork goatskin clothing popular in the north, a simple trousers-and-tunic outfit long associated with those who hunted for a living – nothing baggy to snag on branches in a chase.

"Looks comfortable," said Patch.

At that, Alia came through the door to the kitchen, a glum expression on her face.

"I thought you were helping with the stew?" said Patch.

"I was," said Alia. "As I went to add some mint to the pot, Tobias was so horrified he sent me out." She screwed up her face and put on a mock-Tobias voice: "'*You can't have mint with dermy beans, are you mad?*' I mean, who is he to judge?"

Patch decided it would be wise to keep silent on the matter. While they were in the little cottage on Sorkil Island, Alia's cooking had always had a decidedly *medicinal* taste to it, almost as if she'd taken a potion recipe and thrown in some potatoes. He'd often been unsure whether to *eat* it, or rub it on a rash.

To fill the time, Patch took his Pipe from one of Barver's harness packs, and ran his fingers through some of the patterns Tobias had used in his Healing Songs. Once he had things clear in his mind, he started to play aloud. It seemed like an age since he'd actually *played* anything, and it felt good, like stretching your legs after sitting in one place for too long.

He was pleased with how much he'd remembered from listening to Tobias. The foundations of the Curative Sleep were soon well established, holding together strongly. He added some of the tweaks Tobias had used to adapt the Song for Alkeran. As he played he kept a close eye on Barver, whose sleep had seemed rather uneasy – he'd been shuffling and muttering occasionally, his flight muscles presumably giving him some discomfort.

Sure enough, Patch's Song seemed to help, his friend's agitated sleep becoming more restful. Patch let the Song fade. He'd certainly made a lot of progress, and having a Healing Song tailored to help Barver was a skill he was keen to perfect.

"That's what Tobias played for the griffin," said Alia.

Patch nodded. "I've never spent much time on Healing Songs," he said. "It's good to learn from an expert. I imagine Wren thinks the same, which is why she's so desperate to be your apprentice." He smiled at Wren, but she glared at him.

"Oh, hush!" said Alia, blushing. "I have to admit I'm looking forward to it. I think you'll make a good student, Wren."

200

"Thanks," said Wren. "I'll not let you down."

"You have to wait until you're fifteen," said Alia. "And you'll need permission from your parents, of course." She paused, then frowned and pointed to Wren's face. "You've got a whisker," she said.

Patch looked, and there it was: a great big whisker beside Wren's nose. An extra-large *rat* whisker, he had no doubt. Wren's hand went up to feel it, and right before Patch's eyes it shrank and vanished.

Wren's eyes were wide. "Underath mentioned there might be the occasional glitch," she said, anxious. She turned to Patch and pulled back her upper lip, running her tongue over her teeth. "Do they seem normal to you?" she asked. "Not at all, you know, oversized?"

"*Glitch?*" said Patch, horrified, but Wren shrugged.

"I really do need a book on shape-shifting," she said. "This kind of thing could get embarrassing."

"I'll keep my eye open for something," said Alia. "I know we're supposed to be looking for Ural's missing book, but it's not the only important thing. The background of the woman who kidnapped Alkeran intrigues me too! I'd love to know what she was up to. I think I'll be hunting for any mention of a Bestiary in Ural's notebooks, when we go back down to the Caves after lunch."

Barver opened his eyes and gave a huge yawn. "Did somebody say lunch?"

16

THE UNLIMITED DARK

Patch felt more and more deflated as they made their way back to the Caves of Casimir. After the excitement of their trip with the griffins, and the triumph of Wren's cure, the prospect of looking through the remaining books and papers held no appeal. He didn't share Rundel Stone's confidence that they would find the missing book. Even if they did, would it *really* provide any clues to help track down Casimir's murderer, or the location of the Hamelyn Piper?

Without even a drop of enthusiasm, he sat beside the shrinking pile of books he had yet to look through, knowing that the tall shelves on the walls behind him were still waiting.

That was where Wren stood now, scanning the spines of the books and muttering to herself. She gave a frustrated grunt. "There's bound to be something!" she said; then she looked at the higher shelves towering above her. "Maybe all the way up there... Barver? Any chance you could see if there's a shape-shifting book in that lot?"

"No problem," said Barver. He stepped over to the shelves and started to look. "I see why these are all up so high," he said.

"Because they all sound very exciting and shape-shifty?" said Wren, crossing her fingers.

"No," said Barver. "Because they are *dull, dull, dull!*"

Wren frowned. "It can't be that bad."

"Oh, trust me," said Barver. "It's all boring!" He tapped the spines of each book as he described them: "Almanac for positions of stars; magical uses of herbs; almanac for positions of the moon; a cookery book; telling fortunes from sheep intestines; *another* almanac for star positions." On he went, until he'd gone through every book on the higher shelves. "Nothing on shape-shifting, I'm afraid."

Rundel coughed and glared at them, so Patch and Barver returned to the job in hand. Wren continued her search, but over the next few hours her luck didn't change. It was only when Alia came over, shortly before they left the Caves for the day, that she smiled again.

"Here," said Alia. "Look what I dug up." She handed Wren a slim little book, small enough for a pocket: *The Art and Method of Morphic Transmutation.*

"At least your day was more successful than ours," said Patch.

"That wasn't my only success," said Alia. "I found a single mention of a Bestiary that may be relevant!"

Wren raised an eyebrow. "What did it say?"

"A Bestiary is a book describing exotic or magical animals," said Alia. "But apparently the term is also used to describe a kind of *living* Bestiary – a Sorcerer's collection of live creatures, from where they could get fresh samples for their magic. I mean, Alkeran said he never saw anyone, but maybe there were mornings when he woke and had one less feather, or had lost some blood and didn't know it."

"Kept prisoner so a Sorcerer could use *bits* of him?" said Wren. "That's awful!"

"It is," said Alia. "I didn't find any reference to the symbol tattooed on the woman's wrist, but that will wait until tomorrow."

Then it was time to leave the Caves of Casimir, after another day of failure. Tobias was particularly despondent about their lack of results. They climbed the steps to the surface, and when they reached the top, Barver pulled the lever in the wall.

"How much longer will we spend on this, Rundel?" said Tobias, as the mechanisms above them rumbled and the exit opened.

"We're making progress," said Rundel. "I'm *certain* the book Ural's murderer wanted is within the Caves. We'll find it soon."

"Well, I'm *not* certain, not at all," said Tobias. "And even if it *is* there, it's a thankless task you've set us! How do you find an unusual book, in a library *full* of unusual books?"

A moment later, Patch simply turned and ran, three steps at a time, back towards the Caves.

"Good Lord, what's got into him?" said Alia.

"He can hardly see the steps!" said Wren.

"We've only just got *up* here," complained Tobias. "I'm *not* going back down!"

"Oh, give me that," said Wren, taking the lantern Tobias was carrying. "I'll go back and see what's wrong with him."

Patch didn't have a very high opinion of his ideas, as a rule, but even he had to admit that he occasionally came up with a doozy. Turning the Iron Mask inside out was a particularly good example, of course, but right now he thought he'd had another one.

"Hey!" shouted Wren, catching him up. "What on earth are you doing?"

"I had an idea," said Patch, panting. "It was what Tobias said: how do you find an unusual book, in a library of unusual books?"

"What are you talking about?" said Wren.

"The murderer went through the books in the mansion's library and tore each of them! Even though those books were all just poetry and plays and adventure stories, they tore them! Those books looked *ordinary* on the outside, do you see?"

Wren's puzzled expression vanished, and Patch knew she'd remembered: as Barver had described the books on the high shelves, there had been one that should have jumped out at them right away.

Because in a library of unusual books, an *ordinary* one should stand out.

There was a ladder Erner had been using earlier; Patch carried it over to his and Wren's section, and climbed up to the highest bookshelf.

"If you go to the trouble of disguising a magical book, you make it look as unmagical and run-of-the-mill as possible!" he said, as he looked at each book in turn. "The kind of book anyone might have in their unmagical, run-of-the-mill library."

And there it was. In among the almanacs and the magical herb encyclopedias was a single cookery book. He pulled it free, then came back down the ladder.

Wren cleared a spot on the table, and Patch set the book down. For a moment they both just looked at it, then Wren flipped it open.

The first thing they saw was a loose sheet of paper, the words *Poddle and Poddle, Booksellers* at the top. On the paper was the following:

Sir,
Here is the book you have sought for so long, with a false
cover to hide it from prying eyes. It seems genuine: a
copy of the lost work of Lar-Sennen, called Tharras
Infina Nadus, *or* Thoughts of the Unlimited Dark.
There are rumoured to be only three copies in existence.
I trust it is to your satisfaction.
Yours,
Kondry Poddle

Wren took the letter out and set it to one side, but she seemed wary of touching the first page of the book.

"Go on," said Patch.

"It looks so old!" she said. "I'm afraid of damaging it." She took a deep breath and very carefully turned the page.

There was a detailed picture that looked like some kind of plan or design; on the next page was a sketch of a strange box with a hinged lid, that seemed to match the plan. Underneath was text, written in a curious and unfamiliar alphabet.

She turned to the next page. There was another plan,

of what seemed like jewellery, a kind of intricate necklace; again, an image of the finished item, and writing.

And the next: a pyramid of some form, carved with eyes on each side.

They both looked to the cabinet in the centre of the cavern, then ran over to it to be certain. And there they were: the pyramid, the necklace, the box.

They rushed back to the book and looked through the rest. Page after page: designs, alongside a picture of the finished item, and unintelligible writing.

Magical devices.

Wren turned more pages, and more, and the devices seemed to be getting larger, the designs taking up several pages each, some with human figures to give a sense of their scale.

And then, close to the back of the book, they could only stare at what they saw. After a dozen pages showing detailed plans for long tube-like structures, a full page was devoted to a sketch of the final result. Those tube-like structures rose high above a small human figure beneath, playing on a board of keys.

It was the Obsidiac Organ.

Wren gasped and stepped away from the book, her eyes filled with dread. "Patch," she said. "Go and get the others."

Patch ran.

For the next two hours, Alia studied the book. The others watched from the far side of the cavern.

Waiting was *torture*, Patch thought, but Alia stared at them if they made a sound or approached where she worked. A stare from Alia was more than enough to stop anyone.

At last, she called them to join her.

"I apologize for taking so long," she said. "The writing is in an old runic language that took me a while to get my head around." She opened the book to the first page. "*Tharras Infina Nadus*, or *Thoughts of the Unlimited Dark*," she said. "This book is a collection of devices that are all powered by obsidiac. They start small, but with each page the ambition grows, until we reach what the book calls *the unlimited dark*: what marvels could be created, if you had unlimited obsidiac? As Wren and Patch noticed, several of the items in Ural's collection match illustrations in this book. For example…" She set down a small metal box, which had a kind of clip on the side. Alia turned the pages of the book until she found the matching illustration. "We found this on Imminus Rock. The text describes it as a device to instantly *leap* from one place to another. And this…" She turned to a page with a pair of strange pendants. "This is a device to see from far distances. I've not managed to translate much of the description for that one, so I'm not quite sure what that means." She turned the pages again, coming to a stubby cylinder filled with cogs. "And this, a device for detecting what is called *magical persuasion* – that is, being compelled by magic to do something against your will. Which brings us neatly to the larger items. Most notably, the Obsidiac Organ, a device for magical persuasion on a *huge* scale. Each of its vast Pipes must be coated with a thick layer of powdered obsidiac bound together in resin. There's a smaller persuasion device described earlier, but it claims only to work on the weak-willed, and takes significant time to achieve its goal."

Patch thought of the oddly *empty* people who had helped the Hamelyn Piper in Tiviscan – there had been a few dozen of them, perhaps, and all had escaped with the Hamelyn Piper. "That may have been how he controlled his helpers," he said.

Alia nodded. "The Organ can do the same thing to many hundreds at once, far more quickly, and works on everyone. At least, that's what the book claims, and it's certainly what you three witnessed at Tiviscan. The book keeps making a very clear point, however: these *grandest* of devices are all purely theoretical. They could not be created, as each would need more obsidiac than there was in the whole world."

"Until now," said Rundel. "But how? How did the Hamelyn Piper find enough obsidiac to build that Organ?"

Patch, Wren and Barver looked at one another. For so

long, they had kept that terrible secret to themselves. Barver had sworn to tell only Lord Drevis.

Alia held up the bookseller's note. "We know from this that Ural had been looking for a copy of the book for a long time, and that there may be two others in existence. One is clearly in the hands of the Hamelyn Piper. Now, I want you to look closely at this – the last section of the book consists of thirteen pages, detailing a single design." She turned the pages slowly so that they could all see.

At first it was hard for Patch to make out. The diagrams seemed to be for metal frames of various shapes, and alongside them were pieces of obsidiac that would fit into the metal.

"Are those some form of *spring clip* on the edges?" asked Wren, pointing to the frames.

"I believe so," said Alia. "As with the jewellery earlier in the book, the obsidiac pieces here must be flawless and pure – resin-bound fragments are not enough. Those clips hold the pieces in place."

She continued to turn the pages; there were more and more of the oddly shaped frames, and Patch still couldn't make out what they were, but then the designs began to show how the frames fitted together, to form a larger whole:

A leg.

An arm.

A torso.

And then the full construction. There was no need for a separate human figure in this illustration, because the finished result *was* a human figure.

A figure, wearing a suit of obsidiac armour.

Everyone looked at it, in absolute silence.

"Black armour for the Black Knight!" said Tobias at last. "The ghost armies of the Ortings… That's what you're saying, isn't it? That the Hamelyn Piper has made this, just as he made the Obsidiac Organ?"

"I know it sounds crazy," said Alia. "But the moment I saw this picture, I knew it was true."

"It's impossible!" said Rundel. "You said the armour must be made of pure, flawless pieces of obsidiac. The only pure and flawless obsidiac that's ever been found is the size of *pebbles*. This requires chunks as big as my *head*. No matter what source of obsidiac the Hamelyn Piper has found, pieces like that simply don't exist."

Again, Patch, Wren and Barver shared a look.

"Of *course* it's impossible," said Alia. Then she looked at Barver, and at Patch, and lastly at Wren – a long, uncomfortable look, and Patch suddenly thought: *she knows*. "The three of you went to Tiviscan to tell Lord Drevis something important. You've never given any hint what that was. Yet since you returned to Marwheel Abbey, whenever me and Tobias wondered aloud about the source of the obsidiac used to build that Organ, each of you did *exactly* what you just did when Rundel posed the same question. You became wary, and looked at one another."

And once again they did just that, but this time they gave each other a short nod. Lord Drevis was beyond their reach, yet here were three of the Eight: Alia, Tobias and Rundel.

"My mother told me to tell only Lord Drevis," said Barver. "But I trust you all, and the time has come."

He told them the dark truth: that obsidiac was formed from the bones of dragons, and the bones of dragon children made the best obsidiac of all.

The Hamelyn Piper had murdered a hundred dragon children, to obtain the raw materials to build his Obsidiac Organ.

"And now we know what he did with the purest pieces," said Barver.

Their eyes all went to the picture of the armoured figure in the book.

Alia and Tobias sat in stunned silence; Rundel Stone, though, seemed distraught. He clenched his fist and stood, walking through one of the many tunnels leading to other parts of the Caves of Casimir. A few minutes later, they all heard a distant, muffled sound – an agonized cry of frustration and rage.

Tobias looked up from his misery. "He promised the people of Hamelyn that he would bring their children back," he said. "When we discovered that the children had been murdered – with the Song of Dispersal, no less! – it almost destroyed him. And now…"

"We finally hear the truth," said Alia. "That it was only the dragon children the evil Piper wanted – their bones, left to darken over long years."

"But why take the children of Hamelyn?" said Tobias.

"I can only guess," said Alia. "But without that, the dragons would have blamed all humans for the crime. Their grief and anger would have led to another war between dragons and humans, even more terrible than before. He wouldn't have wanted that. What good would it be to rule over a devastated world?"

"He wanted the dragons to see that humans had suffered too?" said Tobias. "Imagine what kind of mind could think like that."

Patch didn't need to imagine it. He'd met the Hamelyn Piper, face to face, and had seen for himself. "A mind that believes it's better than everyone else," he said. "A mind that must be stopped."

Nobody was going to argue with that.

Alia continued to work on her translation of the text beneath the armour's design, closely watched by Wren.

When Rundel finally returned, he saw the notes Alia

had been making. "You've made good progress," he said. "Do you know what effect the armour has?"

"On its own, it provides significant protection against both Songs and sorcery, and amplifies the power of a Piper," said Alia.

"By how much?" asked Rundel.

"The book suggests tenfold," she said.

Rundel frowned. "I expected more," he said. "I assumed ten *thousand* times at least, for him to think it was worth all his years of evil scheming!"

"There is more," said Alia, and she spoke with such dread in her voice that Patch knew something terrible was coming. "Look at the design of the armour's torso; in the centre of the chest is a space meant for something else. The text on this final page tells of an amulet which it calls the *Vivificantem*, the Life-Giver, an ancient jewel of unique magical properties. Those wielding it, says the book, have the ability to call forth the sun itself and bring life to barren lands. Supposedly Lar-Sennen buried it in one of the Hidden Places. When positioned in the chest of the obsidiac armour, it completes the design. At that point, the wearer of the armour becomes invulnerable to all harm. It makes them *immortal*, Rundel, and gives them unimaginable power."

That took a few seconds to settle in everyone's minds. It sounded *very* much in keeping with the Hamelyn Piper, Patch thought.

"I think it's safe to say that if he'd found *that*, he would have already marched on Tiviscan," said Rundel. "So why is he in the Ortings?"

"The Ortings has a long history associated with magic," said Alia. "One of the Hidden Places was supposedly somewhere in the forests. I think that may be what he's up to. He has his armour, and now he's seeking the Life-Giver. His ghost army, I assume, is made up of his *helpers*. By scaring the locals away, he's cleared the area of prying eyes."

"We can't be certain of *any* of this," said Tobias. "The book *admits* to being theoretical, a flight of fancy! What are the odds that such an ancient design could possibly work?"

"The Obsidiac Organ worked well enough," said Barver.

"One design of many," said Tobias. "That Organ was similar to the great Battle Pipes at Tiviscan, so it's reasonable that it would work. But *immortality*? Nonsense!"

"I know why you don't want to believe it," said Alia. "The possibility terrifies me too. What would convince you?"

"Show me!" he said. "Show me one of these useless trinkets that we found on Imminus Rock a decade ago, these oddities we risked our lives for! Show me it doing *something*, and I'll believe you."

"The only one I've completed the translation for is this,

the 'leap' device I spoke of," she said, patting the box on the table. "Perhaps with a small amount of obsidiac, we could prove that it works, but we have none."

"Actually," said Patch. "That's not quite true."

17

DEVIL PIN BAY

As Alia prepared, Patch couldn't avoid Barver's glare.

It hadn't really been his *fault*, as such.

After all, he'd been *inside* one of the Obsidiac Pipes when Barver had flown into the whole contraption. When he'd emerged from the wreckage, and picked bits of Pipe out of his hair, he'd not thought to go through his pockets carefully and check. By the time he actually *found* the black fragment in a pocket of his coat, he was already in Marwheel Abbey. And what was he supposed to do? *Tell* someone?

Well, *yes*, he realized now, he absolutely *should* have done that, but at the time he didn't want to think about what the obsidiac actually *was* – the bones of murdered dragon children.

Throwing it away seemed both reckless and disrespectful.

That was why he'd wrapped the fragment in a bit of cloth and tucked it deep into a fold at the bottom of one of Barver's harness packs. Then he'd done his best to forget that it existed at all.

And so all this time, Barver had been carrying it around everywhere he went, and he was absolutely *livid* about that.

Alia had been going over the Leap Device's description in the book, making sure that her translation wasn't disastrously wrong, and that she understood how it was supposed to work. At last, she was satisfied.

"What exactly do you plan to do, Alia?" asked Rundel. The fragment of Obsidiac Pipe sat on the table in front of him, a thin shard of darkness two inches long. Rundel hadn't been able to take his eyes off it. Reasonable enough, Patch thought – here was the entire purpose of the Hamelyn Piper's evil deeds, the whole *point* of his horrific actions.

"The device needs an item small enough to clip into this part on the side," said Alia. Along one edge of the device was a spring-hinged piece of copper. "The item must be specific to someone standing near the device when it's operated. They don't need to be the ones who travel, but they will decide the destination."

"Specific in what way?" asked Wren.

"A lock of hair, something like that," said Alia. "The destination will be whatever place is most important for that person – closest to your heart, you might say. So if any of you have a place that pops into your mind right away, that might be…"

"Devil Pin Bay!" cried Barver at once. "Um, it's my favourite place in the world. A vast white-sand beach in the Islands of the Eastern Sea, down in the southern parts where I spent most of my time. The nearby town does the best natter-clumps you'll taste *anywhere*."

Patch found that the thought of natter-clumps made him simultaneously terrified and hungry.

"That seems as good a place as any," said Alia. "A feather should do it, if you would oblige?"

Barver reached to his neck and tugged out a feather, giving it to Alia. As she clipped it to the device, Tobias didn't seem happy.

"Wait," he said. "That seems very risky. How do you know you won't just leap to the Dragon Territories, where Barver was born? Or *anywhere at all*, for that matter? You could end up in danger."

"I'm just going by what the book says," said Alia. "It also makes clear that the obsidiac is *destroyed* by the device, making it a very expensive way to travel."

"So if it works, how do you propose to get back?" said Tobias.

Alia reached to the table and picked up the fragment of Pipe. With some effort she snapped it in two, placing one piece in her pocket. "For the return journey," she said. "All I do is use the device again, and I come back to where I left. Simple!"

"I wish I'd never suggested this," said Tobias.

"There's every chance nothing will happen," said Alia. "Besides, the amount of obsidiac used determines how far you can go. These small pieces might only be enough to transport me somewhere *much* nearer, somewhere else close to Barver's heart."

"The dining room," said Patch and Wren at the same time.

Alia smiled. "Could be," she said. "The instructions state that I place the obsidiac on the ground, and set the device on top." She kneeled, placing the fragment on the stone floor, before setting the Leap Device on top of it. "If you'd all step back, we'll see what happens. The translation is a little difficult to make sense of, but some kind of *ball* should appear in the air, and will grow to a size depending on the amount of obsidiac used. Anyone inside the ball will be instantly transported when the device is activated. To begin, I just pull this little triggering lever." With her forefinger, she pulled back on a copper lever mounted on top of the device. They heard a sound like the slow cracking of glass, an unpleasant *crunching* noise that grated on the teeth. Then, as promised, a ball formed around the device, a sphere with an oddly rippling mirror-like surface. The sphere grew slowly, and started to engulf Alia. Tobias looked horribly anxious. Within moments Alia was gone from sight, fully enclosed by the strange rippling air. Then the sphere stopped growing.

"That's as big as it's going to get, I think," said Alia, her voice sounding rather distant. "I'm going to let the trigger go in three...two...one..."

The sphere suddenly contracted, vanishing completely with a gentle pop and an outrush of air. There were gasps from the others.

Alia was gone.

It was half an hour before she returned, but it felt much longer.

They didn't speak as they waited; with each passing minute it seemed more and more likely that something had gone wrong. Each of them wondered if they would ever see Alia again.

And then they heard the strange sound of crunching glass echoing around the cavern, followed by a short noise like a single *clap*. A moment later, Alia emerged from one of the side tunnels.

She held out her hand in a fist and uncurled her fingers; white sand poured from her grasp.

Everyone let out a sigh of relief.

"Devil Pin Bay is a fabulous place," said Alia. "Apologies for taking so long. I had to find someone to talk to, and confirm where I was, which was harder than I'd expected."

"I told you it was big," said Barver.

"What did it feel like when you travelled?" asked Wren.

"It was too quick to feel anything, really," said Alia. "One moment I was here, and the next I was *there*." She looked at Tobias. "Well, have I done enough to convince you that the book is to be trusted?"

"Yes," said Tobias. "The Black Knight is the Hamelyn Piper. He has his armour. If he'd found his amulet, he'd certainly not be wasting his time causing havoc in the Ortings, so we can assume he's still looking."

Alia nodded. "Heaven help us if he finds it." Tobias tilted his head, and Alia's eyes narrowed. "You still don't quite believe, do you?"

"Not all of it," he said. "A promise of immortality and unlimited power is pure fantasy, but if the Hamelyn Piper wants to chase a fantasy, let him – it means we have a chance to find him, and catch him at last." He looked at Rundel. "Think of it! All these years he's been laughing at us, and now we know where he is. We have him at our mercy!"

"We must tell the Council his location," said Rundel.

"Are you sure?" said Alia. "The meaning of the prophecy is still to be settled. Betrayal is not to be taken lightly.

223

Perhaps it would be better to leave the Council out of it entirely."

"Even so…" said Rundel.

"There's no point!" said Tobias. "Whether you trust them or not, it would take them weeks to act, and we must move quickly!"

"What are you suggesting?" asked Rundel. "We three couldn't hope to take him on again. I can't Pipe! I'd be useless to you, and with whatever additional strengths the armour grants him, he'll be a formidable enemy!"

"The Battle Pipers of Kintner," said Tobias. "I can raise the forces we need. They know me well, and would rally behind one of their most famous colonels – I guarantee it."

Alia saw Wren's puzzlement. "Before he turned to Healing, he was a Battle Piper at the Kintner Bastion," she said. "A decorated commander. Do you have a plan forming, Tobias?"

Tobias nodded, and led them to the globe at the centre of the cavern. There, he found the Ortings, and Patch realized how large the forest was – a whole thumb's width on the globe.

"You said the Black Knight has been leading the attacks, Rundel?" said Tobias.

"That's what survivors reported," said Rundel. "With two dozen or so 'ghostly' soldiers at most."

"That means his forces are small," said Tobias. "If we

had a hundred soldiers, and maybe ten Battle Pipers, we would easily outmatch them. I'd be happier with twice that, of course, but we'll see." He pointed to the north of the forest, where the words "Gossamer Valley" were written in minuscule letters. "This valley is where we'll gather, just outside the Ortings. A good location to prepare, a two-day sail and a day's march from the Kintner Bastion." His finger moved out from the coast and up to an island two hundred miles further north, which bore the label "Kintner". "The problem is *finding* the Black Knight and his soldiers. The Ortings are huge, and we simply can't cover that much territory, either on foot or by horse." He looked at Barver. "We need airborne scouts."

Barver stood to attention and gave a salute. "Barver Knopferkerkle volunteering for duty, *sir*!"

Tobias smiled. "Much appreciated, but we need four, at least. We must be able to quickly lock down their position so we can prevent their escape."

"Perhaps Merta could help?" said Wren, but Barver shook his head, shocked at the suggestion.

"Airborne scouting for an army of Battle Pipers, Wren?" he said. "Remember the Griffin Covenant!"

"But this isn't war!" said Wren. "This is the *Hamelyn Piper* we're talking about."

"I doubt Merta would see it that way," said Barver. "Even *asking* her would be disrespectful."

"We don't need to ask Merta," said Tobias. "When the Eight hunted the Hamelyn Piper before, we were secretly helped by dragon scouts on several occasions. It was invaluable."

Barver nodded. "My aunt's position as a Triumvirate Delegate gives her some authority," he said. "She'll know how to arrange it. I'll go to her in Skamos."

"I'll go with you," said Alia. "If anyone needs convincing, I'm sure I'll be useful."

"And where Barver goes, we go," said Wren, pointing to herself and Patch.

"I shall return to Tiviscan with Erner, and see the Council," said Rundel. "I'll get to the bottom of the prophecy's meaning, and determine where their loyalties lie. I'll tell them nothing of this unless I'm certain they can be trusted."

Alia shook her head. "You're a stubborn man, Rundel."

"I cannot give up on them," he said. "Nor can I give up the hunt for Ural's murderer. Even if the Hamelyn Piper was somehow behind his death, it's unlikely he did the deed in person. I've vowed to bring the killer to justice, and I'll need the assistance of whatever Custodians I can gather."

"We could do with you in the Ortings, Rundel," said Tobias.

"Nonsense," said Rundel. "I told you, I can hardly Pipe!

226

I'd be no use to you out there. We'll reach Tiviscan within five days. With luck, Lord Drevis will have returned by then. If the Council prove trustworthy, I'll make them send help."

"Very well," said Tobias. "By the time you reach Tiviscan, we'll likely be in position. And the hunt can begin!"

They set off at dawn.

Rundel and Erner would begin their travels by horse later that day; Tobias would ride with the others on Barver as far as Essenbach, from where he would sail to Kintner.

Before they took to the air, however, Erner asked Patch if he could speak to him in private. Patch agreed, but he was almost trembling as they stepped out of earshot of the others.

"We've not spoken," said Erner. "Not really. But we must, before we part. I can see it *eating* at you."

"As it should," said Patch.

"Understand your mistake, and learn from it!" said Erner. "That's all any of us can do. To *punish* yourself is damaging. This is a key part of the training for a Custodian Apprentice."

"I know, Erner. I know. I'm sorry for what I did. Do I understand why I did it? I think so – I was overwhelmed by panic and fear. Can I learn? I hope I can. But things between us will be marked by it, always. Nothing either of us can say or do will change that."

"Marked by it, yes," said Erner. He offered out his hand. "But not broken. Never that."

Patch looked at Erner's outstretched hand. He started to bring his own up, but stopped halfway. "You should hate me for what I did," he said.

"I don't hate you," said Erner. He reached further and took Patch's reluctant hand, and they shook at last. "Even if I did try to strangle you." He smiled.

Patch smiled back, but all he could think was that Erner was handling this rather better than he was.

18

A City United

The city of Skamos was ancient.

It had been founded shortly before the first war between humans and dragons, nine hundred years ago, a small human settlement on the very edges of the Dragon Territories. Originally little more than a fort which sat on top of a hill, it had grown until it engulfed the hill and much of the plains at its base. After that first war, in the hopeful peace that followed, dragons joined the residents of the city, and Skamos was given special status: part of the Dragon Territories, yes, but with its own rules so that the dragons and humans who lived there were treated as equals.

Crisis after crisis, it had faced – wars, drought and an encroaching desert. A combination of dragon and human ingenuity had led to the building of a great aqueduct that brought water from a river twenty miles away. Now, that water gave life to the city, and to the land around it; an island of green, in a grey-and-yellow dusty wasteland, with gardens and trees throughout the sandstone and granite of the city's buildings and fortifications.

The central part, built on that old hill, had a vast wall winding around it, up and up to a stone tower at the peak, defences that spoke of a past littered with attacks, sieges and threats, but which were now dotted with windmills.

Skamos: a source of anger for humans who hated dragons, and for dragons who hated humans, yet the city itself had always been peaceful, the two species living side by side in harmony.

They landed outside the city, after almost two days of flying. Barver had taken them into the high windways once more, for speed, and all three passengers – Patch, Wren and Alia – were wrapped up in plenty of extra layers.

When they dismounted, they removed their heavy extras, packing it all into Barver's harness packs ready for their next flight.

"What are the windmills for?" asked Patch, looking at the city walls.

"They aid in the pumping of water," said Alia. "Vast storage tanks lie at the base of the tower, and the water is pumped to wherever it's most needed. Waste water flows out to the surrounding land, as you can see." Even here, well beyond the city's outer wall, tendrils of green extended into the desert, running alongside a channel of water that simply stopped, soaking into the sand.

"It's a wonderful place, Skamos," said Alia. "The Mesyr Desert runs from here to the sea, and south for a hundred miles. It expands some years, contracts others. But the city copes, either way. Ten thousand people and five hundred dragons." She smiled. "I know this city well. I was stationed here for six months as an Apprentice Custodian. Come on, then, follow me!"

They walked through the mudbrick buildings on the outskirts. By and large, they went unnoticed. Those people who did acknowledge them wore wide smiles and waved in greeting. Skamos certainly seemed a happy place.

Sleeping near a water channel was the first dragon they saw close up, a particularly large female, her impressive dorsal spines folded against her back.

"That's Unanda Kellokeen," said Alia. "The city's oldest resident. She's not changed a bit since I was here, what, thirty years ago?" A sly grin spread across Alia's face. "To be honest, she may not have *moved* at all since then…"

At the base of the hill, they reached the city's outer wall. It was the height of three people; the entryways were open gaps, with another small section of wall behind.

"These are the sand walls," said Alia. "In the worst years, they act as a last protection against the desert." Once through, she pointed to a particularly green region where the trees grew surprisingly high. "There," she said. "The residences of the Delegates. That's where your aunt and uncle should live, if everything hasn't changed since I was last here!"

As they drew near, they saw a large shallow pond, in which residents played, adults as well as children, dragon and human both, splashing and laughing.

"Is that *waste* water?" said Patch. He thought back to his time in the dungeons of Tiviscan, where "waste water" meant the rain, washing through the basic sewer system – filthy and stinking. The thought of people swimming in it...

Alia caught the look on his face and understood. "Not that kind!" she said. "Skamos has proper sewers, running under the city itself. Half a mile to the west is a canyon, where the sewers emerge. A lush and magical place, but rather smelly – it gets plenty of water, and plenty of fertilizer! Water that leaves the city through the irrigation channels is fresh. You can have a paddle later, if you like."

Patch, Wren and Barver nodded at each other. They would *definitely* like that, especially after the long journey.

"These are the two Delegate residences," declared Alia, as they approached the buildings. She nodded to the

232

leftmost. "That's where the Custodian Delegate lived, up until the Council summoned them back to Tiviscan." She shook her head, as if she still couldn't quite believe it. "The one on the right is for the Triumvirate Delegate." It was twice the size of the other. Alia led them to the double doorway. It was certainly large, but then most of the doorways they'd walked past were large here – easily wide enough for a dragon, although they would still have to duck a little.

Alia reached to a bell-pull.

"Hang on," said Barver. He straightened his harness straps and ran a hand over the feathers on his neck, flattening them down. "Okay, ready!"

The bell rang, and after a few moments the double doorway opened to reveal a male dragon about Barver's size. The dragon seemed rather tired. "Yes?" he said, looking first at Alia, then at Barver, then back to Alia. Suddenly he looked like he'd woken up, and with a wide smile turned to Barver again.

"Hi, Uncle Zennick," said Barver. "Hope you don't mind me dropping by unannounced?"

"Barver!" cried Zennick, stepping out and giving him a hug. "I can't believe it, after all this time!" He turned his head and called through the door: "Yakesha! Come down! You'll never guess who's here!"

There was movement inside, and Patch almost shrieked:

watching an even *larger* dragon rushing towards you was rather unnerving.

Aunt Yakesha greeted Barver with another hug. "Come on, then," she said. "Introductions, please!"

"Aunt Yakesha, Uncle Zennick, these are my good friends, Patch and Wren. As you see, Wren has found her cure…"

"Patch and Wren!" said Yakesha. "We've heard so many things!"

"You have?" said Wren, somewhat wary.

"I mentioned you in my letter," said Barver. "I left out all the bad stuff, obviously." He winked, ignoring Wren's scowl. "And this is Alia. She's a representative of the Custodians, here on an important mission – the reason we came."

"Custodians?" said Yakesha, with a hopeful smile. "Has the Pipers' Council decided to send a new Delegate?"

"I'm sorry, no," said Alia. "The Council didn't send me. It's a little more complicated than that."

"A shame," said Yakesha, deflated. "It was a shock to us all when they left." She looked at Zennick. "Fetch the little one, my dear." Zennick nodded, and went off to the rear of the building. "Come inside, all of you," said Yakesha. "We can discuss business shortly, but first be at home!"

She showed them to a table, around which were stone benches, some large and low, others small and high, the large ones further from the table. Barver and Yakesha took seats on a low bench, while Alia, Patch and Wren took seats on the higher ones, so that, for once, Barver didn't have to crouch by a table and could sit more comfortably.

Zennick returned, leading a baby dragon by the hand. It was perhaps three feet high, its skin grey with dark green stripes, a rather stubby little body, and wings so tiny they'd have been more at home on a bat. The baby looked around with intense interest as it waddled along. It wore folded cloth around its lower half, which struck Patch as strange – he'd never seen a dragon, or griffin, wearing clothing before – until he realized it was a *nappy*. "Barver, this is your cousin Kerna," said Zennick. "Kerna, this is your cousin Barver. Say hello!"

"Ba Va!" said the baby, holding its arms out and grasping. It wrinkled up its face, and a little glop of snot oozed from its nose. The glop started to swell, forming a bubble. "Bub bub!" said Kerna. The bubble popped, and the snot went on fire, a small flame like that of a candle rising up from the baby's nose.

Patch and Wren stared at the flame; Barver, though, was absolutely smitten. "You are *adorable*, Kerna," he said, as his uncle passed the baby to him. The flame from the baby's nose didn't seem to be subsiding. "Should I wipe that with something?"

"Oh, no need," said Zennick. "Better for it to burn off slowly, really, getting it on a cloth just tends to be…risky."

Zennick and Yakesha shared a wary look, one that contained unspoken tales of near disaster. Patch noticed the same level of deep tiredness in Yakesha's expression as he'd seen on Zennick's. Babies were notorious for leaving parents exhausted. He guessed that *flammable* babies meant a certain extra burden that human parents didn't have to worry about. He glanced around the room, noticing just how few combustible items there were – the furniture was mostly stone, and there were no carpets or rugs.

"I'm keen to learn the reason for your visit, Alia," said Yakesha. "Can you tell me in front of your friends, or should we speak privately?"

"I can tell you now," said Alia. "We have information relating to the location of the Hamelyn Piper. Capturing him requires airborne scouting. We need the help of dragons, as many as possible."

Yakesha frowned. "You want a dragon *army*?"

"Not an army," said Alia. "Four or five would be enough. We have so much ground to cover, and little time to spare. This would purely be scouting. No combat would be involved."

Yakesha's frown merely deepened. "The Triumvirate has been very specific in their instructions. The Pipers' Council have already asked for assistance in their Great Pursuit, and the Triumvirate refused, declaring that dragons would handle this themselves, come what may."

"We're not here on behalf of the Council," said Alia. "I represent a group of Custodians, and we need your help. The situation is urgent. We believe that the Hamelyn Piper is close to gaining power greater than we ever conceived. If he succeeds, he might be impossible to defeat. Any delay will make that more likely."

Yakehsa's frown became a scowl. "I cannot help you," she said, sounding almost *angry*.

Alia was thrown by this, and gave Barver a pleading look.

"Aunt Yakesha..." started Barver, but his aunt stood from the table and stepped away. Zennick watched her, visibly anxious, though he said nothing.

"Forgive me," said Yakesha at last. "It was hard enough when we first heard that the Hamelyn Piper was still alive, and now you bring such a dire warning...but I cannot help you." She looked across at her child, who was pulling faces at Wren; Wren was doing the same back, making the baby giggle. "It was always your mother's fervent wish, Barver, that dragons and humans learned to cooperate. This great city shows how that can be done. Being asked to be the Triumvirate's Delegate for Skamos was the greatest honour I've ever been given. But I'd not truly appreciated the hatred some dragons have for this place – and for what it represents." She shook her head with sorrow. "Those dragons think humans are so worthless that *any* kind of association with them is a disgrace, whatever the circumstances. The attack on Tiviscan was a great victory for them. Their influence has grown significantly. When the Pipers' Council asked for help, those dragons convinced the Triumvirate that no assistance should be given to humans, or accepted *from* humans – that it's a matter of dragon pride to kill the Hamelyn Piper ourselves, alone. Worse yet, they got the Triumvirate to forbid it with a direct Proclamation, the most solemn and binding of all law. The penalties for breaking that law are severe. No dragon is *allowed* to help humans, in any way, in the hunt for the Hamelyn Piper." She sat down again, seeming drained. "Not even me."

"Could you ask the Triumvirate directly?" said Alia.

"I'm sorry," said Yakesha. "Even that would be against the law."

Silence filled the room – silence, and a sense of despair. Baby Kerna, noticing the mood change, frowned at Wren, then sneezed; another dollop of snot emerged, from the other nostril, and now there were two little flames rising.

"Then could *I* ask them?" said Alia. She reached into a pocket and pulled out a small golden ornament, on a fine chain. It was in the shape of a burst of dragon fire, three inches across, and at the heart was a red gem.

Yakesha and Zennick both gasped.

"The Fire of All Days," said Yakesha, astonished. "The highest honour the Triumvirate can give. But how…?"

Alia spoke with obvious reluctance. "I am Alia Corrigan, one of the Eight." Patch, Wren and Barver looked at each other; they knew how fiercely Alia protected her privacy, and disliked revealing her true identity. "Over a decade ago, the Triumvirate honoured us, and told us they were in our debt. Surely that holds weight still?"

"I didn't know the Eight had been paid such a tribute," said Zennick.

"It was done in secret," said Alia. "They knew there would be dragons who hated the idea. Show the Triumvirate this, and see if they'll keep their promise."

Yakesha looked thoughtful. "A direct plea from you to the Triumvirate, to seek special permission…" She nodded. "Yes, it might work. It will take a few days for their response, though."

A few days, Patch thought. By then, if Tobias had succeeded, the Pipers and soldiers he'd recruited should have gathered in Gossamer Valley. If the Triumvirate didn't agree, those soldiers would be waiting in vain for the promised help. But what choice did they have?

"Then we wait," said Alia.

19

A City Divided

"Alia and I will draft the letter to the Triumvirate," said Yakesha. "Once that's done, you can enjoy some Skamos hospitality!"

"A Skamos feast!" said Zennick. "I'll do my roasted harker peas, for anyone brave enough to try."

"We should go and have a splash in that pond," said Barver to Patch and Wren. He tickled Kerna under the chin. "I'm getting some muscle cramps in my shoulders, and it would help."

"Ba Va!" said Kerna.

"That's me!" said Barver, then went into a long oogy-boogy-doogy that made Kerna laugh.

"A swim would be better for you," said Zennick. "You should go to the public bathhouse, while I make dinner."

Kerna grunted and pulled the most curious face, accompanied by an odd gurgling sound.

Wren, who was nearer than Patch, suddenly clamped her hands over her face. "*Oh my God!*" she cried, and backed away.

Patch was bemused, but was suddenly overwhelmed with a stinging pain. "*My eyes!*" he said.

"Ah," said Barver. "I think Kerna needs changing. I can do it, if you like?"

Zennick smiled. "That would be very helpful, Barver! Just through the archway, down the corridor on the right. Everything's there. Pull the lever for water, and I'll check in on you shortly."

Barver picked Kerna up. "Come on, you two," he said. Patch and Wren followed him as best they could. Patch could just about see through his own tears, and Wren didn't seem to be struggling for air quite so much.

"It's okay," Barver told them as they walked through the house. "There's usually a bit of gas that leaks out, but that's the worst of it. Ah ha!" They'd reached a doorway; inside was a large stone bath, and a smaller basin. A pipe stuck out of the wall, with a wooden lever beside it. Barver put a plug in the bath and pulled the lever. Water poured from the pipe into the bath. "See?" said Barver. "Dragons and humans get together, and you have water coming out of the wall whenever you want it!"

241

Patch was impressed. He splashed some water around his eyes and the last of the discomfort went away.

"The ventilation in here seems okay," said Barver. "But it might be best for you two to wait by the door until I've dealt with *the mess.*" He pointed to Kerna's nappy.

Patch and Wren were only too happy to do as he said. They braced themselves as Barver removed the cloth from Kerna's lower half, but there was a surprise waiting.

"Is that…is that *metal*?" said Patch. Sure enough, underneath the cloth was metal, which seemed to be hinged on one side. "A metal *nappy*?"

"Yep," said Barver.

Wren stared. "Why is that necessary?" she said.

"Dragon baby poo," said Barver. "If it gets on things…"

"It tends to leave stains?" said Wren.

"It tends to leave *holes*," said Barver. "Very acidic, dragon baby poo. Improves after the first year, thankfully." He reached down to a large wire basket by his feet, and picked up a jar of a yellow substance. "You put a coating of this stuff on the nappy before you put it on, otherwise it would eat right through the metal. Makes a good seal around the edges, as well."

"You're a bit of an expert at this," said Patch.

"Genasha," said Barver, and Patch could have kicked himself. Of *course* that was how he knew so much about dragon babies – his cousin Genasha, who had died tragically

242

young. "Since my mum was so busy when I was younger, and my dad wasn't around much, I stayed with my aunt and uncle plenty of times. I helped out a lot with Genasha. Watching her grow up, from egg into a young girl…"

"So is Kerna a girl too?" asked Wren.

"No idea," said Barver.

Patch and Wren looked at each other, not quite sure they'd heard right.

"What?" said Wren.

"You can't really tell until dragons reach three or so," said Barver. "When the dorsal spines start to appear, and the girls have a big growth spurt. Not like griffins! With griffins you can tell right off, just by their call." Barver reached over to the water lever and switched off the flow. "Okay, I'm going in!"

He opened the metal nappy, wincing at the smell. Patch and Wren backed away a little more just to be safe.

"How are you getting on?" said Zennick, joining them. "Staying out of the fumes, I see? Very wise! How about you, Barver?"

Barver looked decidedly queasy. "I forgot how bad it was, to be honest. What should I wipe with?"

"Oh, let me show you how we do it here. Running water makes such a difference!" Zennick took the metal nappy and rinsed it in the bath water. There was a great *hiss,* and a cloud of steam rose up. Then he put Kerna in the water too; again, a hiss, and steam. "There we are!" he said. "All perfectly safe now!" He waved to Wren and Patch, and they came in. "So is this your first experience with a dragon baby? What did you think?"

"Acid for poo…" said Wren, slightly in shock. "I didn't expect it to be, well, *actually toxic*."

"I know!" said Zennick. "Babies! Although Kerna won't poo again for at least two days. I understand human babies poo almost constantly? Must be exhausting! Go on, you three, I'll finish up here and get Kerna to bed!"

Their trip to the bathhouse turned out to be just what they needed. Yakesha gave them directions, telling them not to be more than an hour. The bathhouse was an impressive stone structure in the basement of the tower that connected to the aqueduct. It was enormous, with a high vaulted roof above a dozen wide square pools filled with water, ten feet at their deepest point.

Patch and Wren stripped down to their undertunics, and Barver took off his harness and packs. In they went, splashing and laughing and having so much fun that they forgot how *worrying* everything was. When they got out, they saw other bathhouse users standing in a draught of warm air, drying themselves, so they did the same.

Clean and refreshed, they made it back to the Delegate

residence knowing they'd been much longer than the hour they'd been allowed, and they worried about getting a scolding. Yakesha opened the door to them, and they were relieved to see a smile on her face.

"Just in time!" she said, inviting them in. "How was the bathhouse?"

"Amazing," said Wren. "It's *under the ground*!"

Yakesha's smile broadened. "Incredible, isn't it? Dragons and humans, you see! Such achievements! Under our feet, the sewers of this city – four hundred years old! – have kept us free from disease, and able to enjoy the fresh air the Gods send us!"

Inside was a glorious sight: a table absolutely *filled* with delicious-looking food, none of which Patch could recognize. The smell was a heavenly mixture of spice, vinegar and sweetness. Barver actually had to wipe his chin, because he'd started to drool.

"It's the most wonderful thing I've ever laid eyes on," said Wren.

Zennick took a bow. "We may have gone slightly overboard," he said. "But for your first visit to Skamos, you should try all the great dishes of the city!"

And so they did: jackery leaves with kib radish; cheese and orno dumplings; pork and gilla. These and more, all of them full of flavour. When it came to the harker peas, though, Alia urged caution to Patch and Wren. "Take a nibble," she advised. "For humans, they pack quite a punch!"

The peas were white, in a pale yellow sauce. Each pea was about two inches across, and some had been thinly sliced.

Patch took the smallest of bites from the thinnest of slices, but Wren tutted and shook her head at him. "You chicken!" she said, and popped a whole pea in her mouth. Alia seemed horrified.

"That's *really* tasty!" said Wren. "I don't know what you were…"

She stopped talking, her eyes starting to water.

Patch had an idea why: even though he'd only had the tiniest bite, his mouth felt like he was eating *actual fire.*

"It'll pass in a minute, Wren," said Alia, looking concerned. "Just be patient and breathe through the pain…"

As for Barver, he was chomping away at the peas, which were clearly hitting the spot. But then, as he glanced at Wren, his eyes widened; Patch wondered if the peas had got to him at last, but Barver gave a small nod towards Wren's back. Bemused, Patch leaned and saw what Barver had seen: Wren had a *rat's tail* sticking up from the top of her trousers. He wondered if she knew about it, but that was soon answered, as her hand came around and felt it. She coughed.

"I did warn you, those peas are an acquired taste!" said Alia. For a second, Patch wondered if she could see the tail too, but he didn't think so, not from where she was sitting.

"No problem," Wren managed, trying to mask the heat with some of the other dishes. Gradually the tail shrank away.

The three were shown to a guest bedroom. It was a wide room with a raised flat stone at the centre, which was Barver's bed; by the walls were four beds with plush wool-and-straw mattresses, feather-stuffed pillows and soft blankets. Wren tried one out.

"Ahhh!" she said. "This may be the most comfortable bed I've ever slept in!"

"Well, I'm more dragon than griffin when it comes to beds," said Barver. "Griffins do like a bit of padding, but dragons prefer solidity." He patted his chest a few times, then breathed a little fire onto the stone to warm it up. "Especially when it's hot!" He removed his harness and curled up on the heated stone, wincing a few times as he tucked his wings in.

"Muscle cramps?" asked Patch.

"The bathhouse helped," said Barver. "But, yes, the cramps are still there."

Patch hunted in one of the harness packs, and took out his Pipe. "Would you like me to play, see if it helps?"

Barver nodded, so Patch began the Curative Sleep, building it up the way he'd done before. As he played, Wren got off her bed and came over. She looked in another of Barver's packs and took out *The Art and Method of Morphic Transmutation,* the book Alia had found for her.

"How much have you read?" asked Barver.

"I've only had time for a quick skim," she said. "It makes for hard reading, but I'll get there. I mean, I need to, given today…"

"Does the book mention spicy food giving you a tail?" said Barver.

"Oh, *don't*," she said. "I was so embarrassed!"

"Nobody saw," said Barver. "If they'd seen it, they probably would've yelled *snake*. It's all fine now, no need to fret."

Patch scowled at them both. "Really, you two need to be quiet! I'm trying to play!"

"Sorry," said Barver. "I do appreciate it, Patch. When we fly to our rendezvous in Gossamer Valley I don't want to have to spend time resting, I'll have work to do!"

Wren looked worried. "What if we don't get permission?" she said. "I mean, Alia's medal should go a long way, but what if it's not enough?"

"Then I'll do my best, alone," said Barver.

"Doesn't the Triumvirate's Proclamation apply to you?" said Wren. "I don't want you to get into trouble."

"Oh, don't worry about me," he said. "The dragons don't count me as a proper dragon, and the griffins don't count me as a proper griffin, so…" He blew a massive raspberry. "I can do what I like. No Proclamation to worry about, and no Covenant to break."

"I have it!" said Wren. "Dracogriffs! There must be others like you, right? They wouldn't be forbidden either!"

Barver shook his head. "I only know of two other dracogriffs. Both of them live way over in Yekarn, about as far east as you can get in the Dragon Territories, in a religious retreat. They're *highers*. You know about highers and lowers?"

Wren nodded. "The highers are pretty, but fragile; the lowers…aren't."

"Yep," said Barver. "Well, these two would break if you so much as *looked* at them, I heard."

"So, what if it *is* only you?" said Wren. "What if you're our only scout?"

"Then I'll do my best," said Barver. "But we'd be relying on luck more than anything. The whole point is to take them by surprise and make sure their escape is impossible, or they'll be off, and the Hamelyn Piper can hide again and bide his time!"

Patch had had enough of all this chatter. "Can you both be quiet? I'm *healing* here!"

✶
✶ ★

Patch's bed certainly was comfortable. He woke from wonderful dreams (dancing with his mother, always his favourite) to a gentle knocking on the bedroom door.

The door opened, and in came Yakesha and Zennick. They looked rather tired.

"Sorry to wake you early," said Yakesha. "But you don't happen to have seen little Kerna?"

Patch and Wren shook their heads.

Suddenly, from under Barver's wing, the baby's head appeared, and Kerna stood up. "Ba Va!" Barver opened his eyes and yawned, then noticed Kerna. "Uh…morning," he said. "How long have *you* been there, little one?" He gave his aunt and uncle a confused look.

"Sorry," said Yakesha. "We do try our best, but Kerna is a bit of an escape artist."

"You should see what we've had to do to the cot," said Zennick. "But no harm done, this time!"

"Ba Va!" said Kerna again.

Wren sat up. "Hi, Kerna, can you say Wren? *Wren?*"

"Wen!" said Kerna.

"And what about Patch?" said Patch.

"Bub bub!" said Kerna, smiling. Snot oozed from both nostrils, catching alight a moment later.

Patch ignored the giggles from Barver and Wren.

The doorbell rang. "I'll go and see who that is," said Yakesha. "How about some lop-root tea, dear?"

Zennick nodded. "A good idea." He turned to Barver as he left. "Don't let Kerna run around in here. Too many flammable materials!"

Barver nodded and picked the baby up.

"Everyone sleep as well as I did?" asked Patch.

"Absolutely," said Barver, between goo-gooing at Kerna. "Well enough that I didn't notice our escape-artist guest sneak in!"

"How are your muscle cramps?" said Patch.

Barver grinned. "Are you fishing for compliments about your Healing Song? Although if you are, they'd be well-deserved. I think it really helped."

"What about you, Wren?" said Patch. "Discover anything in your shape-shifting book?"

"Bits and pieces," she said. "I tried to learn some of the exercises. It does mention sudden uncontrolled changes like my tail. Glitches like that are how children first discover their ability. Mostly harmless, it says. Stress is one thing that can bring it on, and the risk of inversion is slim."

"Inversion?" said Barver. He and Patch shared a wary look.

"That's when it's bad," said Wren. "It didn't go into too much detail, though. Reckon you'd know it when you saw it. On the positive side, glitches are a sign of strong shape-shifting ability. Even if it takes years, I really think it'll happen!"

"And then you can work on becoming a tiny shark," said Barver.

At that, Alia poked her head into the room. "Something's up," she said. She looked decidedly worried. "Get dressed and come on."

Every citizen was watching.

Yakesha stood at the outskirts of the city. Beside her were the elected City Elders: one dragon and one human.

And in the distance, a darkness of dragons was approaching.

"Not again," muttered Patch. They were standing a little back from Yakesha and the Elders. Zennick had remained at home – Yakesha hadn't wanted Kerna anywhere near this, whatever *this* turned out to be.

"At least it's not as big as last time," said Wren, and she was right. It was nowhere *near* as huge as the army that had besieged Tiviscan; even so, there were more dragons in the sky than there were dragons resident in Skamos.

"They're taking their time to get here," said Barver. "A classic show of strength. I don't like it."

"I don't like it either," said Alia. She stepped forward to catch Yakesha's ear. "What is this, Yakesha? Could they be here because of me, and the request?"

Yakesha shook her head. "The letter won't reach the

252

Triumvirate until this evening at the earliest," she said. "Besides, an army like that takes time to assemble. They would have been on their way even before we'd *written* your letter, Alia."

The dragons landed over a mile away. Once settled, a solitary dragon took off and flew towards them.

"Ooh, a messenger," said Wren. She nudged Barver. "That used to be your job, didn't it?"

"Don't remind me," he said.

The messenger didn't take long to reach them. "For the Triumvirate Delegate of Skamos!" he announced, holding out a scroll.

Yakesha stepped forward. "I am Yakesha Knopferkerkle, Delegate," she said, taking it. She stared at the messenger, who was just standing there.

"I await a response," he said.

Yakesha glared at him. "Well, wait further away, lad," she said, her authority clear. "Give us privacy."

The messenger flew off a little distance, and waited.

Yakesha unrolled the scroll, and read aloud: "*The commanding officer of these forces, General Yem Kasterkan, seeks a private audience with the Triumvirate Delegate of Skamos, so that he may give instructions as to the nature of a new Triumvirate Proclamation.*" She rolled the scroll up again, frowning. "Whatever this is about, I don't like it."

"Aunt Yakesha?" said Barver. "I know Kasterkan. He was

in the army that attacked Tiviscan, although he was just a captain then."

"Quite a promotion to general," said Yakesha. "Do you *like* him?"

"He's only a year older than me, and I knew him as a child," said Barver. "Even then, I didn't like him *at all*. Self-serving and nasty. He led the aerial bombardment units at Tiviscan, in charge of the rocks that destroyed the dungeon walls."

"He did a particularly good job of that," muttered Patch, thinking back to the horror of it – the walls of his dungeon cell exploding as the rocks hit, almost killing both him and Wren.

Yakesha turned to the City Elders. "He wants a private meeting, but whatever the general has to say, he can say it to us all. Agreed?"

"Agreed!" said the Elders, as one.

Yakesha summoned the messenger. "Tell your general I'll grant an audience, here with the leaders and citizens of Skamos. Tell him the people of this city stand together!"

The messenger returned to the army. Soon, a small group set off back towards the city – the general and four soldiers. They landed a short distance away, and the general strode out. There was contempt in his expression, Patch saw.

"Delegate," said the general. Yakesha nodded. "You dispense with a formal audience. Perhaps that's for the best.

It saves us time. The Triumvirate has spoken. The city of Skamos has long been a splinter in the eye of all dragons."

"All?" said Yakesha. "I beg to differ. We have five hundred dragons here who have a very different opinion, for a start!"

The general ignored her. "It was never meant to be this way. An unnatural state, for dragons to sully themselves with the vermin humans! But the time has come for dragon and human to be sundered, pulled apart. Separation is the only way to restore the pride of dragons!" The general smiled a cold, terrible smile. "Dragon and human will no longer live together in the city. Separation! That is the order of the Triumvirate."

"The Triumvirate means to divide us?" said Yakesha. "Nonsense! Skamos has been a shared home for centuries. How can you draw a border in a city where we all live as one?"

"There will be no border," said the general, raising his voice as shouts of protest came from the crowds of citizens.

Yakesha looked exasperated. "Then who is to be evicted? The citizens of Skamos will not stand by while our friends are expelled!"

The general glared at her. "You ask meaningless questions," he said. "There will be no border, because there will be no longer be a city. We have come to destroy it!"

255

20

SKAMOS EVACUATED

Yakesha stared at the general. "Destroy the city?" she said. "The Triumvirate would *never* authorize that!"

General Kasterkan offered a paper document, sealed with wax. "Read out the Proclamation," he said. "The citizens shall be evacuated to safety, but the city will be *obliterated*."

Yakesha took the papers and carefully examined them. "The official seal of the Triumvirate," she said. She broke the seal and read aloud: "*The shared ownership of the city of Skamos, and the cohabitation of dragons with humans, will come to an end. General Yem Kasterkan, leader of the forces so tasked, is to achieve this aim by any means deemed necessary.*" She looked up at the general, who had a satisfied expression on his face. "This is madness," she said. "The Triumvirate can't mean you to destroy the city, to turn thousands out of their homes!"

"*By any means deemed necessary*, it says," sneered General Kasterkan. "I deem it necessary. Therefore it's within the law. Humans are vermin, and dragons will no longer tolerate them. Is it so hard to understand? The Triumvirate has decided that involvement with the world of humans is pointless. How better to demonstrate their resolve than the end of Skamos itself?"

Beside Yakesha, the dragon Elder shook his head. "This city will never give in to oppressors!" he said.

"Never!" cried the human Elder. She spat on the ground. "We can hold out for as long as it takes, just as our ancestors did!"

"I know the history of this city, just as well as you," said the general. "You could try and hold out for a few days, long enough for an army of Pipers to reach you. That was how it happened in the past, yes? But this time, things are different. The Pipers have their attention elsewhere. There's no army coming to your aid, even if you could get the word out about your situation. Which you cannot: my soldiers are faster than any of you."

"We will defeat you," said the dragon Elder. "Human and dragon citizens, standing as one!"

Kasterkan shook his head. "I told you, I know this city's history. Every time a dragon army besieged Skamos, the

257

citizens did exactly as you say. They stood side by side. And every besieging army had the same dilemma: a soldier can face down a fellow soldier in combat, but to kill a *civilian* dragon, who's defending their own city? To some, that would be cold-blooded murder. No dragon soldier would follow an order to *murder* a fellow dragon."

He gestured across the plains to where his army was building their camp, and Patch could see a wooden frame of some kind, easily twenty feet high, from which hung a huge bell; behind the bell, the soldiers were busy building other things, which Patch couldn't make out.

General Kasterkan continued: "You all heard what happened to the walls of Tiviscan Castle? Rocks, larger than any a normal catapult could launch, hurled with skill by dragons who've trained long and hard to perfect their aim. But even for them, there's a limit, and so a new weapon is called for. Out there, my forces are building the largest, strongest catapults ever devised. One hundred of them. They will be capable of destruction on a scale you cannot conceive, released by the pull of a simple wooden lever." He smiled a cold smile. "It's one thing to kill a fellow dragon eye to eye: to see their blood spilled, and the life vanish from their eyes. It's quite another thing to merely *pull a lever*. A rock, launched into the air, becomes a matter for the Gods to decide. No soldier would think that was cold-blooded murder, not any more. The human and dragon

258

citizens of Skamos can choose to stand together, as they have done many times before. But be in no doubt: this time, if they do that they will die."

The bell that the dragons had built began to ring out. Patch counted twelve strikes.

"Twelve now, one less each hour," said Kasterkan. "The bell counts down the life of Skamos. At the zero hour, it will ring out continuously, and the destruction of the city shall begin! We'll allow you to evacuate, but be assured: when the bell rings for the last time, anyone who remains in the city will perish, whether human or dragon."

"The Pipers will punish you for this!" said Yakesha.

The general shook his head. "I think not. By the time they hear of it, it'll be too late to prevent. Humans can be rallied to a cause, yes, but not if the cause is already lost! What are they to do? Start another war with dragons? No. They will be very loud in their protests, and very quiet in their actions. Besides, there's a truth you must accept, Delegate: many humans hate Skamos too, and will be secretly pleased with its destruction."

"We will not go!" said Yakesha. "You're just trying to scare us!"

He stepped closer. "Skamos dies today," he said. "I've dreamed of this moment for as long as I can remember. You wouldn't *believe* the things I've had to do to make it happen. I've not come this far just to stop now. I will see it through, whatever the cost. I will kill every living creature in this city if I must, Delegate."

She looked into his eyes and saw something terrifying. It wasn't *madness* that she saw; it was far worse than that. She saw *certainty*. Kasterkan wouldn't hesitate to give the order, no matter how many would perish.

Yakesha felt all hope drain from her.

"At last you understand," said the general. "The only thing in your power is to decide how many of your precious citizens die between now and nightfall. Now I have other matters to attend to. My corporals will oversee the evacuation." He took to the air, and flew back towards his army.

Yakesha closed her eyes. Behind her, the city was silent.

When they returned to the Delegate residence, Zennick was waiting at the door, holding a tearful Kerna in his arms. He said nothing, and just leaned forward, head bowed; Yakesha did the same, and the tops of their heads came gently together, a display of love and support that left Patch with a lump in his throat. They stayed like that for a short while, in silence – even Kerna stopped crying.

When they separated, Yakesha took Kerna, hugging the baby close.

"Young Hannul told me what happened," said Zennick.

"Is there really nothing we can do?"

"We have no choice," said Yakesha. "We must pack what we can carry, and make certain we have everything Kerna will need. The army gave instructions." She told Zennick the details: a camp was being set up for the city's refugees, close to the dragon army. From there, each dragon citizen would be given a free choice of where in the Dragon Territories they would make their new home, and everything would be provided for them.

The humans, however, would have to fend for themselves.

"We can't abandon our fellow citizens," Zennick said.

"We won't abandon them," said Yakesha. "I proposed to the Elders that the contents of the city treasury should be divided among the human citizens, to help them resettle. It won't be much once shared out among ten thousand, but it'll be something. The first requirement will be to hire ships to transport them from the camp to safety. Only once that's done should *any* dragon agree to move on."

"No!" cried a voice, and everyone turned to Wren, who was distraught. "I can't believe how you're talking! This isn't right, this isn't fair! You have to *fight*…"

Alia put her hand on Wren's shoulder. "Wren, this is not a time to fight."

Wren stared at her, baffled. "But you of all people, you can… You can…"

261

"I can what?" said Alia. "Take down a dragon soldier? Yes. Maybe ten! Maybe fifty!" She shook her head, slow and sorrowful. "They would fire their weapons, killing thousands, and say it was self-defence!"

"Listen to me, Wren," said Yakesha. "The city will stand. What can they do? Bombard it, as they did Tiviscan? Yet Tiviscan is repaired! Destroy the aqueduct, as many have done before? We'll build another! The walls, the buildings, these are only bricks. Only stone. Let them do their worst. Because the city *will stand*."

Wren, tearful, shook her head. "I don't know what you mean…"

Yakesha was also tearful, but she smiled, a smile that held courage, and defiance, and despair, and hope; seeing it, Wren felt her heart both break and soar, all at once. "The city of Skamos is the people, Wren," said Yakesha. "Humans and dragons, together! And one day we *will* return. Skamos will rise again."

The City Elders came to the Delegate residence, to help organize the evacuation. The dragon corporals had given them until the next bell tolled to present a plan, while the citizens in every home had to make agonizing choices about what to take with them. The army's instructions had said, "take only essential things, easily carried"; how could

262

a lifetime, or a family history, be distilled into just a few items?

"We must bring supplies out of the city first, before all else," said Elder Inia, the human. "Food, medicine and materials for building shelters. And gold, of course, to help with resettlement."

Elder Rafal, the dragon, nodded. "The wealth of the city, carefully managed. The army has sworn not to steal from us. Can we trust them?"

"Trust soldiers with gold?" said Yakesha. "Never. We have the grain stores to empty too. Hide bags of gold in the sacks of grain."

"Once the supplies have been removed, the citizens will be evacuated together, as one," said Rafal. "We'll need every hand to help prepare. I suggest the children should go to their schools, to free up the adults."

Yakesha looked across the room to the table where Barver sat. Little Kerna was on his lap, the baby's nose alight. "Nurseries too," she said. "It would be best for the children to be with each other, rather than see the fear and anger on their parents' faces."

Elder Rafal wiped tears from his eyes. "And to let dragon and human friends play together one last time," he said, before giving a brief sob. "I'm sorry. It feels like it's the end of the world."

They set about planning the details. Transporting the

necessary supplies would take eight of the remaining eleven hours. This would leave three for the citizens to leave the city.

The distant bell sounded eleven times. Yakesha and the Elders stood and left, going to see if their plan was acceptable to the corporals.

"Ba Va!" cried Kerna, clearly confused by how miserable everyone was.

"Kerna's taken a shine to you," Zennick told Barver. "Perhaps you could stay in the nursery, and keep the little one company?"

"No," said Barver. "Much as I'd like to, I'll be far more use helping to move supplies." He looked to Patch, Wren and Alia. "You three can look after Kerna, can't you? They'll take all the help they can get at the nursery, I imagine."

"Perhaps," said Alia. "Although I was going to offer my assistance at the city infirmary instead."

Zennick nodded. "They would appreciate that," he said. "So, what of you, Patch and Wren? Will you take Kerna to the nursery, and help shield *all* the little ones from this trauma?"

"Of course we will," said Wren. She leaned over to Patch and whispered: "We're babysitters now."

Patch said nothing. There were worse things to be, here at the end of the world.

21

THE CONVOY

"That doesn't look good," said Wren.

They were walking along a cobbled street, halfway up the great hill on which Skamos had grown. The street led straight down the hill, and on the plains in the distance, the activities of the dragon army were clear to see: many of the vast catapults had been completed already.

Patch thought back to the attack on Tiviscan – groups of dragons coming towards them, huge boulders hanging from nets beneath, reaching incredible speeds before launching their missiles…

He shivered.

He was carrying Kerna now, having swapped with Wren five minutes before. The baby was heavier than he'd expected, and his arms were already starting to complain, but the scenes around them put everything into perspective. The people of the city, dragons and humans both, were working hard to enact the plan that the Elders and Yakesha had put in place, even though behind every pair of eyes the tragedy and injustice was clear.

As they turned a corner, the bell in the dragon camp started to ring. Patch and Wren looked at each other, baffled – it wasn't long since it had last rung, and now it was ringing quickly, not the slow count of before.

It had to be a warning.

A panicked voice shouted out: "They're attacking already!"

Screams came from far and near, with cries of "Look out!" and "Take cover!" as people started running to get out of the street.

Patch and Wren hurried to the nearest building and stood pressed against the wall, waiting; Kerna burst into tears.

Seconds later, they heard a distant crash, and more screams. Then silence.

Kerna was crying even harder, reaching out to Wren as she and Patch held their breath, expecting more crashes to come. But none did. People stepped back into the road, wary.

"They're saying it was a misfire!" shouted someone. "Just a single misfire!"

Wren scowled. "Misfire, my *backside*," she muttered.

"You don't think…" said Patch.

"The dragons want us to know they mean business," she said. "Anyone who was considering just *staying* in the city will be thinking twice now."

"I hope nobody was hurt," said Patch. They kept going up the hill, and soon he got the answer. A building a few streets on had been destroyed by the catapulted boulder, which was visible in the midst of the devastation. Some dragons were searching the wreckage, while a small group of humans, covered in dust, stood in shock nearby. Patch and Wren stopped, as did many others; a small crowd was watching the rescue, in total silence.

At last a call came up, and a limp human body was pulled from under the building's rubble; urgent shouts followed, and one of the dragons took to the air with the victim.

"Taking him to the infirmary," said a man in the crowd, next to Wren. "It's a miracle no one was killed!"

As the remaining dragons cleared the debris from the street, Patch felt the ground beneath him rumble. Around them, the gathered crowd backed away, and someone pointed out a great crack in the road itself. One dragon moved towards the crack, and the crowd gasped as part of the road visibly tilted.

"The impact has left the ground unstable," shouted the dragon. "We need to get everyone clear, and rope it off!"

"But this is part of the the evacuation route," came a shout from the crowd.

"They'll have to reroute it, then!" said the dragon, looking at the ground uneasily. "The main sewer runs right under here. The slabs could give way at any time. It's too dangerous!"

The crowd began to disperse, people getting back to their preparations. Patch took one last look at the crack in the road.

The evacuation hadn't really begun yet, but Skamos was already broken.

When Patch and Wren arrived at the nursery, the chaos and panic of the supposedly misfired boulder was still having an effect. All the children – forty human and five dragon – were inconsolable. Kerna, who had settled down by then, started crying again.

The nursery staff were red-eyed. Patch couldn't imagine how terrible this day must be for the people of the city, losing everything at once – their homes, their jobs, their friends. Even so, the staff knew what to do, and soon the children were playing, laughter replacing the tears. Kerna was happy to join in, and seemed to forget that Patch and Wren were even there.

"I wonder what they do when Kerna's nose lights up,"

said Wren to Patch. They were in a corner, trying to keep out of the way. When they'd offered to help, the staff had politely made it clear that, really, staying out of the way would be the most helpful thing they could do. This was entirely acceptable to them both.

Wren took the little shape-shifting book from her pocket, and also produced a small notebook. She opened the notebook and started reading.

"Can I look at the shape-shifting one?" asked Patch.

"Be careful with it," she said, handing it over.

"I will," said Patch. He pointed to her notebook. "What do you have there?"

"Interesting things I found in Casimir's books," she said. "I jotted them down before we left. I found lots of barrier spells, for a start. Alia's speciality in Piping was barriers, so I thought she might be impressed if I taught myself some spells that did similar things."

"Anything else?"

"Oh, lots," grinned Wren. "Plant magic caught my eye. It's a bit like the stuff your Arable Pipers do, only hugely more impressive. When the time comes, I'll knock Alia's socks off with what I've learned!"

Every hour, the great bell rang, counting down the remaining time. Outside, carts rolled by as supplies were gathered and moved out. Patch and Wren helped with the children now and again, with simple things like gathering

269

up cups or toys. They shared a simple meal, a water-and-grain stew that was rather like porridge but with a pleasing crunch to it.

"Can we help wash the dishes?" offered Patch.

The staff member he asked – the only dragon among them, a male called Hagen – shook his head. "What would be the point?" he said, looking lost. What *would* be the point, washing dishes they weren't intending to bring when they left?

When the bell rang four times, meaning only four hours were left, there was a knock at the nursery door. It was one of the city guards, asking how many there were inside, then telling them the plan for the actual evacuation: carts would come in one hour, and the city would evacuate in a convoy. Once all the citizens were clear, the city guards would scour the streets as a final check that the evacuation was complete, and that everyone was safe.

And then...

Then the catapults would come alive.

The hour that followed was an agonizing wait. The nursery staff made sure the children had everything they'd brought with them. All those with favourite toys had their precious woollen teddies, ducks and squid tied to their wrists for safekeeping. Patch tried to read the shape-shifting book, but the words just sat on the page and stubbornly refused to make sense. Wren studied her notebook, her lips moving as she recited the spells to herself, though as the last few minutes drew closer even she couldn't concentrate.

The three-hour bells rang, and there was a knock at the door.

"It's time," said a city guard, and out they went. It was quite a sight – the road was full, up the hill and down. The citizens of Skamos stood, carrying what they intended to bring, ready to begin the long walk that would take them out of the city. Here and there, carts waited, dragons at the front, ready to transport those too infirm to walk, or – as with the nursery – too young.

There were two carts for the nursery, and both looked like they were normally used for transporting livestock, with high bars around the sides. The nursery staff made a game of it, even though their heartbreak was clear for all to see. The children got aboard, and there was just enough room for them and some of the staff. Patch and Wren would walk, and stood behind the second cart. Kerna was at the bars, waving at them.

Shouts rippled up from below, and soon the long convoy began to move. Apart from the crunch of cartwheel on stone, the shuffle of feet, and a gentle rumble of movement, there was almost no sound at all. From time to time, the procession would halt briefly before continuing.

Patch and Wren took each other's hand, missing Barver terribly, and Alia too.

A little further on, they came to the reason for the stop-start motion. The convoy was being made to take two tight corners, through an alleyway and onto a smaller road that twisted and turned. Some of the carts struggled with the tight bends.

A city guard passed by, and Wren asked him what had happened. "It's because of the building that was brought down, and the damaged road," he said. "We have to miss that whole street, and this is the only other way."

The convoy halted again; the cart three in front of them was having real difficulty getting around a bend, even with dragons helping at both sides. The minutes ticked by, and then Wren put her hand to her mouth, with a look of such horror that Patch expected to turn and see the Hamelyn Piper himself standing there.

Instead, Wren was staring through a narrow passageway that was shrouded in shadow, horrified by precisely nothing. Nothing that Patch could make out, anyway.

"What is it?" he said, and Wren pointed.

"I can't bear it," she said, tears in her eyes. And, without another word, off she went through the passageway.

Patch, open-mouthed, looked at the passage, and looked at the cart ahead. It would be stuck for a while yet, he reckoned. He chased after Wren, and before his eyes could adjust to the shade, he walked right into her.

"Careful!" she said. "I just wanted to catch it, there was no need for you to come."

"Catch what?" said Patch, but then he could see it: a black cat, bewildered by the activity, was in the middle of the passage ahead of them. It meowed and scampered away.

Wren ran after it, and Patch followed. The passageway opened out a little, and bright sunlight lay ahead. There was the cat, cleaning its bottom as if nothing was remotely wrong.

"We can't just leave it," said Wren. "The poor thing!"

"We should go back," said Patch. "It doesn't look like it *wants* to be rescued."

Wren took a step nearer the cat, and off it went, not a care in the world. Wren followed behind, calling, "Puss cat! Puss cat!" again and again, all her attention on the animal.

Patch emerged from the passageway into a wide street, bright and empty. He could feel a slight tremble through his feet, and assumed the evacuation line was moving again. "Come on, Wren. Leave the cat. It can look after itself."

"Poo tat!" said a voice beside him.

With a quiet dread, Patch looked to his left. Six feet away, little Kerna was smiling up at him.

"Oh, *no*," said Patch. "How on earth did you sneak away?" He thought back to Yakesha, telling them what a little escapologist Kerna was. He kneeled down and offered

273

a hand out. "Come here," he said. Kerna blew a raspberry at him.

"Poo tat!" said the baby, scampering off towards Wren with surprising speed. Patch caught up halfway across the street, though, and got a hand on the child's arm.

Kerna gave him a stern look. "Poo tat!"

"Enough, Kerna," he said. "The pussy cat will have to find its way without us. Let's get back to the cart. Wren? Come on, let it go!"

Wren ignored him. She was still trying to coax the cat nearer, but whenever she took a step towards it, it slunk back.

And then, two things happened at once. First, Patch noticed the ropes tied from one side of the street to the other, a little way up. And second, he felt the ground wobble again.

The ropes suddenly made sense.

He turned around. There it was, in plain sight: the building next-but-one to the passageway was a collapsed ruin, the great rock from the catapult still clear to see, and a huge crack running through the road ten feet from where he stood. It was a *larger* crack now, he realized, stretching right across the street, and the road on one side of the crack was noticeably higher.

As he looked at it, he could *swear* that he saw it rise a little more, as the ground wobbled under him again. He remembered what the dragon had said, the one who'd ordered the street to be roped off: *the slabs could give way at any time.*

"Wren…" he said, his mouth feeling very dry indeed. "This is important. Can you turn around, really carefully? *Wren!*"

The cat had had enough, and ran off. Wren turned, irritation on her face. "You scared it away!" she said. "I was so close to…" She saw the baby. "Kerna!" she said. "What on earth are *you* doing here?" Instinct taking over, she hurried towards them, and Patch had just enough time to raise a hand, ready to shout "Stop!", before two great slabs of stone suddenly tipped up in the road, opening a great dark hole and sending all three of them down into the black.

And a short distance away, the evacuation line kept on going without them.

22

THE MISSING

Barver had never felt so proud of his dragon heritage.

It was an odd feeling, of course, because it was dragons who had *caused* this catastrophe, but those weren't the dragons he felt a kinship with. General Kasterkan's hatred of humans was shared by many, but not by the dragons of Skamos. Each and every one had the same outlook that Barver's mother had tried so hard to encourage – that cooperation was to the benefit of all.

As the hours were counted down, Barver had helped distribute supplies and equipment in the evacuation area near the army encampment. A vast field of simple tents started to grow.

He'd felt sick witnessing that terrible catapult launch, the bell ringing repeatedly as a warning. The soldiers claimed it had been an accident, but Barver could see a hint of shame in the eyes of some of them. Not all of Kasterkan's soldiers were entirely comfortable with what was happening, it seemed.

Eventually, the time came for the citizens to leave the city. Before the convoy assembled, the patients and staff of the city infirmary were brought out to the evacuation area. Barver saw Alia, and hurried over to her.

"Any news?" he said.

"Patch, Wren and Kerna are all well," she said. "I asked after them. They're in Kerna's nursery, safe. You saw the launch, I assume? The *misfire*, one of their soldiers called it, but I doubt that. Perhaps they were just making sure of their range…"

Barver nodded, frowning. "I heard there was one serious injury – an old man." He looked at the patients, fifty or so of them; some walked with help, others were laid flat in the back of wide carts.

"Yes, he's in among them," said Alia. "Crushed in the wreckage of his own house. Both legs broken, and an arm. A few others hurt too, but his was the worst of it."

Barver looked out to the city. He could see the streets filling, as the convoy started to form. The long, slow walk from Skamos would soon begin. "A tragic sight," he said. "But I'm grateful to be here."

"You are?" said Alia.

Barver nodded. "When it mattered most."

Alia went with the infirmary group, heading to the largest of the tents that had been erected, while Barver took up his position.

When the convoy reached the edges of the evacuation area, the citizens were directed to one of twelve sections. Barver's role was to organize arrivals to section nine, making sure everyone took their time and left enough space around them, especially near the many toilet pits that had been dug. It was almost unbearable to see the lost looks on every face, the empty stares, the tears; he expected questions about food and water, but the people moved in a silence that was broken only by the crying of children.

The sections filled, and soon the end of the convoy was visible. A final sweep of the city began, small groups of citizens and city guards with handbells urgently checking every street, every building.

The last to be moved was Unanda Kellokeen, the oldest resident of them all.

Barver's section was close to the dragon army camp, and he could hear two dragon soldiers laughing about her. "I heard that she's not moved from that spot in decades," said one.

"Well, *I* heard she hasn't taken wing in over a century!" laughed the other, before spitting on the ground. "That waste of space calls herself a dragon. That's the problem

278

with this city, that's why it has to die."

"They're *infected*," said the first soldier in disgust, as the second nodded. "Infected with human ideas and human laziness. The world is for the strong, not the weak!"

Barver tried not to look at them; he knew they would see the anger in his eyes, and it might cause trouble. And what could he say? That dragons and humans were more alike than they thought?

That was certainly true, because there was no shortage of humans who believed the same thing they did – that *strength* was the only virtue that mattered, and that any signs of weakness were to be treated with contempt.

That *needing help* was a sin, and *giving help* a crime.

With the evacuation complete, the people were coming out of their daze and asking the questions he'd expected before – about where to go to the toilet and how much water they were allowed to take from the nearest barrels. But the most common question was one he'd not expected. Again and again, he was given names, and asked if he'd seen them. People from other streets, relatives who'd become separated while leaving the city.

"If they're not close by, they're in another section," was all he could say in reply, but Barver's own anxiety grew a little each time he said it. Patch, Wren and little Kerna were safe and well, he told himself.

And then he saw his uncle, hurrying towards him.

"Your friends," said Zennick. "Where are they? I can't find them!"

"With Kerna's nursery group," said Barver. "Alia checked earlier. Be calm, Uncle. Everyone's looking for everyone at the moment!"

But Zennick shook his head slowly, and Barver had a sudden cold feeling in his guts. "I've spoken to the nursery staff," said Zennick. "Kerna isn't with them. They assumed your friends were taking care of the baby, but I can't find them either!"

Barver thought for a moment. "Alia!" he said. "That'll be it. They'll have gone to find Alia, in the infirmary tent." Zennick's gaze was darting everywhere, his growing desperation visible. "Please, Uncle, people will see your fear. You could start a panic! The final sweep of the city has been made. Everyone's safe." Yet even as he spoke, he felt his own panic rise. He took to the air, off towards the infirmary tent with his uncle close behind. There, he spotted Alia and waved her over.

"Patch and Wren," he said, keeping a low voice. "Are they with you?"

She shook her head. "They were at the nursery," she said. "I told you."

"The nursery staff don't know where they are." He nodded to his uncle, who was at the edge of the tent, searching every face. "Kerna's missing too. Uncle Zennick's terrified."

"Look around, Barver," said Alia. "The whole city is here! We'll find them. How long do we have until the deadline?"

"Twenty minutes or so," said Barver.

"Well, then, time enough," she said. She thought for a moment. "Barver, have you anything of Patch's, or Wren's? Something important to them. I'll see if I can get a rough bearing, we'll have them in no time."

"Right," said Barver, and he rummaged in a harness pack. "Here," he said, bringing out a Fox and Owls playing piece. "It's the cross-eyed owl, Wren's favourite."

Alia took it. "Good. This'll just take a minute." She held the piece tightly and closed her eyes, then turned on the spot for a few seconds. She paused and frowned, muttering something before trying again.

Zennick came over. "We're wasting time!" he said. "We should find Yakesha. Kerna could still be…" He looked to the empty city.

"Okay," said Barver, sensing his uncle was on the verge of panic. "Alia, keep trying."

"Of course," said Alia, her eyes still closed.

Zennick was already in the air. It was Barver's turn to follow, as Zennick spotted Yakesha at the front of the army encampment, beside the great bell. General Kasterkan was with her. Seeing them approach, a group of soldiers armed with pikes formed a line and called for them to turn back.

Yakesha spoke to the general, and a moment later the soldiers stepped down.

Zennick was the first to speak. "Kerna is missing," he said.

Yakesha looked to Barver. "What about your friends?"

"Missing too," said Barver.

Yakesha turned to the general. "You can wait, surely? Until all citizens are accounted for?"

The general scowled and pointed to the base of the bell, where a large hourglass sat, more than two-thirds through. "You have until the sand is gone," he said. "That's the end of the last hour."

"But my child is missing!" cried Yakesha.

"Your child is out there!" shouted the general, gesturing to the evacuated citizens. "There, among the masses, hidden in the crawling pestilence of the *humans* you wanted to share your lives with!"

"You must be *sure*," said Yakesha. "Before you begin your attack, be *sure* no one is left in the city, I beg you!"

"Your motive is *transparent*," the general scoffed. "A delaying tactic, nothing more!" He picked up the hourglass. "If you want reassurance, I suggest you use your time more wisely." He raised the hourglass to his face, almost gleeful as he watched the sand fall. "It runs through so quickly…"

"You think we'd lie about this?" said Barver.

"Watch your mouth, Knopferkerkle," said Kasterkan.

282

"Why would we lie?" said Barver. "To put the inevitable back a few more minutes? What would be the point? These are *lives* at stake, Yem..."

The use of his first name didn't please the general one bit. "You will address me as General, or General Kasterkan."

"Oh, *shut up*, Yem!" said Barver, overwhelmed by how petty this dragon was being. "This is more important than your stupid *title*."

The general gasped; Yakesha and Zennick both looked shocked. Barver knew at once that he'd gone too far. He may have known Yem Kasterkan as a child, but that counted for nothing here.

"I'm sorry," said Barver. "Forgive my outburst, I..."

Kasterkan, his face full of rage, threw the hourglass to the ground and smashed it. "Our time is up, it seems," he snarled, before turning to his troops. "Prepare to fire!"

Yakesha kneeled at his feet, begging. "You can't... please... They may be in the city!"

"Then you should have taken better care of them," said the general. With a nod, the soldiers nearby stepped forward and seized the three of them. Barver struggled, almost breaking free; it took four soldiers to hold him still.

And then Barver noticed what the soldiers by the catapults were doing – breathing fire at the rear of each boulder, until a cloud of white smoke began to rise above the loaded rock.

He noticed something else: each boulder was smooth, an almost-perfect sphere.

"Those aren't rocks..." he said, breathless after his struggle.

The general grinned, and picked up a long metal bar that hung beside the bell. "At my signal!" he cried. After a moment's pause, he struck the bell repeatedly. First one, then two, then all the catapults launched their cargo into the air. Anguished cries came from the people of Skamos.

"No, those are not rocks," sneered the general. "After the Tiviscan assault, I put all my efforts into maximizing our capacity for destruction. Those efforts bore fruit."

Barver watched the spheres as they flew, leaving trails of smoke in their wakes, converging on the city ahead. "They lit them...like fireworks."

The general gave him a satisfied smile. "Nothing gets past you, does it? Yes, these are very similar to fireworks; but less colourful, and much louder. And I promise you, the spectacle will be something to behold. Watch!"

23

IN THE SEWERS

Patch woke from a dream of bells and shouting.

He hurt all over. High above him, he could see a chunk of sky through a hole ten feet across; there was just enough light to reveal his surroundings.

It was a *sewer*. Arched columns supported the roof, part of which had collapsed.

He sat up, his hand splashing in a puddle of liquid beside him. He didn't want to look. The smell down here was awful enough without *seeing* what they'd fallen into.

Wren's voice startled him. "Did you hear the handbells?" she said.

He turned and saw her sitting at the wall of the tunnel. Kerna was in her lap, looking scared. "Handbells?" he said. He remembered his dream. "I suppose so."

"It was the last check of the city," she said. "When I came to, I could just about hear them, so I yelled as loud as I could… Nothing. They must have already passed by. How's your head? You've got a big old egg risen up there."

Patch put his hand to the side of his head, wincing at the pain that shot through his skull. "What about you and Kerna?" he said. "Are you hurt?"

"Not really," she said. "Cuts and bruises, that's all. Kerna's been quiet. I think dragon babies are tough little things, though. Can you walk?"

He stood carefully and went over to her, relieved to find that his body didn't announce any new and excruciating pains. He pulled a face at Kerna, trying for a smile, but the baby looked on the verge of tears.

"Poo tat," said Kerna, in the saddest possible voice.

Wren pushed herself up to her feet, grimacing as she wiped muck off her hand. "It's a good thing adult dragons don't have the same acidic poo as their babies," she said. "Or we'd probably have dissolved by now."

Then came the distant sound of the great bell – a single strike.

"One hour," said Wren. "And nobody knows we're here."

Patch gestured to the hole in the roof. "Can we climb up?" he said.

"No," said Wren. "It's too high, and even if we could

286

reach it, all that masonry is unstable. We'd just bring it down on top of us."

"Then what do we do?" said Patch.

"Remember what Alia told us?" she said. "About the canyon to the west?"

"The canyon…" said Patch. "Where the sewers lead to!"

"Exactly," said Wren. "We just follow the flow. It'll take us deeper under the city, safe from the dragons' rocks. Eventually, we'll make it to the canyon."

Patch looked up to the hole above them, tantalizingly near. Then he looked to the gloom of the tunnel that led downhill, the floor glistening with unmentionable fluids. Even with the city abandoned, there was a steady trickle of waste water – the constant run-off from the water stores and the public pools, that had kept the Skamos sewage system running for centuries. "Sounds like a plan," he said. "Smelly and disgusting, but a plan."

"Poo tat," said Kerna.

They'd not gone far before a snag in the plan materialized. Even as their eyes adapted to the dim light, the further they got from the hole in the roof, the darker everything became. At first it was possible to avoid deeper puddles and dodge the occasional mound of squelchy nastiness, but soon there was so little light that almost every step resulted in Patch's foot going up to the ankle in something unpleasant.

"We can hardly see," he said. "Soon it'll be pitch black!" He looked at Wren. "You can do something, surely?" He wriggled his fingers in a bad impression of a Sorcerer. "You must have a useful spell in your little notebook. You need to read it now, before we're in total darkness!"

Wren frowned. "I wish I could do that finger lightning thing that Alia does," she said. "But I can't. As for my notebook...I copied the spells that interested me, or ones I thought might impress Alia. Barriers, shielding spells, that kind of thing." She looked thoughtful, and passed Kerna over to Patch. "There is *one* that might help..." With a snap of her fingers, a tiny ball of flame appeared and hovered in the air. It burned bright and brief, then vanished. "It's the basic fireball," she said. "For beginners."

"Good!" said Patch. "Keep doing that! I mean *constantly*. Like a lantern!"

Wren nodded. She snapped her fingers again, and another tiny fireball appeared. This one was smaller, dimmer, and lasted less than a second. "Well, *that's* no good," she said, despairing. "At this rate we'll be lucky to get ten feet before I'm all spent."

Then Patch had an idea.

"Kerna?" he said. "Bub bub! Can you do a bub bub?" Kerna tensed slightly in his arms. There was a gloopy sound, and then a little pop...

And there!

Kerna's nose was alight, illuminating the sewer tunnel. Ahead, Patch noticed a few rats scampering away, darting down small inlet pipes that dotted the tunnel wall.

"Clever baby!" said Patch, and Kerna giggled.

With the tunnel lit clearly, they made rapid progress. The slope was gradual for the most part, but occasionally it grew steeper. More than once did Patch or Wren slip and fall, coming face to face with disgusting debris too stubborn to be washed away. One fall led to Kerna being briefly submerged in a grim and murky puddle. Tears followed. It was a worrying moment for Wren and Patch too, as Kerna's nose was extinguished, but the tears soon led to a fresh supply of flammable snot, and light returned.

"How long left, do you think?" said Patch. "Before the catapults begin? It feels like we've been down here for *weeks*."

"Oh, there's ages yet," said Wren. "We might even reach the canyon before…"

She stopped. Just at the very edge of hearing was a deep, steady ringing. It *had* to be the great bell of the dragon army.

Time was up.

Patch thought of the gap between hearing the cries of "Take cover!" earlier, and the arrival of the catapulted boulder. In his head, he started to count, as he and Wren instinctively crouched. Kerna, now in Wren's arms, sensed their fear and whimpered gently.

One…two… counted Patch.

"It won't be so bad," Wren told the baby. "We're so far down now, it'll just be a rumble, that's all."

Six…seven…eight…

Nine.

It did *start* as a rumble, but the noise grew and grew until it was overwhelming. As the tunnel shook violently, they both clamped their hands over their ears, looking around in dismay as dirt and dust fell from the roof. Even Kerna's wailing was lost under the noise.

"*Should we run?*" shouted Patch.

Wren shook her head, switching to Merisax: *Wait for it to end*, she signed.

Patch nodded, realizing that the ground was shaking so badly they would find it hard to even stand, let alone run.

They both looked up, thinking of the city above them and the horrifying assault it was suffering.

At last the noise died back, and the shuddering gradually reduced. Kerna was sobbing. Patch and Wren just stared at each other.

"What could have done that?" said Wren. "It can't have just been *rocks*…"

"We need to keep moving," said Patch.

On they went. Time after time, the walls of the tunnel shuddered. Chunks of the roof would fall down, ahead of them and behind.

And then they felt a movement in the air around them, almost a *breeze*.

"Wait," said Wren. She set Kerna on the ground, and blew hard at the baby's nose, extinguishing the flame.

"What are you doing?" cried Patch, but in a moment he saw. The tunnel up ahead wasn't completely dark.

He could see *light*.

A moment later Kerna's nose spontaneously relit; Patch and Wren grinned at each other.

"Not far now!" cried Wren. "Ten more minutes and we're out! Come on!"

Patch took Kerna, and they picked up their pace, hope surging through them.

But then came a sound: a deep and ominous *crack* that Patch felt in his kidneys, like the earth itself had fractured. Patch and Wren froze and looked at each other, their grins gone.

"What was that?" said Patch.

Wren shook her head, and as she was about to reply she frowned and turned, looking up the tunnel at where they'd come from. Patch turned too, because he could hear it now – a curious noise, like a thousand people whispering in a church.

"There!" said Wren. She pointed: in the tunnel, at the edge of their vision, the *floor* was moving.

"What is it?" said Patch, terrified.

"I can't tell," said Wren. But it wasn't long before they could see – rats, carpeting the tunnel floor, rushing towards them. "Stay by the wall!" cried Wren. The noise grew, a maddening cacophony of panicked chittering, as thousands of rats abandoned the city.

The tide of rodents threatened to take Patch's feet from under him. He just managed to stay upright. Wren slipped, falling against the wall as the rat horde tore past. "They're terrified!" she cried.

"I am too!" said Patch, but the huge rat pack started to thin out, the last stragglers coming past now. And then a strange thing: one of them, as it ran across Wren's lap, stopped and looked right at her. Wren stared back, as if…

As if she's seen a ghost, thought Patch. But a moment later, the rat squeaked and set off again. Wren stood up, in a daze.

Slowly, she and Patch turned once more to look up the tunnel. For there was yet another sound approaching, one that explained why the rats were running for their lives. Patch realized that the steady trickle of water in the sewer had suddenly increased; he thought of the pool they'd swum in, and about the water supplies being large enough to allow Skamos to hold out in a siege, even if the aqueduct was destroyed.

And that vast *cracking* sound.

"The reservoirs," said Wren, almost in a whisper.

They could see movement again, far up the tunnel, but this time it wasn't rats. It was *water,* surging towards them.

Patch looked down to the tunnel's end. "Can we make it?" he said, knowing even as the words left his mouth that there was no time.

"*Kerna,*" said Wren, and when Patch gaped at her in confusion she scowled at him. "Hold the baby up!" she cried. "I need the nose light to see my notebook!"

Patch held Kerna up, as Wren took her notebook and flicked through the pages.

A spell! thought Patch. "What do you have?" he said.

"Let me look!" snapped Wren, but an instant later she seemed to have found it. "I'm not sure what it does," she said. "*A shield against catastrophe*, it was called, and that caught my eye. *Use only when no other options remain*, it said." She paused, and they could both hear a terrible roar, as the contents of the reservoirs of Skamos grew ever closer.

"I think no options remain," said Patch. "Go for it!"

"Stand right behind me," said Wren. "Whatever happens, stay there! Don't move an inch!"

Patch held Kerna so the baby's light shone on Wren's notes. Wren began to chant, the words ancient and mysterious, and very similar to those that Alia had chanted back in Gemspar a lifetime ago.

"*Tee skarra tee garra,*" said Wren. "*Hin yessa hin vessa, skee tow, skee tow! Pak hansa pak! Pak hansa tak!*" She waved a hand carefully, in a gesture that Patch could see was described in the notes.

He looked up: the full torrent burst into sight, floor to ceiling, the noise growing every second.

Wren had to shout now. "*Tee skarra tee garra,*" she yelled. "*Hin yessa hin vessa, skee tow, skee tow! Pak hansa pak! Pak hansa tak!*" She waved her hand again, but nothing. Patch could feel the frustration in his friend, as she started to repeat the words faster, faster, and the water came closer, closer…

And then: he felt something take hold of his foot. He looked down and saw dark vines wrapping around his leg. *Don't move,* he told himself, as Wren's chanting became so rapid he wondered how she was managing it.

The vines spread, covering his legs, engulfing his torso, and Kerna too.

"Wren…" he said, all courage gone. Kerna let out a howl of fear, and as the vines crept over his face the last thing Patch saw was a wall of angry water about to hit them.

24

THE OUTLET

Alia had watched the catapults fire, and knew all was lost.

With the cross-eyed owl playing piece clutched tightly in her hand, she'd been trying her best to locate Wren. Somewhere out there, among the tents and the hopelessness, Wren and Patch and little Kerna were surely waiting to be found. Eyes closed, Alia had recited the simple words of the Sensing Enchantment, one of the oldest spells she knew. Hands outstretched, turning slowly, she waited for a *tug* that would indicate Wren's position.

A tug that didn't come.

And then the bell had sounded, and the catapults had launched…

All she could do was watch. Seeing the smoke trails that

the "rocks" left behind, she knew at once that this was different. Here was a new technology, a fearsome advance. The explosions ripped through Skamos: stone shattering, buildings crumbling, clouds of dust engulfing the fabric of the city.

A cry of horror and disbelief came from the citizens, watching those terrible spheres detonate. Watching their city *crumble*. But soon the echoes of the detonations turned to silence. Long seconds passed; then it began to rain sand and grit, the death of a city pouring down from the skies.

And as she watched, she realized with dismay that she felt a *tug* – facing the ruined city, she felt a sign of Wren. She looked for Barver, seeing him standing by the great bell. "Barver!" she cried, breaking the silence. He took wing, and was with her in seconds.

His face was heartbreak. "What is it?" he said.

Alia pointed to the city. "Wren's out there," she said. "*But alive!*" She climbed onto his back. "Go!"

Barver flew. Together, they approached Skamos. It was dying still, structures that had somchow withstood the barrage now disintegrating.

Alia held the cross-eyed owl; she focused until she felt the tug again. But it was weak, difficult to pin down.

"Well?" said Barver, desperate. "Where are they? How can they be alive in all of *that*?"

Alia directed him to the western edge of the city, and the

tug grew a little stronger. She suddenly understood: down! Down, beyond the wall!

Wren was in the sewers!

It was at that very moment that the sound came, like the earth itself breaking in two. The tower connected to the vast aqueduct began to collapse, water surging out across the devastated streets.

She knew where else that water would go; she knew what it meant for Wren.

"To the canyon!" she ordered, and Barver flew. There: the outlet from the sewer, a pipe the height of a large dragon. Only a slow trickle of fluid came from it at first, but soon there was a torrent!

In that water, sensed Alia, were lives – small, terrified, some doomed but all clinging to hope.

And then something larger, half-filling the tunnel. It burst out, falling to the canyon floor, where it was swept along by the flow.

"There!" yelled Alia. "Get it out of the water!"

Barver flew down, keeping close. It was like an enormous walnut – a bizarre thing, the surface twisted and intricate, but Alia knew exactly what it was.

And she was more proud than she'd ever felt in her life.

It was carried along on the white-foaming surface of the surging water, tossed around too violently for Barver to be able to grab it. Further down the canyon, the water calmed slightly; he managed to get enough grip on part of it to lift the whole thing clear. He flew high, returning to the plains above and setting it down.

"Give me room," said Alia. As Barver stepped back, purple light flickered around Alia's fingers; she released a careful flash at the walnut. Seeing where part of it broke, she worked at the weak point and opened a wider fracture. She looked to Barver, who seemed dazed. "Tear it open," she told him. "But be careful. If I'm right, they're inside!"

The words snapped Barver to action. He pulled at the curious walnut, and away came things that seemed to be branches, and vines, and bark, until he saw something that brought tears to his eyes, hot and uncontrolled: Wren's face, and Patch's, and Kerna's, as each of them took a gasping breath and let out a great sob.

Barver couldn't speak. Nor could Alia, or Wren, or Patch.

It was left to little Kerna to break the silence.

"Ba Va!" cried the baby, as Barver wrenched the last of the vines aside and took the child in his arms. Wren and Patch fell from the strange plant-formed sphere, coughing and exhausted.

Barver hugged Kerna tightly.

"Poo tat?" said Kerna. Baffled, Barver smiled, the tears not stopping. He looked to Patch for an explanation.

"Long story," said Patch, catching his breath at last.

In the distance, they saw some of the dragons of Skamos flying towards them, Yakesha and Zennick at the head.

Alia offered Wren her hand, and helped her up. "I see you've been studying, little Sorcerer," said the Witch of Gemspar. Then she gave Wren a long hug.

25

THE GRIFFIN EYRIE

Night came, and fires were lit to keep the cold at bay.

Patch and his friends discussed what they would do next. If Tobias had managed to convince the Pipers of Kintner to come to the forests of the Ortings and hunt down the Black Knight, they might already be on their way to Gossamer Valley. Without dragons to provide the airborne scouting needed, there was only one option left if the mission was to have any chance of success: find Merta Strife, and see if griffins would step in and help where dragons would not.

"It may be impossible," said Barver. "I don't know enough about the Griffin Covenant, but as a Pila, Merta can tell us if there's any way it could work."

Alia left them for the night, and went to the infirmary

tents to help out. Patch and Wren took warm clothing from Barver's packs, and all three of them were soon asleep.

When Patch woke, the smell of cooking filled the air. Beside him, Wren and Barver still slept.

He ached all over, and kept finding new bits of vegetation in his hair, up his sleeves, or elsewhere; tiny twigs and leaves, leftovers from the protective shell Wren had conjured up to save their lives. But it was his heart that ached most of all, at the sight of the citizens of Skamos, trying so hard not to seem defeated. Everywhere he looked he saw forced smiles beneath anguished eyes. The journey ahead of them all would be long.

Food was shared out freely as it was cooked in the camp, everyone making sure those around them were looked after. Patch nudged Wren and Barver from their slumber, and they ate a small meal of eggs and chicken.

As they were finishing, Alia returned.

"How were things at the infirmary?" asked Wren.

"Busy," said Alia. "I did what I could, before we depart. Which we should do right away! Barver, we must find your aunt and uncle, and bid them farewell."

They found Yakesha, Zennick and little Kerna at the edge of the camp nearest the devastated city. Seeing them approach, Kerna began to yelp with excitement.

Barver gave his aunt and uncle a hug. "It's time for us to set off," he said.

"I knew you'd be going as soon as you could," said Yakesha. "Kasterkan's forces aren't preventing people leaving any more – they allowed us to send out envoys at first light, to begin the discussions needed to resettle the human population."

"I wish I could stay and help," said Barver. "But people are relying on us."

"I know," said Yakesha. "Your mother would be so proud of you. Just as proud as *we* are. We'll all miss you – Kerna especially."

The baby reached out to Barver, insisting on being held by him. "Ba Va!" said Kerna, giggling as Barver made faces.

Zennick looked lovingly at his child. "I thought yesterday's little adventure might have left a mark, but Kerna slept soundly. And this morning, not a single tear."

Yakesha nodded. "I want to thank you two again," she said to Patch and Wren. "For keeping our little one safe."

Patch and Wren muttered a thank you, although they felt more than a little guilty at Kerna being in danger in the first place.

Barver tried to pass Kerna back to Zennick, but the baby kicked up a fuss. "Wen Wen!" said Kerna, and so Barver passed the child to Wren instead, and *she* made faces for a time. And then, as Wren went to pass Kerna back, the baby did something that brought a tear to Patch's eye.

"Pat Pat!" said Kerna, reaching out to him.

"You *do* know my name!" he said, taking the baby. He started making faces too, getting a riot of laughter in return, but after a few seconds a curious rumbling sound started to come from Kerna's belly.

With a calm urgency, Zennick reached over and turned Kerna's head to one side. Suddenly a great burst of intense flame came rocketing out of Kerna's wide-open mouth, filling the empty air to Patch's left – which was far preferable to it incinerating his *very shocked* face.

When the flames stopped, Zennick took Kerna from Patch, and gave him an apologetic smile. "Babies, eh?" he said.

Patch whimpered.

Barver flew them higher than before, seeking the fastest airflows. He was getting more and more used to the cold thin air, something dragons struggled with. And while Barver's wings were more dragon than griffin, they seemed to have just enough griffin in them to cope with higher altitude flying.

Their destination was Sullimer Forest, the region Merta Strife had said was her home. After nine hours of flight, Barver spotted a vast mountain ridge close to the coast. He began to descend.

"That must be Sullimer Knife," he told his riders. "Now we just have to find Merta!" He let out a huge *scrawwww*, a deafening call that drew complaints from those on his back.

"A bit of warning next time!" complained Wren, her hands clamped firmly over her ears.

Barver kept repeating his call as he followed the ridge, and soon enough there was a reply. "There!" he cried. "At the base of that crag!"

He circled, and they could all see it now: in a sheer cliff face was a cave entrance, and there was Merta, wings spread. They landed, and Merta led them into the cave where a very welcome fire burned. Patch and Wren took position in front of it.

"How numb are your feet?" said Wren.

"Not as numb as my fingers," said Patch.

Barver explained the situation to Merta, and told her of the events at Skamos. As he spoke, she grew visibly wary.

"If we had any other choice, I wouldn't have come to you," said Barver. "We're due to meet our forces in Gossamer Valley, and without scouts in the air, finding the Hamelyn Piper will be impossible! I know what I'm asking is difficult, but…"

Merta stared at him. "*Difficult?*" she said. "It isn't *difficult* to break the Covenant, Barver. It's impossible! I fear you don't understand the Griffin Covenant at *all*."

"How could I?" said Barver. "Neither griffin nor dragon

304

seem to count me as their own. My father taught me a little, but…"

Merta nodded. "He thought he had more time," she said. "You cannot blame him. There are things that griffins aren't told until they come of age. Things they are sworn to secrecy about. I will tell you what I can. At the heart of the Griffin Covenant is a simple idea: lives are precious, and *conscious* beings are most precious of all. The mindful species of this world – that's to say, the griffins, dragons and humans – have a sacred duty. We are the means by which the universe *itself* thinks."

Wren frowned, looking at Barver. "I thought griffins didn't *do* religion?"

Merta laughed gently. "We don't," she said. "I mean nothing mystical by it." She reached to the cave floor, picking up a handful of dirt and rubbing it, letting it fall from her hand as she spoke. "This *stuff*, this *soil,* is not alive. But from it, plants grow – life emerges. You don't need to see *gods* in everything to find that miraculous! And then, in only our three species, life gives form to another miracle, that of *reason,* the means to look at what exists, and find beauty in it. The universe can see itself, and discover wonder, through *us!*"

Wren caught Patch's eye; she was clearly unimpressed, but Patch quite liked the notion.

"That," said Merta, "is at the heart of the Covenant.

305

Respect for each other, be it griffin, human, or dragon, because whatever differs between us, there's more that connects us. To endanger such life is a terrible thing!"

"But griffin pilots risk their lives all the time," said Barver.

"You misunderstand me," said Merta. "Risking your *own* life, especially to save another, is an honourable act of courage. But to actively seek to *endanger* lives? Do you know what blasphemy is, Barver?"

"Of course," he said. "In a religion, blasphemy is an offence against whatever gods you believe in. Not showing respect to something sacred. For dragons, using black diamond is blasphemy against the Gods of Fire and Scale."

"Exactly!" said Merta. "And while griffins have no gods, to us the lives of the mindful species are sacred. To disrespect them is blasphemy. And the greatest blasphemy of all? Surely that's obvious?"

"War," said Barver.

"Yes," she said. "Griffins despise war, above all else."

"But I'm not asking griffins to fight in a war," said Barver. "I'm asking them to help stop an evil man gaining more power than any of us can imagine! As a Pila, I know you can give a griffin leniency with their Covenant. The griffins working as Protectors needed that."

"This is *not* the same thing," said Merta. "Not at all! You want griffins to enter disputed territory, where neighbouring nations are rumoured to be preparing their armies! It may not be a war now, but you're asking us to risk *triggering* one! A Pila can give a griffin leniency with their Covenant, as you said. But this is too serious even for a Pila to decide."

"It couldn't be *more* serious!" said Barver. "My mother taught me about the End of the Skies, Merta – where black diamond leads to chaos, and the destruction of everything. If the Hamelyn Piper's plan succeeds, that's exactly what would happen. Every creature in this world would have to bend to his will. Human, dragon and griffin. All of us, slaves!"

Merta nodded. "Slavery *is* a kind of death," she said. She folded her wings tightly, and closed her eyes, deep in thought. At last, she opened her eyes again. "There is a way," she said. "A higher authority you can appeal to, higher even than the Pilas, but the journey will be perilous and difficult. Can you withstand the cold, Barver? The high airways don't seem to trouble you much, the way they trouble dragons, but there is another pathway in the skies, higher still, and even colder. Have you heard of the lacherbrooks?" Barver shook his head. "The highest and fastest of all the windways! Up there, the winds are so fast and unpredictable, they can gather up an unwary flier and break every bone in their body – or freeze them to death in an instant! No dragon can navigate them, and even if they could, the cold thin air would quickly render them unconscious. Yet there are places in the world that can only be reached by using them, and we must go to one such place. Just us two, mind – the lacherbrooks are unsurvivable for human passengers. I warn you, you must make every turn I make, and match my speed at all times, or else the lacherbrooks will have you for their dinner…"

"You don't have to do this, Barver!" said Wren. "It sounds too dangerous!"

"She's right," said Patch. "There must be another way."

Alia scowled. "Where are you taking him, Merta?" she said.

Merta looked at them all. "This is Barver's choice, and his alone," she said. "It *is* dangerous, but if you want the help of griffins, this is the only way."

All eyes turned to Barver. "I have to try," he said.

"Wait here," Merta told the three humans. "We'll return by sunset tomorrow." She turned to Barver. "Follow me," she said.

She led him out of the cave and into the sky. As he was about to take wing he signed to Patch and Wren, the simplest of Merisax signs: an open palm, as if about to wave, becoming a closing fist, like catching a moth; then, bringing the closed fist to his heart. They repeated it back to him, as did Alia. It was a sign that meant many things, like *good luck* and *be safe*, but it meant one thing most of all.

Friendship.

Up they flew, higher than Barver had flown in his life, up where the thin air made each breath a struggle, and the cold wind threatened to freeze the blood in his wings. This was no place for a dragon, certainly; only a griffin could make use of the currents this far up, and Barver wondered if there was enough griffin in him to cope.

They would stay in a current for only minutes at a time before Merta would take them to a different one. These were dangerous winds they were navigating, but Merta knew them well, calling out a warning when she turned sharply to one side to avoid turbulent air – invisible to Barver, although the signs must have been there for Merta to know.

He knew he was flying faster than he'd ever gone in his life, but it was the currents themselves that were the cause of the speed.

Merta fell back a little to join his side. "How are your wings?" she called. "A dragon's wings would have seized up long before they reached these heights."

"They feel like they're about to cramp," he replied. "I'm not sure I can go much further."

"A normal reaction," said Merta. "Try this!" She folded her wings to her side, then rapidly pushed them back out, the action fast enough to avoid much loss of height. Barver tried it, and although he wasn't quite as graceful, he could feel his wings loosen up. "The greatest danger here is loss of consciousness," said Merta. "If you feel that happening, call out! I'll guide you down to a lower current until you're ready to ascend again!"

North they went, for hour after hour: then, far below, he saw the frozen wastelands of the Jennum Desert – a desert of ice rather than sand, that was as far north as any human had ever ventured. On and on, beyond the range of humans; beyond the range of dragons. And they did not stop. The ice below was soon replaced by the dark grey of old volcanic rock, and ahead a range of mountains rose from the flat plains.

Barver thought of the globe in the Caves of Casimir, and of every map he'd ever seen. There weren't supposed to be mountains here, only desolate plains. Ice for a thousand miles.

"How is this possible?" he cried. "How can nobody know of this place?"

"Because they cannot reach it!" said Merta. "Yet for a Pila, it's easy to reach."

"Easy?" said Barver. "If I tried this alone I'd be dead fifty times over!"

"True enough!" she said. "Transition to the wrong current, and you'd always get a surprise! Frozen solid in

310

a minute, or hurtling to the ground! That's as it should be, Barver. All griffins are brought here when they come of age. To become a Pila, you must be able to find the way here alone."

She led him down through the currents, slowing with each change, and soon they were out of the lacherbrooks, and even out of the high windways.

Sudden gusts buffeted them as they approached those impossible mountains, flying towards one peak in particular. It was not the largest of them, certainly, but it was a strange formation, oddly flat at the top.

"Keep close," cried Merta. "The winds swirl here in ways you've never experienced."

They flew closer to the strange mountain, and her warnings of dangerous swirls were borne out. Never before had Barver fought the wind so hard to stay aloft; never before had it felt like the air itself had a vendetta against him.

When they landed, he was so out of breath that it took him a full minute to notice what he should have seen in an instant.

They had landed on an outcrop halfway up the mountain, at the base of a cliff face of near-flat rock, and in that rock was a *door,* at the centre of a vast carving in the rock itself. The carving rose for three hundred feet above them, symmetrical patterns of incredible intricacy. And within those patterns, Barver could see holes – *windows* – and he thought of Tiviscan Castle, and the oldest, deepest parts, which had been carved from the rock thousands of years ago.

In awe, he walked to the door – a double doorway, perhaps eighty feet high and the same in width. Merta was beside him.

"Is this…" he said, struggling for words. "Is this a *castle*?"

"Castle?" said Merta. She seemed amused by the thought. "You'll see, soon enough." And with that, Merta let out a great griffin call, then stood in silence, waiting.

Barver was overflowing with questions, but he held his tongue. The huge doors began to open, with no sound save the howling wind accompanying them. Merta strode forward, and Barver did the same.

Inside the doors was a long corridor, as tall and wide as the doorway. As they walked along it, Barver could see entryways to other passages on each side, but those passages were in darkness and he couldn't tell how deep they went. Ahead was a second set of vast doors, shut tight.

"How big is it?" he asked. "This building, carved into the mountain?"

"Answers will come," said Merta. "The chamber we are about to enter, we call the *Eyrie*." When they reached the Eyrie's entrance, the outer doors swung shut behind them.

They were in total darkness. "The Eyrie is a secret place, where the oldest Pila have come to live, withdrawn from the world. When any Pila faces a question of great importance, they come here to consult with the wisest of us all. It's also where griffins are brought when they come of age, to take the Covenant."

Minutes passed. Barver was sure he could hear movement from beyond the door ahead. Movement, and voices.

At last those other doors opened, revealing a bright chamber, a wide circle and a domed ceiling. The dome and the floor were carved in the same kind of intricate pattern that had covered the cliff face.

"Stand here," said Merta. "You can plead your case when the time comes, but there will be business to attend to first. I must go ahead, and the doors will close again, so be patient."

"What do I do?"

"You'll hear us call – a ceremonial call, there'll be no mistaking it! These doors will open again. Then you must enter, and stand in the centre of the Eyrie. Show reverence, and answer the questions put to you. Good luck!"

Barver nodded. He watched as Merta entered the Eyrie and the doors closed, plunging him back into darkness. He could hear the muffled sounds of speech; a long discussion, some of it angry. Then the ceremonial call began. As Merta had promised, it was unmistakable.

One by one, the individual calls came: the high screeches of griffins, yes, but each call was a note, and the combination was a song, of sorts – a single drawn-out chord, each griffin's call lasting as long as the breath, then beginning again once a new breath was taken. There was sorrow in the sound: a deep melancholy. Yet there were other things there too. Beauty, and courage, and joy. These feelings grew in Barver's heart, and he could not explain how they could be brought about by such a simple combination of calls, five in all – *no, six*, he realized.

Then, as each call faded, instead of a breath and beginning again, the callers fell silent. Soon there was only the sound of the wind playing among the rocks outside.

And the doorway began to open.

26

THE VANISHING

B arver walked into the Eyrie.

Above him, the domed roof had three large circles open to the sky. He stared at the holes, baffled; given their position deep in the rock halfway up a mountain, he'd assumed that the light came from lanterns of some form, or had a magical source like the Caves of Casimir. How was the *sky* visible?

Ahead of him, five griffins were crouched in recesses carved into rock. None of them looked particularly old, but that was the way with griffins. Beyond a certain time of life, they tended not to age outwardly, the way humans and dragons did. Only when they moved or spoke would an old griffin give away any problems that their age had wrought.

Merta was standing at the far left of the gathered griffins, a welcome familiar face. Barver took his position in the centre of the chamber.

"Merta Strife," said the blue-grey female in the middle of the five. "Please make your introductions."

"I will," said Merta. "This is Barver Knopferkerkle, son of Gaverry Tenso, griffin, and Lykeffa Knopferkerkle, dragon. He has come here with an urgent request for assistance, in a situation that would be considered a breach of Covenant for any griffin who comes to his aid. He seeks a ruling from the Eyrie on the matter."

The blue-grey female looked at Barver. "Make your plea."

The rightmost griffin, a green male, scoffed. "You're no griffin, boy. The Covenant is not for you, yet you dare to ask for others to be released from their oath? Why should we even hear you out?"

"He has come to the Eyrie," said Merta. "The law says his request must be considered."

"Nonsense!" said the green male. "The law applies to griffins, and griffins alone!"

Another of them, a grey-and-black male, laughed gently. "Merta's right," he said. "The law says that anyone who flies here to stand in the Eyrie must be heard. It makes no mention of them being a griffin."

"A technicality!" said the green male. "The lawmakers saw no need to state it, but that was clearly what they meant! If not, where do you draw the line? Would you listen to a *dragon*?"

"Barver is not a dragon," said Merta, her voice calm. "He flew here, something no dragon could do! He has the right to be heard. He is *half*-dragon, yes, but would you tell him to disown his mother, before you listen?"

The griffins leaned over to one another, discussing in whispers. At last, the blue-grey female spoke again. "Very well," she said. "Go ahead, Barver."

Barver told them about the Hamelyn Piper's obsidiac armour; he told them how all dragons were forbidden from helping them; he told them of how Skamos had been destroyed.

Throughout all this, the griffins listened in silence. But when he explained the need for griffins to act as military scouts, there were gasps. He saw a look of outrage on the green griffin's face, and the griffins began their whispers again, the discussions growing ever louder, becoming *arguments,* the noise filling the chamber.

"There is a dragon legend," said Barver, almost shouting to be heard. "The End of the Skies!" At that, the arguments subsided and the griffins listened to him once more. "It tells of black diamond, freed from the earth, and how all life is destroyed in the chaos that follows."

"Dragons and griffins share many myths," said the grey-and-black male. "There are differences, of course, but the most ancient of our tales are almost identical. The Lords of the Night Kingdoms. The End of the Skies."

"*The End of the Skies is upon us!*" said Barver. "The world – this whole world, dragon, human, griffin – will fall to evil. The Hamelyn Piper seeks absolute power."

"Wars come and go," said the green male. "So do rulers."

"He seeks immortality," said Barver.

"Then he's not the first to try," said the green male. "And he'll fail, as all before him have failed. You draw us into a pointless fight, based on guesswork. Fights become wars. All wars are evil."

"This is not war," said Barver. "This is survival! I look to a future where the Hamelyn Piper holds sway, and I'm *frightened*. But not for myself. I'm frightened for the friends I already had, and for the new friends I've made." He looked over to Merta. "I think of my aunt and uncle, and their new baby – my cousin, Kerna. I think of Kerna growing up in a world that knows only cruelty, a world without hope. Merta taught me about the mindful species – griffins, dragons and humans. We are the same, more than we are different. We are *equals*. We share this world, and we must fight for its future – in whatever way we can."

He tried to think of something more to say, something that would convince them, but nothing came.

The blue-grey female nodded. "We will make our decision.

You and Merta must wait in the passageway." She gestured to the doors they'd entered by.

"Before you decide, I have a request of my own," said Merta. All eyes turned to her. "As Barver said, we must embrace one another as equals. Barver may only be half-griffin, but he deserves to be shown respect, and told the truth of this place. He deserves to know our heritage, for it's his heritage too." She gestured towards a different set of doors, on the far side of the Eyrie.

The discussion among the griffins was brief. "You may show him, while we make our decision," said the blue-grey female. "*If* he swears to secrecy." Merta nodded, and the blue-grey griffin turned to Barver. "Barver Knopferkerkle," she said. "Do you swear to hold secret the truths that will be revealed?"

The griffin had a sombre tone to her voice that struck Barver as odd. "I swear," he said.

"Then take him through, Merta," said the blue-grey female. "Let him see."

The doors opened, and Merta led Barver through. His mouth fell open in shock at what he saw: a vast expanse open to the sky, encircled by steep rock. It explained how he could see daylight through the holes in the roof of the Eyrie – the mountain was *hollow*.

"An ancient volcano," said Merta, as the doors closed behind them. "Long extinct, its core collapsed. A wondrous sight, yes?" Barver nodded, but Merta put her hand on his shoulder. "Look again," she said.

He looked out at the mountain's interior, and saw *structures*, carved into rock, both on the floor of the massive crater, and on the edifice that encircled it all. He could see holes that were surely doorways, windows; higher up the sides were prominences, on which were rectangular areas that seemed *green,* surely an impossibility given the temperature.

But the temperature, he realized, was far milder than it should have been. The wind, likewise, was little more than a breeze. He looked at Merta, confused.

"There is shelter here from the bitter ice," she said. "Just enough sun reaches inside for plants to grow – mosses hardy enough for the terrain, good grazing for sheep and goats. And even though the volcano is long silent, there's still heat from the deep earth, rising through the rock."

"What is this place?" asked Barver.

"This is *Pripax*, Barver. The greatest griffin city that has ever existed."

Speechless, Barver looked out, his emotions in disarray. His heart soared at the very sound of the words *griffin city*, but he knew why Merta's eyes had been filled with sorrow all this time.

Griffins didn't fill the sky here; their calls didn't echo from the ridges that enclosed this haven.

320

Pripax, however glorious a sight it might be, was dead, and Barver suspected that it had been that way for a very long time indeed.

He turned to Merta. "What happened here?" he asked.

"Most believe that the first war between humans and dragons was nine hundred years ago," she said. "But that is not quite true. There was an even older conflict, lost to legend. Six thousand years ago, the *true* first war between humans and dragons. All wars bring the same horrors. They bring death. They bring destruction. They bring famine. And they bring *disease*. New plagues emerge in the chaos, and as war rages on, those plagues can spread unchecked."

Merta led him further out from the doors, to the edge of the wide outcrop on which they stood. The floor of the crater was perhaps five hundred feet below them.

She continued. "Wild birds were affected first, and then the livestock – the chickens and geese. Humans and dragons paid little attention to it. The disease didn't infect either of them, and only a small part of their food supplies was impacted. So, the war continued, with no effort made to contain the plague. The chance to stop it was missed. And then a griffin fell ill. By the time the war between humans and dragons ended, it was already too late. The disease had spread to all four griffin cities."

"Four?" said Barver.

"Yes, four," said Merta. "The plague was devastating.

From the moment a griffin showed symptoms, death was certain. Certain, and painful. The griffin cities cut themselves off, hoping to limit the spread, but the cities died one by one. In time, their ruins were lost to jungle and sea, forgotten by human and dragon, just as the war itself was forgotten. Only Pripax still stands. A monument to when griffins gathered together and lived side by side in their thousands. A testimony to when griffins almost vanished from the world."

Barver stared at her, stunned.

"You see," said Merta. "The only ones who survived were those who lived alone, in remote places. Those who shied away from company. They are the ancestors of us all, Barver. That is why most griffins seek solitude to this day. That is why there are so few of us. And it is why we hate war so much. Humans and dragons fought, but it was griffins who were changed for ever."

Merta and Barver waited for the griffins of the Eyrie to make their decision, and for the doors to open again.

"They're going to say no," said Barver. "Aren't they?"

"I honestly can't tell," said Merta. "But I do know this: I saw the look in their eyes as you spoke. They listened to you, Barver, and your words carried weight. If you didn't convince them, I don't think anyone could have."

The doors opened. Barver and Merta walked to the centre of the chamber.

They both looked to the blue-grey female, but it was the green griffin who addressed them first.

"What do you believe you are, Barver Knopferkerkle?" he said. "Are you griffin? Are you dragon? Where are your loyalties? Spending so long with humans, are you part-human too, dracogriff? When the humans and dragons fought, whose side would you have taken?"

"I am *me*," said Barver. "What others choose to call me, I don't care. Where are my loyalties? With what is right. I'll never be given the Griffin Covenant, but I already *have* my Covenant. Here." He placed a hand over his heart. "Whose side would I have taken? The side of my friends."

The green griffin's expression was stern, but he turned to the blue-grey female and nodded; she nodded back, then stood. "Barver Knopferkerkle," she said. "Your father showed courage and honour throughout his life, and also in his death. We see that same courage in you. We see that same *honour* in you. You are your father's son, and we will grant you the respect that Merta spoke of. Our decision is this: any griffin who volunteers to help you can do so without breaking Covenant, as long as their activities are restricted to scouting. There is one other condition: Merta herself must personally ensure that this restriction is observed. She must go with you."

Barver looked at Merta, who smiled at him. "It would be my honour," she said.

"Thank you!" Barver told her. Then he turned to the griffins: "Thank you all!"

The blue-grey female nodded. "All you need now are volunteers," she said.

"I know who to ask," said Merta. "And we shall gather them on the way."

27

A Rumble
of Thunder

They saw the tents in Gossamer Valley and knew at once that Tobias had been successful in his mission. Drawing closer, they could see dozens of horses and a few hundred soldiers.

They landed to cheers, and the sight of them was extraordinary: Barver, Merta, Cramber and Wintel, touching down just outside the edge of camp.

Patch, Wren and Alia dismounted as Tobias rushed to greet them. "Word reached us of the disaster at Skamos," said Tobias. "I feared the worst."

Alia nodded. "*The worst* is a good summary," she said. "We were there when it happened. But we've found our scouts, as you can see! And you've raised quite significant help yourself."

"Kintner Bastion decided to send almost half of its forces on an exercise," said Tobias, smiling. "Fifty Pipers, three hundred soldiers, forty cavalry."

"An *exercise*," said Alia. "An interesting term for it. I also note there are no uniforms being worn."

"Of course," said Tobias. "Calling it an exercise draws less attention. Same for the lack of uniforms. Officially, this is a training expedition."

"And who is in command of this…training expedition?" she said.

Tobias smiled. "They would have none but me," he said.

"A *monk*?" said Alia. "I thought your fighting days were behind you?"

"The Bastion wouldn't have agreed to it any other way," he said. "Until this venture is concluded, I am Brother Tobias no more. I am Colonel Palafox, as I used to be. Our airborne scouts should rest ahead of their night's work. I'll take you through our plans soon enough."

Dusk was approaching by the time Tobias summoned them to the command tent. The tent sides were folded up to allow Barver and the griffins access; in the middle of the tent was a large canvas sheet, on which a rough map of the region had been drawn.

With Tobias were two majors, one in charge of the soldiers, and the other in charge of the Battle Pipers.

"The Ortings," Tobias began. "Ten miles south, it begins: a huge area of forest, scrub, marsh, bog and grass. Somewhere within that expanse, the Black Knight moves around with his forces and causes chaos. We estimate that those forces number a few dozen, but as you saw we're taking no chances. And although our enemy has great skills with the Pipe, which may be boosted by his armour, we have fifty of the best Battle Pipers in the world. Our problem is *finding* this foe. The Ortings is vast, parts of it are extremely dense. We have to locate our enemy quickly, without them knowing, and then make sure we can cut off their escape. Then we bring the Hamelyn Piper to justice at last." He gave Barver and the griffins their instructions, each being assigned an area to scout overnight under the cover of darkness. "If the skies stay clear," he said, "we should discover the location of the Black Knight's forces within three days."

Merta looked to the sky and sniffed the air. "It will rain tomorrow," she said. "But it will be clear until dawn." She looked to the others. "Are we ready for the hunt, my friends?"

Cramber, Wintel and Barver all shouted together: "We are!"

Merta smiled. "Then let us take to the skies and find the villain!"

Morning came with no sign of the rain Merta had predicted. Instead, patchy sunshine warmed them all. The griffins slept peacefully, tired after their night of scouting. Barver slept too, but peaceful wasn't quite the word to use – he was on his back, and his snores were loud enough to frighten the horses on the far side of camp.

Patch and Wren had stayed up into the early hours, as a show of solidarity with Barver, but had fallen asleep long before he'd returned. They'd woken early, the camp busy around them. Weapons were being cleaned, horses tended, and wherever they looked pairs of soldiers were engaged in combat practice. They wandered over to the command tent, to see if anything interesting had been learned from the night's scouting. Hanging around at the mouth of the tent, they listened to the conversation within.

The voice of Tobias was the first they heard: "…which cuts out all of the southern marshes," he said. "Wintel's coverage of the western section here will have to continue tonight, but she's ruled out a significant part."

Alia spoke next, and she sounded unusually cheerful. "If the skies are clear again after dark, I think the chances are good that we'll spot our prey much sooner than we'd expected!"

"Merta said there'd be wet weather today," said Tobias. "But she thought it would clear by nightfall. We can draw up some possible scenarios for containing the enemy, now that we've limited the kinds of terrain we'll be facing."

Losing interest, Wren gave Patch a nudge.

"What say we go and see if we can scrounge a bite to eat?" she said.

"Absolutely!" said Patch.

"Watch this," Wren told him as they neared the mess tent. She gathered herself a little, and then feigned an expression of such utter misery that, for a moment, Patch thought it had to be genuine. Then she grinned. "Think I can get us something with *that*?"

Patch stayed back and watched a master at work. Wren stuck out her lower lip, strode into the tent, and returned with a handful of dried apple slices and a cup of hot tea. They sat and shared it, before walking back to the snoring Barver.

Soon after they'd returned, Barver stirred from his sleep. He rolled onto his front and stretched. "Did someone say there was food?" he asked, still groggy.

"Not for an hour or two," said Wren. "Although, really, you and the griffins could just march in and take whatever you fancied."

"That wouldn't be polite," grinned Barver. A short way off, the three griffins were also rousing from their sleep. Cramber gave Barver a nod.

"On you go," said Wren. "See how everyone's doing after your long night of excitement!"

Barver didn't need any encouragement.

"I'm glad he gets on with his new friends," said Patch.

"Yes," said Wren. "It'll do him the world of good."

They both frowned and looked at each other.

"We sound like we're his parents," said Patch, and they burst into laughter. As they laughed, a great thunderclap filled the valley.

"That'll be the rain Merta promised," said Wren, but they both looked to the sky in confusion. There were only the lightest of clouds – no sign whatsoever of rain, let alone a storm. Even so, a second thunderclap echoed around them.

Patch noticed that everyone in the camp was stopping what they were doing, and looking around warily. The griffins seemed particularly apprehensive; Barver looked back to Patch and Wren, clearly anxious. He signed to them: *Something's wrong.*

The thunder came again, but this time it kept going, rolling on and on, crossing over itself in a curious way. From within it came recognizable sounds, and suddenly it resolved into a *voice.* Deep and unnaturally loud, it seemed to resonate inside Patch's skull.

"*Good morning to you all,*" said the voice. "*I think you were looking for me?*"

Patch felt a knot tighten in his stomach, because he knew that voice. It had haunted his nightmares for months.

330

And there, on the crest of the hill nearest them, a figure walked into view. A figure wearing a suit of armour, dark as night, which even from this distance glinted in the sun.

The Hamelyn Piper had found them.

As the thunder-voice continued, Alia and Tobias emerged from the command tent, looking utterly stunned.

"*I expected more than this ragtag militia,*" said the voice. "*I expected the Council to send a proper army! It's hardly a fair fight, but so be it.*"

The thunder faded.

Once it was gone there was silence. Barver and the griffins had their heads huddled close together, and Merta was talking rapidly. Patch could see, in the face of every soldier around them, a grim look of expectation.

"He thinks the Pipers' Council sent us," said Tobias. "Why would he think that? Unless…"

"Unless he wanted them to come," said Alia. "Good Lord, Tobias…was this a trap all along?"

"If it was, we're the ones who've fallen into it," said Tobias. His face fell. "Does this mean he's found the amulet? Did he want to lure an army here, just to show off his strength?"

Alia said nothing, but the worry on her face spoke volumes.

There came a distant sound, of rhythmic footfall and shouts, which grew louder with each second. Cresting the hill behind the Hamelyn Piper was a line of soldiers. Patch watched in horror as the same thing happened on every hill around them.

"There must be eight hundred at least," said Tobias. "Who *knows* how many more there are behind the hills!"

"Surrounded," said Wren.

"Outnumbered," said Patch.

But then, in a flurry of feather and wing, it became suddenly clear why Merta had been whispering so feverishly to Barver, Cramber and Wintel: all four launched themselves into the air!

Barver flew high and hard to the west, buoyed by cheering from the camp behind him. The Hamelyn Piper was due south; Merta was going east, Cramber north, all three of them heading straight for the Black Knight's forces.

That left Wintel, who was going straight *up*.

Barver snuck quick glances to see how they were doing, but he had to stay focused on his own task. *The world needs to know what's happening here*, Merta had told them. *We need to get word out*. Wintel was best placed for that, and so the other three would try and distract while Wintel gained enough height to take her out of the range of any weapon.

But distraction wasn't their only task. Perhaps the Hamelyn Piper had already found the amulet, and the power the armour gave him was enough to destroy them all; if that was the case, they stood no chance. If not, though, they had to know what they were up against. Seeing over the tops of those hills was crucial – seeing, and reporting back. They only needed Wintel to escape. Whatever defence they hoped to mount, two griffins and a dracogriff might still prove invaluable.

Barver heard a griffin's call and looked to see Cramber come under a barrage of arrow-fire. Cramber swerved sharply, but then larger black streaks flew right at him – the shots of bolt-throwers. Cramber was hit: his wings folded in, and he plunged towards the earth below. Barely managing to regain control, he turned back towards camp. From the way he flew, Barver could tell he was badly hurt.

Merta was next to make it into range of their weapons, and again they unleashed volley after volley, though Barver couldn't watch her – he was closing on the hill ahead, still far too low for his liking. He put all his effort into getting higher, but the image of Cramber being hit kept filling his mind, and he found himself getting *angrier* with every beat of his wings.

And *there* was the Black Knight, on the other hill. The Hamelyn Piper, standing well in front of his troops, so arrogant that he had left himself exposed…

Barver looked ahead, to the hill he was flying towards, the archers on top notching their arrows and pulling back their bows.

He remembered, back at Monash Hollow all that time ago, suggesting to Patch that he just *burned* the evil Piper: just crept up on him as he played his Obsidiac Organ, and released all the fire Barver had in his throat. And with that memory, his plan changed. The moment a volley of arrows headed his way, he folded up his wings and dropped, feigning injury.

Gaining *speed*.

As the ground loomed, he stretched his wings back out, catching the air and converting all the speed of his descent into horizontal motion; he hurtled over the land now, blisteringly quick, and he only had one target in his sights: *the Black Knight himself.*

Harder, he pushed. *Faster.*

In a flash he was at the base of the southerly hill, hugging the ground. Up the slope of the hill, he flew, maintaining his speed, and *there* was the Black Knight, arms by his side, too sure of himself to move even as Barver drew near, readying his fire.

28

THE PIPERS OF KINTNER

Patch's heart was in his mouth.

Everyone had started cheering the moment they saw Barver and the griffins take to the air. When Cramber had been hit, the cheers had faltered as they watched him fall; he'd just managed to make it back to camp, a large bolt lodged in his side.

Then Merta had come under attack, and had been forced to turn towards camp again. She seemed unscathed, and headed for Cramber.

Barver, though...

Patch felt sick as he watched, Barver seeming to tumble down under a hail of arrow-fire, plummeting to earth, but then – with no sign of injury – he pulled out of his fall, changing his direction and travelling at incredible speed.

Flying directly towards the Hamelyn Piper.

Oh, no, though Patch. *Barver, what are you doing?*

His speed was astonishing, and Patch sensed a sudden resurgence of hope in the soldiers of the camp, that maybe the Hamelyn Piper had underestimated, and his arrogance would be his downfall.

But no.

Patch could feel it as it built, even from this distance. A *melody,* deep and complex, and he knew at once what it was – one of the many Push Songs, about to be released. The air around the Hamelyn Piper began to shimmer, and a moment later the shimmer exploded outwards at Barver, sending him hurtling back, out of control.

Barver fell, tumbling down the hillside to the valley floor. He came to a halt and was utterly still.

Everyone's eyes turned up, to the last of the four: Wintel had spent all this time gaining height, and now she was little more than a dot above them, surely out of range. But Patch felt the Push building again, even greater than before, and he thought: *the Black Knight has been toying with us.*

When the Push was released this time, its power was beyond anything Patch had ever witnessed. He thought of the great Battle Pipes that had defended Tiviscan Castle against the dragon attack, but even those seemed pitiful in comparison.

This time, the air around the Hamelyn Piper darkened considerably as the Song exploded outwards and up, and they could see it closing on Wintel, closing without seeming to lose any of its terrible force.

In seconds it was on her, throwing her around as if she was a leaf in a storm. The thundering sound that had preceded the Hamelyn Piper's voice returned; but this time it wasn't *words* that they heard. It was *laughter*, growing louder as Wintel struggled. Then the laughter faded: Wintel had ridden out the turbulence, and was flying again.

"*No...*" they all heard from the thunder-voice, before it died away.

Patch felt another Push being readied, but by now Wintel was flying due north to safety, beyond the Hamelyn Piper's reach. The Push was still building, though, and just as Patch wondered what the Hamelyn Piper was about to do with it, the ground a little downhill suddenly exploded.

The Black Knight was venting his frustration.

"The attempt to bring down Wintel clearly weakened him," said Alia. "He *can't* have the amulet, surely."

The sound of horns echoed across the valley.

"He may not have the amulet," said Tobias. "But he has an army, and he plans to use it. Look!" He pointed to the hilltops to the east. Horses galloped over the crest, a hundred or more; then, the same number came over from the west. "Cavalry assault. They hope to swamp us." He

337

turned to the majors. "Ready pikes! Prepare shields! Take sword until the order is given!"

Their soldiers hurried to an armoury tent, where long pikes, swords and bows were handed out. Those with swords created a circle around the main tents of the camp and the horse enclosure; those with bows took position within the circle, while those with pikes created a second circle outside the first, and kneeled ready to defend against any cavalry reaching them.

"Aren't they going to use their Pipes?" said Wren.

"Just wait," said Patch. *Take sword*, Tobias had ordered: it meant that the Battle Pipers would mix among those with swords, to hide their numbers.

Patch felt the ground rumble under his feet as the enemy horses grew nearer. He could see how the riders were armed now – many carried bows, some had spears.

Horseback archers loosed a volley of arrows, and Wren's mouth fell open in horror.

"Wait for it," said Patch.

"Shield ready!" called one of the majors, and some of the soldiers sheathed swords and took Pipe in hand, beginning to play. In seconds, their Songs were complete; one by one they let them go, creating a shield that covered the entire camp in pulsing waves, the loosed arrows knocked back and falling to the ground shattered, the Pipers preparing their Songs again so the shield could be maintained.

The rest of the horses were charging at them now on all sides, seeming unperturbed.

"Charger Shrill at two hundred yards," ordered Tobias. "Long Fives at one hundred!"

Wren looked to Patch for explanation, but Patch just wanted to watch the Pipers in action. This was the career the tutors at Tiviscan had suggested he follow – as part of the Battle Elite, much of his apprenticeship would have been spent at Kintner Bastion. This could have been his life, if the thought of battle hadn't turned his stomach.

But here, now: he was fascinated.

As the charging cavalry closed in, some of the Battle Pipers began a new Song. This was the Charger Shrill, and when it was released the sound was extraordinary – a horrible, high-pitched cacophony that hurt the ear, but which was intended for the horses themselves. Patch could see the wavefront hitting the charging animals, the noise creating fear in all and panic in many.

One third of them stopped or turned, riders holding on for dear life as their steeds became uncontrollable.

Then came the Long Fives, a form of Push Song that kept the force of the Song focused at distance, blasting chunks of mud into the air around the horses and creating even more panic.

"Head Level Strike," called Tobias. "Maximum spread!"

And now all the Pipers joined together in the same

Song, and a blast of air spread out from the circle, hitting the closest riders with such force they were left unconscious or dead, still strapped to their fleeing horses.

The few riders left in control thought better of it, and started to turn back.

From the hilltops, horns sounded again.

"A recall," said Tobias. He looked at Alia and smiled. "He underestimated us, by a long way."

The thunder rumbled once more, and the voice of the Black Knight reached them: "Enough!" it said. "Why waste the lives of good fighters? I will grant you a choice! Fight for *me*, not for the old world. I will change the ways of every nation in these lands. Never before has the world seen a King so honourable, or so *just*! Rich and poor, all will be equal under my sight!"

"Aye," muttered Alia. "All slaves are equal, aren't they?"

"I will grant you two hours to decide," said the voice. "Those who wish to join my forces, and swear allegiance to me as their new lord and master, will be welcomed into our ranks without prejudice. As for the rest of you…there is only one fate that awaits those who oppose me. The rest of you will *die*." The thunder-voice faded, then the Hamelyn Piper walked back over the crest of the hill, out of sight.

Patch looked to where Barver lay, distant and still. "What

was he thinking?" he said, turning back to Wren as his eyes filled with tears. Wren was silent. She hugged him, but a few seconds later she spoke again.

"You should probably ask him yourself," she said, and her tone was bright. She pointed, and Patch turned to look: Barver was in the air now, more or less, flying back to them in short hops, landing every few seconds. His left wing wasn't holding shape properly, and each time he took off he needed a run-up.

When he reached them, he was grinning, and it was a dreadful sight. His teeth were bloody, his face marked with small cuts; his right eyelid was swollen.

Patch was too relieved to speak, but Wren went to Barver, scowling. "*What on earth were you thinking?*" she snapped.

"I was *thinking* about incinerating him," said Barver. "I got pretty close too! Close enough to see he didn't have the amulet in his chest."

This, at least, was good news, but it didn't defuse Wren's anger.

"You got close because he *let* you get close!" she said. "He was showing off!"

"But Wintel got away," said Barver, smiling. "When I flew at him, he ignored Wintel completely. It may only have been a few seconds, but those seconds were precious."

Wren's scowl faded, and she nodded. "They were," she said. "By the time the Hamelyn Piper took action, he'd left it too late. Which means he's not as powerful as he thinks he is." She shook her head. "But one of these days, Barver, you might find you aren't as *indestructible* as you think you are."

"Maybe," said Barver. "But not today." He stretched out his left wing to its full extent, wincing a little. "Although it does smart."

Barver, Patch and Wren stood nearby as, with Merta's assistance, Tobias removed the bolt from Cramber's side. Cramber was clearly in agony, and cried out in pain when the bolt came free. Tobias began to play his Healing Songs; soon Cramber was asleep.

"Will he live?" asked Merta.

"He should," said Tobias. "The injury is serious, but not as bad as I first feared."

Alia came. "Merta and Barver, did you see what other forces lie over those hills?"

"I had a brief sight before they fired at me," said Merta. "I estimate their army is two thousand strong. Most of those who stood on the hilltop were archers, and they have dozens of large bolt-throwers. Their cavalry is perhaps double what they attacked with. Some things were covered, though. *Camouflaged.* Even in daylight, it was difficult to see…" She shook her head. "Even so, how could we have missed them last night? As we flew out to scout, and as we flew back? How could we miss an army on our *doorstep*?"

"For a Sorcerer, there are ways to hide things," Alia suggested. "To make the eye glide off them, unseen. Perhaps the Hamelyn Piper is as powerful a Sorcerer as he is a Piper…"

"They had no need of sorcery," said Tobias. "You didn't see them, Merta, because they knew we were here and knew how to hide from us."

"Well, at least one thing is explained," said Alia. "The rumour of mercenaries heading to the Ortings was absolutely true. Gastyl and Pard weren't hiring soldiers, but it's clear who *was*."

"An army of this size would cost a small fortune," said Tobias.

"It would," said Alia. "Though remember: obsidiac is vastly more valuable than gold, and there are plenty of rich Sorcerers who'd be willing to buy it without asking questions. I suspect he's been building up that fortune over the last few years." She turned to Barver. "And you, scaring us all half to death with your antics… What can you tell us of the Hamelyn Piper? Wren told me you saw his chest, and there was no sign of the amulet."

"Just a hole in the armour," said Barver. "Also, he used no Pipe. When he played his Song to attack me, he was just whistling it."

"Lip-playing," said Alia. "The armour *itself* takes the role of a Pipe to amplify the Song. It tired him quickly, though. The armour drains him. Without the amulet, he weakens fast."

"With an army like that, does it matter?" said Barver. "How long can we repel it?"

Alia looked to the sky, in the direction Wintel had flown. "All our hopes rest with her."

"Any help will come too late," said Merta. "But Wintel's escape will let the world know what happened here."

"Perhaps things aren't as bleak as you think," said Tobias. "The Hamelyn Piper didn't expect us to fend off his attack, and now he's holding back from all-out assault. He must fear that we have more surprises for him."

"Well, we do!" said Alia. "I'll not show my hand until I have to, but the sparks will fly, I promise."

"I know they will," said Tobias. "My point is this: he has a mercenary army, and if he spends their lives cheaply they may abandon him. He can't afford heavy losses, even if he's sure to kill us all in the end. His offer to spare those who join him is a way to assess our strength before he attacks. If anyone defects to his forces, he'll know we're weak and will attack us at once. But if *nobody* defects, it shows him we're confident of victory. If we hold strong, we'll earn more time."

"Then we must hold strong," said Merta.

29

THE BLACK KNIGHT

Tobias began playing his Healing Song for Cramber again, making Merta and Barver sit next to him so that their own injuries would benefit too.

As the Hamelyn Piper's deadline approached, Patch offered to take over from him.

"Let's hear you, then," said Tobias. He listened as Patch began to play, and nodded. "You learned quickly," he said. "Play a fraction more slowly, and I think you've got it."

Tobias and Alia went to the command tent; Wren followed them, as she wanted to know the truth about their situation. She listened, and none of it was good. For all the planning of where and when to place Push Songs and their more destructive relatives, the moment the Hamelyn Piper felt confident about an all-out assault, their chances of victory were non-existent.

But with forty minutes left, a call came up from within the camp. Soon, all eyes were fixed on the sky to the north.

Patch stopped Piping and looked. It was barely a dot in the sky, but Merta's eyes widened, as did Barver's.

"She did it," said Merta. "*She did it!*"

"Did what?" said Patch.

Barver had a tear in his eye as he spoke. "Dragons have answered the call!" he said. "A dozen at least!"

"Is Wintel with them, Barver?" asked Patch. "Can you see her?"

Barver shook his head. "I can only see dragons, but she might be behind them."

Cheering began within the camp. Patch saw Wren over by the command tent, celebrating with the rest of them.

"They're flying in pairs, and each pair carries netting beneath it," said Merta. "I can't make out what's inside."

"I can," said Barver.

The dragons were flying in a line that was spread out considerably – the furthest back were still some distance away, but the nearest pair was soon close enough for Patch to see that the nets were filled with grey spheres. "Are those what I think they are?" he said.

Barver nodded. "The same kind of explosive devices

they fired at Skamos. The Hamelyn Piper's army will be decimated!"

Patch wasn't sure what to think – they were saved, yes, but the slaughter would be horrifying.

"Barver…" said Merta, sounding anxious. She gestured to the Hamelyn Piper's forces, still standing on the hilltops around them. "They're not *moving*," she said. "They must be able to see the dragons approach, but they're making no preparation to defend themselves."

She was right. The dragons began to break away from their line, flying to the hills, but as they approached the enemy army there was no reaction at all. The first pair of dragons reached a hilltop. Unchallenged, they flew above the soldiers, disappearing behind the crest of the hill. They reappeared a moment later without their nets.

Patch's blood ran cold. "They're not here to help *us*," he said. "They're here to help *them.*" The cheering around the camp stopped as the realization sank in.

The two dragons flew back the way they'd come; they had delivered their cargo, and didn't seem to want any further part.

"Perhaps that's why they've been putting off their assault," said Barver. "They were waiting for this."

"But why?" said Patch. "Why help the Hamelyn Piper?"

"Kasterkan," said Barver. "It has to be his doing."

Patch thought back to what General Kasterkan had said

to Yakesha at Skamos: *You wouldn't believe the things I've had to do to make it happen.* He wondered what deal the general had made with the Hamelyn Piper, but it didn't seem to matter any more. He wouldn't be around long enough to find out.

One by one, each dragon pair did the same thing, flying to a different hill and delivering their deadly cargo. The pair furthest back kept heading towards the camp, however. Suddenly Barver gasped, pointing to them: "I see Wintel," he said. *"She's in their net."*

"Barver!" snapped Merta. "With me!"

She took to the air and Barver followed. Patch didn't understood what they were doing, until the dragons carrying Wintel simply *dropped* her from a thousand feet. It was impossible to tell if Wintel was conscious or not – entangled in the netting, she tumbled through the air as she fell.

Barver was struggling to keep up with Merta, his injuries clearly hindering him. He managed it, though, and as one, the griffin and the dracogriff seized the net as it hurtled down. The weight of it dragged them down too; they pushed out their wings hard, fighting the air to slow their fall, and at last they pulled up.

They brought the netting back and set it beside Cramber, then began to carefully untangle Wintel. Tobias rushed over to help as Merta checked the unconscious griffin.

"She's alive," said Merta. She took each wing, carefully feeling along the length. "Nothing's broken. No torn flesh, and no blood. Though see the swelling here, on the side of her head? It would take a forceful blow to do that."

Wintel let out a cry of pain. Her eyes flickered open, but she was clearly dazed.

Barver crouched next to her and hung his head in sorrow. "I can't bear to think of her, asking them for help, and realizing there was no help to be found."

Wintel reached out and took his hand. "Don't...don't leave me, Cramber," she said, her eyes closing again.

Barver opened his mouth, ready to correct her; then he simply squeezed her hand, giving her what comfort he could. "It's okay," he said. "I'm here."

Over by the command tent, soldiers were gathered, the two majors giving out hurried instructions. Patch could see Alia and Wren, and he could have sworn they were *arguing*, their expressions irate – Wren almost storming off at one point, Alia putting a hand on her shoulder to stop her.

Patch knew it was over now. The Hamelyn Piper had no need to risk his soldiers when he could destroy his enemy from a distance. It didn't surprise him when a warning cry came out. A catapult shot had appeared from behind a hill, trailing smoke.

"Take cover!" cried Tobias.

Patch watched it pass high over their heads, feeling an odd detachment as he saw soldiers crouch on the ground. He stayed standing; only at the last moment did he think to cover his ears.

It landed six hundred feet from the camp, the explosion throwing mud into the air, terrifying the camp's horses – they pulled at their staked leashes, but none tore free. There was a look of horror on every face around the camp. They may have *heard* about what had happened to Skamos, but seeing it with their own eyes was a different thing entirely.

No more shots came. Not yet.

Patch thought of the rock fired before Skamos had been evacuated. It hadn't been an accident; it had been fired to ensure nobody doubted what would happen if they stayed.

"I don't understand," said Merta. "I thought they would keep firing them until they wiped us out! No amount of Piping or sorcery could withstand it!"

"Well, Tobias?" asked Barver. "What can the Battle Pipers do? And Alia?"

"Even the best Shielding Songs would count for little against those," said Tobias. "Alia could take some of them out as they fly, igniting the explosives early, but not enough."

"And then they'll launch more," said Merta.

"Look!" said Patch. The Hamelyn Piper, in his dark armour, walked into view on the hilltop once more. The

350

rumbling of thunder began, engulfing them all, resolving slowly into the voice Patch despised.

"*You see what awaits you*," said the voice. "*Fight for me. Swear your allegiance, and your life will be spared. Your time is up. Make your choice.*"

"He has victory within his grasp," said Merta. "Why does he delay?"

Patch thought of when he confronted the Hamelyn Piper, in front of the Obsidiac Organ, and at least *this* was a question he could answer. "He thinks he's worthy of being King," he said. "That all the evil things he's done were justified. He made his offer, and he's going to honour it – because then it's *our* fault when he kills us, not his."

"*You have five seconds,*" said the Hamelyn Piper.

"I would rather die," said Merta.

"*Four!*"

First one, then a second soldier began to move, walking to the edge of the camp.

Tobias saw them. "We have to hold firm," he said, and then he shouted it: "*We have to hold firm!*"

"*Three!*"

More started to move, their heads low, unwilling to make eye contact with the others. Calls came up: "You can't trust him!" "Shame on you!" "Traitor!"

"*Two!*"

What had begun as a trickle was now a torrent. More

and more were joining the deserters. Patch could see some dropping Pipes – Battle Pipers hoping to hide as ordinary soldiers.

"*One*," said the voice.

There were eighty, perhaps, walking out of the camp.

"Go, then!" cried Tobias, outraged. "If you're willing to fight for the Hamelyn Piper, go. But make no mistake. You will *belong* to him!"

Patch couldn't watch. He looked away, focusing on the dark-armoured shape high on the hill.

"*Good*," said the thunder-voice. "*It takes courage to join the right side! Come to me, and pledge your loyalty! If I judge it to be genuine, then you will be welcome!*"

The voice faded, the rumble echoing to nothing.

"I must rejoin Alia," said Tobias. He looked horribly shaken. "We'll see what our shields can do. We'll see if there's still damage we can inflict. We stand and fight, come what may."

But Patch wasn't listening to Tobias. He couldn't believe what he was seeing.

Walking with the deserters, near the back of the group, was Wren.

30

A LAST FAREWELL

Patch ran to catch up with her. "Stop!" he cried, breathless. "Wren, stop!" He put a hand on her shoulder.

She spun round, eyes flashing with anger. "Let me go," she said, brushing off his hand.

"You can't do this," pleaded Patch. "You know you can't."

She scowled at him. "Can't do what? Stay alive?" She gestured to the camp. "Look at what's happening here, Patch. You think the Battle Pipers can defend you? That Alia can whip up shields to save everyone, or knock fifty catapult shots out of the sky?"

"They can try!" he said. "And maybe they'll succeed!"

Wren shook her head. There were tears in her eyes, just

as there were in Patch's. "It would take a miracle," she said. "I want to go home, Patch. I want to see my parents again. All this time I've been putting off going back, and now it's all I can think of…I have to do this."

"Fight for the Hamelyn Piper?"

"I'm just a child," she said, almost to herself. "I'm no threat to him." She looked at Patch again. "Go back to camp."

"No!" said Patch, gripping her arm. "I won't let you go!"

"You won't *let* me?" she said, wrenching herself from his grasp. "This is my decision to make!" Her tears were flowing freely now. "Whatever happens, remember this was *my* decision. You don't get to have a say." She looked to the group of deserters making their way to the hill, already some distance ahead. She started walking again.

Patch grabbed her arm, more tightly this time. "Please, Wren…" he sobbed; she stared at him, enraged. "This is a mistake. I won't let…"

He heard a *sparking* sound and felt a sudden, searing pain throughout his body; his legs buckled under him and he fell to the ground, unable to move. He was barely able to *breathe,* as the pain continued.

"I'm sorry," said Wren, and then she walked away.

It was almost a minute before the pain subsided and he could move once more. He sat up. Wren had reached the other deserters again. She gave him one last sorrowful look.

Patch felt a heaviness in his heart so great he thought he would never get up again.

At the centre of camp, Barver had been watching. He went to move, but Alia stepped in front of him.

"Let her go," she said. "Wren's made her choice."

And Barver, like Patch, could only watch as the line of deserters made their way up the hillside towards the figure of the Black Knight. For both, it felt like part of them was dying.

As Wren walked, the first spots of rain started to fall.

Her fingers ached from what she'd done to Patch. It was a simple little spell she'd found in Casimir's notebooks. She hoped it hadn't hurt him too much, but she'd panicked.

None of the deserters could even look at each other. Their footsteps were heavy, and slow; ahead of them, at the top of the hill, two rows of the Hamelyn Piper's soldiers formed a corridor ten feet across, leading to the Black Knight himself.

As they entered the corridor, the deserters fell into a rough narrow column. The soldiers of the Black Knight leered at them as they passed, offering sarcastic welcomes. When they were fifty feet away from the Hamelyn Piper, one of the soldiers stepped out and held up his hands.

"That's far enough," he said.

The rain was getting heavier now, and Wren could hear sounds coming from over the hill – calls of "Keep those shots dry!" and "Cover them up!"

The Black Knight's armour was exactly like the diagrams in the ancient book – his arms, legs and torso encased in black, with no helmet. The sight of his face chilled her to the core. She'd last seen it while riding on Barver's back, with the Obsidiac Organ looming above them, and Barver under the Hamelyn Piper's control.

"Begin!" announced the Black Knight.

The soldier pointed to the deserters nearest him. "You five go first! Step forward!" The deserters did as they were told. "Now repeat after me, loud enough so our lord and master, the Black Knight, can hear! I swear on my life that I will renounce all previous loyalties, allegiances and fidelities!" He waited, as the deserters repeated the words, before continuing: "And I give my life to the service of my new lord and master, the Black Knight, for whom no undertaking shall be refused!" Once the deserters had repeated everything, he turned to the Black Knight, expectant.

The Black Knight gave a slow nod.

"Your oaths are accepted," said the soldier. He pointed to the left, where, at the hill's crest, a man stood with a black-and-white flag. "Go to the standard bearer, he'll give you instructions. Next!"

Again and again, small groups of deserters were asked

to state the oath of allegiance, and were sent to join the Black Knight's forces.

And then the sixth group stepped forward. The deserter in the middle wore a long leather coat, and as the oath was recited, he kicked out at the soldier and charged. From under his coat he produced a sword, and ran at the Hamelyn Piper, bellowing a battle cry.

None of the Black Knight's troops moved a muscle, and Wren felt sick at what she knew was coming. A look of utter arrogance was on the Hamelyn Piper's face as he pursed his lips and began to whistle a Song.

The deserter bore down on him with his sword raised. Five feet from his target, he was struck down by the Piper: the Song was released, and the deserter's head snapped backwards horribly. He fell. His sword, now in two pieces, landed beside him.

"Continue," called the Hamelyn Piper.

Wren sensed an uneasiness around her, and wondered how many others in the line had planned to try the same thing. They would surely not attempt it now.

Gradually the line grew shorter. With ten deserters behind her, it came to be Wren's turn, and as she stepped forward, the soldier stared at her.

"Dear God, girl, what age are you?" he said.

She started to cry. "Please, sire…" she sobbed. "I want to speak with the Black Knight. Please…"

The soldier shook his head and sighed. "What kind of people bring a child to a battlefield?" he said. "You can work in the mess tents, I suppose. Ready, girl?"

But Wren shook her head, the tears still flowing. "I'll swear directly to the Black Knight, or not at all," she said, defiant. "He says he's honourable, he says he'll be a just King. I must hear it from him, face to face!" She blew her nose on her sleeve.

The soldier looked to the skies. "Oh, good *grief*," he said. "Lass, just say the oath."

Wren folded her arms and shook her head, then burst out sobbing again.

"Send her forward, Captain, or we'll be here all day," said the Hamelyn Piper. "If she must hear my *sincere* pledge to be an honourable and just King, then so be it!"

"Very well, sire," said the soldier, giving Wren a shove. "Off you go."

Wren approached warily. The Hamelyn Piper had seen her once before, on Barver's back; if he recognized her now, she had no idea what he would do.

He frowned as she came closer, but there was no sign of recognition in his eyes. And then she was standing right before him.

"Child," he said. "I swear to you that I will be an honourable and just King."

"I beg you, sire!" Wren burst out. "Spare my friends!"

She fell to her knees and grabbed his leg, speaking through sobs. "You say you are honourable and just! Show me! Show all of us, and spare my friends!"

"Get *up*, girl," he said. There was barely disguised contempt in his voice.

Wren stayed where shex was. She gripped his leg tighter, and her sobs grew even louder. "Sire, I know you'll be a good King, a *great* King, as you said. Give them another chance!"

She heard the soldier approach. "Lord, should I *remove* her...?"

"*No*," barked the Hamelyn Piper, clearly irritated. "I'll deal with it." The soldier walked away again. "Child, I've given them all the chances I can. It's their choice to stay and die. You've made a good decision, and they have not. Now, please, take your place in my ranks. There are things to be done."

It was a relief to Wren that the Hamelyn Piper seemed fond of his own voice. She wasn't sure if she could keep the crying going much longer. "You are so wise, sire," she threw in, hoping he'd keep talking.

He did: "They believe they can win, and they are mistaken. You have seen the truth, and your reward is to live."

And at that moment, there was a *click*. A small sound, barely audible even to Wren; she had found the mechanism for the clasp, not an easy thing when you couldn't see it. She'd been beginning to think that her memory of the armour's design hadn't been good enough, or worse – that the actual construction differed from those ancient diagrams.

But no. It had taken her longer than she'd hoped, but she'd managed it.

She sensed a change, though, a sudden tension in the Hamelyn Piper. A realization that something was *wrong*.

What came next happened in less than a second.

She lifted the freed piece of obsidiac armour from the Hamelyn Piper's left calf; she rose and turned, speaking the brief incantation Alia had taught her. She felt the energy in her fingertips, and a rush of power. The piece of armour – *pure obsidiac* – shot out from her grasp, hurtling over the heads of the Black Knight's forces and the remaining deserters, flying out towards the camp. And then it changed direction mid-air as Alia's own spell caught it, drawing it towards her at an impossible speed, vanishing from sight. The sound it left in its wake was an extraordinary *crack*.

At first, nobody moved. Wren, standing next to the Hamelyn Piper, could scarcely believe it had worked.

"What have you done?" said the Black Knight, staring at her. Then he almost screamed: "*What have you done?*"

The soldier ran to her, and put his sword to her throat. "Give me the word, sire," he said.

"Little *witch*!" sneered the Hamelyn Piper. "Captain, there are manacles in my saddlebag. Send for them."

"I have manacles here, Lord," said the captain, and he did – hanging from his belt.

"Not like *mine*, you don't," said the Black Knight. "Send for them! They're painted red, and of a design specially for holding those with *sorcery* in their blood. I didn't expect to need them for a *child*…"

The captain nodded, and caught the eye of another soldier, who set off to fetch them.

The Hamelyn Piper shook his head at Wren. "You think stripping me of a piece of armour will make a difference?" he said. "You have courage, yes, but not an ounce of sense in your head!"

"My lord, look to the field!" called the captain. "Look!"

The Hamelyn Piper looked.

He had never felt such anger in his life.

Watching Wren leave had been the hardest thing Alia had ever done. The plan had been Wren's idea, and however Alia had argued against it, Wren had held firm.

"Let me go instead," Alia had told her.

"He'll never let you get close enough," Wren said. "I'm just a child. I'm not a threat to him. And you're the only one who's used the Leap Device before."

"We don't know if this will work!" said Alia.

"It's a chance," Wren said. "And there are no others left."

And so it had been decided.

Nobody else could know their plan. Alia watched from the camp as the deserters took their oath. When it was Wren's turn, Alia prepared herself: standing firm, ready for when the moment came. Tobias looked at her, and was about to speak, but she shook her head. His demeanour changed, then – he didn't know what, but he knew she was planning *something*.

When Wren sent the piece of armour towards her, she was ready to catch it in her own spell and pull it down to her. It shot through the air, coming to a halt the instant it was in her hands.

And there it was: a perfect chunk of pure obsidiac.

She wasted no time. She kneeled and set the obsidiac on the ground, then took the Leap Device from her pocket, with Barver's feather still clipped to it. She looked at Tobias, who was staring in astonishment.

"Fingers crossed," she said, then placed the Leap Device on the obsidiac and pulled back the trigger.

The sound that had come before came again, like the slow cracking of glass, but this was magnified a thousandfold. With the sound came the rippling sphere, growing slowly out from the device, engulfing first her, then Tobias, and Barver, then the griffins…

Within the boundary, sounds were muffled, echoing back; the world beyond was dim, hard to see through the rippling surface.

This had never been done before, Alia knew, not at this scale. This device that Lar-Sennen had created over a thousand years ago had, surely, only been used rarely, with the smallest of pieces of black diamond. Even so, it seemed to be working.

Wren's plan was working.

Soon it would cover the whole of the camp, and she could release the trigger. Soon, they would all be gone to the safety of Devil Pin Bay.

All but one.

Even with the captain's sword at her throat, Wren laughed as she saw the rippling shell grow.

The Hamelyn Piper sneered at her. "What is this?" he said. "Some kind of *shield*?"

But then his expression changed. "No," he said. "*No*." He turned to the captain. "Prepare to fire everything we have! Obliterate them!"

"Lord, if we fire everything and it *is* a shield…"

"It's no shield, Captain. Give the order. Fire everything. *Now!*"

The captain nodded. "Corporal!" he called. "Signal all catapult units to fire on my command!"

"Aye, sir!" came the reply.

In the valley, the shell kept growing, and with it Wren's hope grew too. It covered a quarter of the camp already, and soon it would…

It stopped. It was as big as it was going to get.

She heard the cries from the camp: *Draw closer! Get inside the shell!* The soldiers in the camp started rushing to the outer edge, horses led warily through the boundary, everyone running now.

Then Wren saw: in the valley, one was furthest of all, having trailed after the deserters and stayed, defeated, where he'd fallen. Stayed, watching *her*. And only now was he standing; only now was he running back to camp.

Patch.

"*Fire!*" cried the captain, and from behind every hilltop the catapults loosed their projectiles, twenty at least, smoke trailing in their wake.

When the sphere had stopped growing outwards, it had left most of their people on the wrong side of the boundary. Alia, kneeling by the obsidiac chunk, was squeezing the trigger so tightly that her finger was cramping, but she had to hold it until all of their forces reached safety.

"Get everyone inside!" she cried, and her instructions were passed on. More and more soldiers came through the rippling border, along with frightened horses, the noise growing with each moment. Soon enough it was chaos all around them. The dimming effect of the sphere's boundary made it difficult to see what was happening beyond.

"Where's Patch?" said Barver suddenly, fear in his voice. Calling his friend's name, he moved against the flow of people and horses, too many around him to let him take to the air.

"Alia!" yelled Tobias. "They've launched!"

She looked up, and against the sky she saw the shadowy outlines of death coming for them. "Is everyone inside?" she cried. The noise was unbearable – shouts from the soldiers, and the panicked whinnies of the horses, all echoing inside the rippling sphere. "Tobias, tell me! *Is everyone inside?*" She didn't dare take her eyes from the approaching projectiles.

"I don't know!" said Tobias, unable to see past the chaos around him. "There's no time! Do it now!"

She wrenched her eyes from the sky and looked for herself; she thought she could see Barver's feet through the legs of the crowd around her, but he was still heading away from them, towards the rippling boundary. Patch still had to be outside.

"*Alia!*"

She snapped her eyes back to the sky, and her heart sank. The projectiles were almost upon them.

Time had run out.

Alia closed her eyes and released the trigger.

31
GONE

The Hamelyn Piper watched in silence as the rippling shell suddenly contracted. Wren watched too. The captain was beside her, his sword still pressed to her throat.

The shell collapsed in an instant. In the Caves of Casimir, there had been a gentle *pop* when Alia had vanished, and an outrush of air. Here, the *pop* became a *boom,* and when the outrush of air met the incoming projectiles, all of them exploded together – a vast detonation that drew a gasp of horror from the captain.

The shockwave spread out rapidly, and when it reached the top of the hill it hit them like a sudden gale, strong enough for the Hamelyn Piper to be pushed back a step, and for the captain's sword to nick Wren's skin.

The Hamelyn Piper turned and looked at her.

Even though she could feel blood dripping down her throat, Wren couldn't help but grin at the Black Knight. For she had seen something, in that instant before the shell had contracted: seen a flying dracogriff burst through and take hold of Patch Brightwater, before turning and disappearing back inside.

In the valley below was a devastated camp, tents in ruins. But there were no *bodies*, because the army had escaped.

The Hamelyn Piper screamed, his rage a terrible thing to witness. The thundering that had filled the camp before now echoed around the hills, his cries of anger delivered to all of his forces at once. When it finally subsided, the Hamelyn Piper stared at Wren again. *This is it*, she thought. This victory would cost Wren her life, but she didn't regret it at all.

A soldier came, holding a pair of red-painted manacles, two metals bands joined by a chain. With grim satisfaction, the Hamelyn Piper took the manacles and clamped them around Wren's wrists.

"Shouldn't I kill her, Lord?" asked the captain, sword raised.

"No," said the Black Knight, staring at Wren as he spoke. "I want the little witch to see it, when I find her friends, when I *kill* them in the worst ways I can think of. I want her to live, and know that their pain is because of *her*. Place a guard of four on her at all times. The manacles never come off. Feed her scraps enough to keep her alive, and let no harm come to her. Not *yet*."

"Yes, sire," said the captain.

And although Wren *knew* it was foolish, she kept smiling. She couldn't help it. She pictured Barver vanishing behind the rippling mirror, with Patch in his arms, and her smile couldn't be stopped.

The Black Knight's eyes narrowed. He lashed out, striking her across the face with a gauntlet-clad hand. She fell to the ground, and the Hamelyn Piper strode off.

From where she lay, Wren could still see the devastated camp in the valley. And now, with blood running down her neck and a split lip, all she could think of was Patch and Barver on a beach of pure white sand.

"Have some natter-clumps and remember me," she whispered, as the captain dragged her away.

32

NOT A BEACH

The arrival was instant.

One moment Patch was running for his life towards the mirror sheen ahead of him, and the next he was being yanked into the air, landing in deep meadow-grass with a blazing sun overhead.

He got to his feet. Barver was beside him, staring around.

"This is *not* a beach," said Barver.

"Were you expecting one?" said Patch.

"Yes! I saw Alia using the Leap Device, and my feather was in it. This should be the white-sand beach of Devil Pin Bay! Instead…" He looked around. "It's whatever *this* is."

And *this*, Patch thought, was a decidedly odd place. They were in a large meadow, roughly square. On three sides, tall trees rose – curious things, of a kind he'd never laid eyes on before. And *ugly*, their trunks resembling leg bones, the branches bare. Over the treetops, the only thing visible was a distant hill, or possibly a mountain. He couldn't tell how far away or how big it was, as the air had a strange haze to it.

On the fourth side of the meadow were trees that were much more welcoming – sycamores, with healthy green foliage and entirely normal trunks.

The rest of the travellers were packed closely together, having arrived in a dense jumble after their panicked dash for safety. Now they were starting to spread out; all of them, horses included, seemed rather dazed.

Merta was kneeling beside Cramber and Wintel; Tobias was there too, beginning to play his Healing Song for the unconscious griffins.

Patch caught sight of Alia heading their way. When she reached them, she hugged Patch, and then did the same to Barver. All three of them were in tears.

"Wren asked me to do that, on her behalf," said Alia.

They were silent for a while. Patch wanted to say something, but nothing seemed right – or *enough*. He wanted Alia to tell him Wren would be okay, though it would surely be a cruel thing, to make her tell such a lie.

Alia took out a handkerchief and blew her nose. "Now, Barver, a very important question. Where are we?" She looked at him with intense expectation.

"I have no idea," said Barver. "Honestly, no idea at all."

"Your feather brought us here!" said Alia. "Something links you to this place – something *strong*. Stronger than your connection to Devil Pin Bay. The sheer power of such a large, pure piece of obsidiac allowed so many of us to travel at once, but it also meant we travelled much further than we'd expected – we could be anywhere in the entire *world*. Think, Barver!"

"I'm sorry," said Barver. "I don't recognize where we are."

Alia frowned and looked up to the sky. "We can probably determine our location from the position of the sun, but I'm too exhausted to think about it right now. At least we're safe."

Patch was exhausted too – and numb, unable to deal with Wren's sacrifice. He was about to suggest that they go over to Tobias and the griffins, when a disturbance to their right caught their attention. One of the horses was whinnying and pulling on the reins its handler was leading it by.

"Something's spooked it," said Barver. The other horses seemed skittish too, but none were as bad. Suddenly the horse pulled free and galloped off in panic, heading for the tall bone-trees. It hardly slowed as it passed the treeline and disappeared from sight.

"Probably just the disorienting effect of the Leap," said Alia. "I mean, even for us it was…"

She didn't get to finish, as the air was filled with the horrifying sound of the horse's screams. Patch saw the tops of the trees swaying slightly, near where the horse had vanished. Then, abruptly, the screams were silenced.

Wide-eyed, the soldiers in the meadow stood in readiness; the Battle Pipers among them took their Pipes in their hands, prepared to defend against whatever might emerge.

But there were no more sounds, and the trees stopped swaying.

The beating of wings came from behind them, and they turned to see Merta approach, low to the ground. "I'll see what I can see from the air," she said, and started to climb, but when she was barely fifty feet up she faltered and crashed to the grass. Barver unfurled his wings, preparing to fly to where she'd fallen.

"Stop!" cried Alia. "Run to her, Barver. Don't fly." She was looking at the very air above them with what seemed like *suspicion*.

They hurried over to Merta, and her eyes flickered open. "What…" she said. "What happened?"

"You lost consciousness," said Alia. "Did you notice an odour, Merta? A *smell*?"

Merta frowned at first, but then her eyes widened. "Apples," she said. "I could smell *apples*."

Alia nodded. "Something is very wrong with this place," she said.

"What does it mean?" Barver asked.

"I'm not sure," said Alia, looking up again at the air above, as if she simply didn't *trust* it. "None of you should fly to any height, though, and perhaps not fly at all."

Everyone decided to keep as far from the bone-trees as they could.

A stream ran out of the sycamores, and one soldier was brave enough – or thirsty enough – to try it. It seemed safe, although most decided they could wait a while longer before consuming anything from this place. The death cries of the horse still filled their thoughts.

Several groups were organized to investigate the sycamores themselves. While the bone-trees inspired dread, the sycamores created no such feeling. One group went first, and came back with tales of fruit-laden bushes, and rabbits scampering.

"Did the rabbits have fangs?" Patch muttered to Barver. "I wouldn't be surprised if they did."

After a second group had ventured safely in and out of the sycamores, Barver decided he was going to take a look for himself. As Patch tried to dissuade him, they walked along the edge of the trees.

"Come on," said Barver. "Just a little explore, we'll not lose sight of the meadow."

They'd opened up quite a gap to everyone else. "No," said Patch. And then he saw something through the trunks ahead of them. "Is that what I think it is?" he said, and curiosity took over.

It was a *fence*, not very far in from the treeline. They reached it quickly, and it was a curious thing; the fence-posts ran between the trees, and were carved into spiral patterns, with only a single piece of rope strung between the posts. Further in, the trees seemed to thin out a little.

"It's like a boundary marker," said Patch. "It certainly wouldn't keep anything in or out."

"A fence of any kind means there are people here," said Barver. "They can tell us where we are!" He stepped over the rope.

"Don't!" said Patch. "You get back here at once! We should tell the others before we go any further."

But Barver was already off, heading to the right.

Patch stood where he was, quietly wishing he'd not ventured into the trees at all. He was torn between going back to tell the others, and waiting in case Barver suddenly needed help. Barver was almost out of sight, though; Patch decided to wait it out. "I'll just stay here, then, shall I?" he called.

As he stood waiting, he noticed something through the trees to the left: a hint of distant blue, that was surely water. Curiosity won the day again. *A quick look won't hurt,* he thought. A short walk took him down a gentle slope that wound around a small hillock, and there it was:

The *sea*.

The sea was far lower down, so he knew there was a cliff-edge up ahead. Patch wasn't willing to get much closer for now, so he turned around, intending to call for Barver.

An enormous griffin was right in front of him, giving him a very hostile stare.

"What's all this noise?" said the griffin. "Who are you people? Are you real?"

It stepped forward and prodded Patch's chest, knocking him to the ground before pinning him down with one hand. "You *seem* real!" said the griffin. "Can you talk?"

Patch noticed that the creature had a collar around its neck, attached to a length of chain. The chain trailed back towards the hillock, and now Patch realized there was a rocky opening there: a *cave*.

The griffin pressed its hand down harder on his chest, and Patch could hardly breathe. As he was on the verge of passing out, the griffin seemed to understand and took some of the weight off. Patch gulped a lungful of air, and let out a tremendous scream.

The griffin scowled. "So *loud*!" it said. "Wait, if my ears hurt, that means I'm not imagining things again!"

And then it stopped talking. It looked up from Patch, staring to its right.

Barver was rushing back between the trees.

Distracted, the griffin's weight on Patch grew again.

"Stop!" cried Barver. "You're hurting him!"

The griffin looked down, then took its hand off Patch and backed off.

Patch stood and hurried to Barver, standing behind his friend for protection.

"You can't be..." said the griffin. "*You* can't be real..."

"I am real," said Barver, and Patch saw that great tears were falling from the dracogriff's eyes, just as tears were falling from the *griffin's* eyes. Barver walked closer and put his hand on the griffin's beak, and the griffin nuzzled up to it, eyes closed.

"What's going on?" said Patch, bewildered.

Barver seemed just as bewildered as Patch was. "This... this is Gaverry Tenso, Patch," he said. "This is my father."

Barver and his father retreated to the cave in the hillock to talk. It had been Patch's suggestion, to give father and son some time alone before telling the others about their discovery.

Patch stood as close to the cliff's edge as he dared, watching the sea far below – a sea that stretched out to the horizon with no sign of land, no hints at where in the world they'd found themselves.

After an hour, Barver came out of the cave. He and Patch returned to the meadow, and took Tobias and Alia to one side to explain what they'd found.

"Your *father* is what links you to this place," said Alia. "He's the reason the Leap Device brought us here. But only a large piece of pure obsidiac was powerful enough to actually make it happen. He and Alkeran vanished at the same time. The collar you mentioned confirms it: this is where Alkeran was held captive, and clearly the same thing happened to your father. This is the Bestiary."

Patch had known from the moment he'd seen that collar, but to hear Alia say it aloud made it real, and terrible.

For the Bestiary was a prison. They had escaped certain death at the hands of the Hamelyn Piper, only to find themselves *trapped*.

"Dad says that the meadow's safe by day," said Barver. "But this place changes in the dark. At night, things come out of the bone-trees to feed. There's a fence within the sycamores, beyond which it's safe. Everyone should be on the other side of that before nightfall."

"What, *everyone*?" said Tobias. "Two hundred and sixty humans, thirty-nine horses, one dracogriff and three griffins!"

"Four griffins," corrected Barver.

"Yes, yes, four griffins, including your father," said Tobias. "We still have the problem of food to deal with. How can we possibly feed them all?"

"There's more than enough space, and Dad says there's plenty of food," said Barver. "Bushes produce fruit all year round, and replenish overnight. The rabbits are plentiful, and are slow and easy to catch. He said..." Barver paused, wary of what he was about to say. "It may just be that he's been alone for so long, but Dad said this place is *alive.* Alkeran said he never saw a jailer. Dad says this place *is* the jailer. And it caters well for its prisoners."

Long before darkness fell, everyone had moved from the meadow into the promised safety of the sycamores, and the glades within. Cramber and Wintel still slept, nursed by the Curative Sleep. Patch and Tobias shared the duties on that.

Fires were lit, but the night was mild.

Patch sat by one of the fires, alone; Barver was spending time talking with his father in his cave. Alia came and sat with him.

"Will you be able to remove the collar from Barver's father?" he asked.

"Underath managed it for Alkeran, somehow," she said. "So it must be possible."

"And will you be able to free *us*?"

She said nothing for a few seconds. "It took the pure obsidiac of the Black Knight's armour to break through the magic that guards this place, Patch. The Leap Device used it all up to bring us here."

"That sounds like the kind of challenge Wren would have relished," he said, and that, at least, won a smile.

"Here," said Alia. "I forgot I had this. It was how I found you in Skamos."

She placed the cross-eyed owl in Patch's hand. For a while, he simply held it, unable to speak.

He sat in the warmth from the fire, thinking of Barver and his father, and of his own grandparents. He thought of Erner and Rundel, who would surely be nearing Tiviscan by now.

Most of all, he held tightly to the cross-eyed owl and thought of Wren.

On returning from his father's cave, Barver sat with him. Seeing what Patch was holding, he put his hands on Patch's, then began to sing.

It was an old song, famous throughout the world. A song that was at once sad, and proud; mournful, yet a celebration. It was sung to remember those close to you, who had gone.

It was called "The Lament for Fallen Friends".

Patch's tears flowed freely as he joined in. Soon, the entire camp was singing for Wren.

380

As they sang, two horses rode on the Collosson Highway, fifty miles from Tiviscan Castle. On their backs sat Virtus Rundel Stone and his apprentice Erner Whitlock, heading to Tiviscan in the hope that the Pipers' Council would help their friends in the Ortings, oblivious to the disaster that had already befallen them.

They were just as oblivious to the dangers that waited for them both in Tiviscan.

And in a forest deep within the Ortings sat a girl.

She was kept in the open, near the middle of the camp, her manacles fastened by a short chain to a stake hammered deep into the ground.

Four guards sat nearby, the corners of a square. The guards didn't pay her much attention. All she ever did, it seemed, was sit. She took the scraps of food she was given, and ate them in silence; she took the water she was given, and drank it without fuss. And if the guards grew bored and shouted things at her to relieve the tedium, the girl would look forlorn, and allow the tears to come; the guards, finding some shame buried deep inside them, would stop.

And so, Wren could practise. The manacles robbed her of sorcery, that was true, but they didn't seem to strip her of *all* magic.

The exercises she'd memorized were silent, so all she

did was close her eyes and concentrate. For days, it seemed futile. Nothing happened, and she despaired, thinking that nothing would *ever* happen.

But then, one night, she gave herself a tail. It was just like the tail she'd had in Skamos, sitting at the table in the home of Barver's aunt and uncle.

It was uncomfortable, of course, bunched up under her clothes, but it was *there*. She had taken her first real step. The tail disappeared a few minutes later.

Underath had warned her that perfecting this new skill would take time. A *long* time, perhaps.

Then again, she had nothing better to do.

Acknowledgements

Huge thanks to my editors Anne Finnis and Sarah Stewart. When my son asked me what editors do, I told him to imagine making a meal, but you've not added any salt to your soup, or sugar to your cake, and you entirely forgot to put the oven on. Dinner would be hot murky water, raw chicken, and strange fluffy bread. Yet think how different it would be, if there was someone to point these things out to you! The meal wouldn't just be improved, it'd be transformed. Editors are like that, but with words.

Thanks also to Rebecca Hill and the rest of the Usborne team – their unwavering support has got me through more than one difficult patch, and I'm indebted to you all.

My thanks too to George Ermos, for yet another wonderful cover. And to my agent Luigi Bonomi, who nudged me down the path of writing for children in the first place – I wasn't sure I could do it, but now that I'm here, I never felt more at home.

Finally, my thanks go to my wife Laura, and to my kids. They occasionally get to see me when I emerge from my dark hideaway, as I mutter about mysterious things that they won't get to read for months and months. I thank you for your patience, which has been sorely tested. I promise to be quicker in future!

Will the three friends ever see each other again? Can they finally beat the evil Piper of Hamelyn or is he just too powerful?

Look out for the third and final SONGS OF MAGIC adventure that will determine the fate of the world!

Coming in 2022

Check here for news:

@Usborne

@SethPatrickUK

@usborne_books

facebook.com/usbornepublishing

#ADarknessOfDragons
#AVanishingOfGriffins #SongsOfMagic